Praise for *New York Times* bestselling author

JOAN JOHNSTON

"[Joan Johnston] does short contemporary westerns to perfection."
—*Publishers Weekly*

"A guaranteed good read..."
—*New York Times* bestselling author
Heather Graham

* * *

Praise for national bestselling author

CAROLYN ZANE

"Readers enjoy Ms. Zane's zippy writing style and touches of humor..."
—*Romantic Times*

"Carolyn Zane provides readers with very funny scenes and lighthearted banter that will surely put a smile on your face."
—*Romantic Times*

JOAN JOHNSTON

New York Times bestselling author Joan Johnston started reading romances to escape the stress of being an attorney with a major national law firm. She soon discovered that writing romances was a lot more fun than writing legal bond indentures. Since then, she has published a number of historical and contemporary romances. In addition to being an author, Joan is the mother of two children. In her spare time, she enjoys sailing, horseback riding and camping.

CAROLYN ZANE

lives with her husband, Matt, their preschool daughter, Madeline, and their latest addition, baby daughter Olivia, in the rolling countryside near Portland, Oregon's Willamette River. Like Chevy Chase's character in the movie *Funny Farm*, Carolyn finally decided to trade in a decade of city dwelling and producing local television commercials for the quaint country life of a novelist. And even though they have bitten off decidedly more than they can chew in the remodeling of their hundred-year-plus old farmhouse, life is somewhat saner for her than for poor Chevy. The neighbors are friendly, the mail carrier actually stops at the box, and the dog, Bob Barker, sticks close to home.

The Bluest Eyes in Texas

JOAN JOHNSTON

Wife in Name Only

CAROLYN ZANE

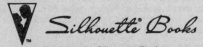

Published by Silhouette Books
America's Publisher of Contemporary Romance

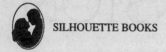 SILHOUETTE BOOKS

Copyright in the collection:
© 2002 by Harlequin Books S.A.

ISBN 0-373-48474-7

The publisher acknowledges the copyright holders of the individual works as follows:

THE BLUEST EYES IN TEXAS
Copyright © 1995 by Joan Mertens Johnston

WIFE IN NAME ONLY
Copyright © 1994 by Carolyn Suzanne Pizzuti

This edition published by arrangement with Harlequin Books S.A.

Visit Silhouette at www.eHarlequin.com

Printed in U.S.A.

THE BLUEST EYES IN TEXAS

Joan Johnston

Dear Reader,

Seven years after writing *The Bluest Eyes in Texas*, I'm still writing about Texas Rangers and making them my heroes. They're a fascinating, elite breed, modern-day lawmen who remain renegades and lone wolves. Burr Covington is one of my favorites!

I have no trouble picturing "the bluest eyes in Texas"—because my heroine's eyes aren't really blue, they're the color of Texas bluebonnets, which aren't blue, either, but a striking lavender color. I have pictures of my children playing among those Texas wildflowers, which blanket the hill country around Austin in the spring.

I invite you along as Burr Covington, a Texas Ranger from the wrong side of the tracks, rescues the governor's "ice princess" daughter from kidnappers, and then falls head over heels for *The Bluest Eyes in Texas*.

As always, happy trails to you and those dear to you.

Joan Johnston

Chapter One

Lindsey Major pressed her fingers against her temples to ease some of the awful pressure, then rolled onto her side, hoping that would relieve the pain in her head. As she did, her skirt wrapped around her legs. That was odd, because she slept in men's pajamas and had since she was a teenager and thought it was a cool thing to do. She reached a hand down to untangle the yards of material and realized it wasn't just any old skirt, it was ankle-length taffeta. She was still wearing her ballgown!

Lindsey sat up abruptly, which set her head to pounding ferociously and brought a wave of nausea. She fought the sick feeling, sliding her feet onto the floor and carefully pushing herself upright on the edge of the bed. Which was when she realized she wasn't in her own bed upstairs in the Texas governor's mansion. She was…somewhere else.

It wasn't a dream. I was kidnapped right off the front porch of the mansion. I've been drugged. That's why my head hurts.

Lindsey caught a glimpse of herself in the mirror across the room and was appalled at what she found. Her tawny golden hair had fallen from its sleek

French twist. The makeup she had sparingly applied to what the press had labeled "the bluest eyes in Texas" was so badly smudged that she looked like a raccoon on a binge. And her beautiful strapless taffeta dress—a glorious shade of lavender that rivaled the remarkable color of her eyes—was crumpled from having been slept in. Lindsey tried to remember what had happened after the struggle on the porch, but drew a blank.

There was no window in the room, no route of escape. She crossed to the only door and slowly, silently, tried the knob. It was locked. She pressed her ear against it, hoping to get some clue as to who had kidnapped her and what terms they were demanding for her release. She could actually make out voices in the next room. Two men were arguing. What they said sent a cold chill down her spine.

"I say we might as well enjoy her while we can. Hector ain't gonna let her go even if the governor commutes the Turk's sentence like he asked and the Turk goes free."

The Turk! Lindsey thought with despair. *I should have known!*

Turk Valerio, the man who had accidentally shot and killed her mother in his abortive assassination attempt on her father five years ago, had been sentenced to die for his crime. The Turk had boasted that he would never be executed, that the Texas Mafia, headed by Hector Martinez, would find a way to set him free. Lindsey had the sinking feeling that she had become a pawn in a very deadly game.

"I want to know what it feels like to do a lady,"

the man said. "And I sure as hell want to see them blue eyes when I'm pumping into her—before Hector does what he threatened, I mean." The kidnapper made a disgusted sound in his throat. "She's gonna be a mess after that."

"I can see the governor's face when he read that note," a second voice, one with a distinct Texas drawl, said. "'Commute Turk Valerio's sentence by noon tomorrow, or I'm gonna blind the bluest eyes in Texas.' Bet the man turned white as a ghost!" A high-pitched, almost girlish giggle followed.

"Hector won't like it if you touch the girl," a third voice said flatly.

"Well, Hector ain't here," the man with the deep Texas accent retorted. "I agree with Epifanio. I say we enjoy the girl now, while we can. Only, I want her first."

"I get her first, Tex," Epifanio countered. "It was my idea."

"You're too hard on women," Tex complained. "There won't be any left for me."

"I'm telling you both, leave the girl alone," the third voice said.

"Hell, Burr, you wouldn't spoil our fun, would you? Besides, me and Tex together, we're bigger 'n you. I don't think you could stop us all by your lonesome." That horrible, high-pitched laugh resounded again.

"Make a move toward that door and we'll see," the man called Burr replied in a steely voice.

Lindsey's heart was thumping loud and hard in response to the fight-or-flight instinct that had taken over when she realized her peril. They planned to blind her! But they were going to rape her first! Any minute she expected Epifanio and Tex to come bursting through the door—right past the man called Burr, who was all that stood between her and immediate disaster. And good old Burr hadn't said anything about protecting her from the man who wanted to blind her, only from the two men intent on rape.

Lindsey looked around for a weapon. Her eyes alighted on the lamp beside the bed, which had a porcelain base. It ought to make a good club. She quickly pulled the plug from the wall and stripped the lamp of its shade, then dragged a chair over to one side of the door and climbed onto it so the lamp could be wielded from above. She waited, terror stealing her breath and making her suck air in harsh gasps. How much time did she have? How long before she was fighting for her life?

Lindsey watched in breathless horror as the doorknob began to turn.

She brought the lamp down on the head of the first man through the door, who collapsed at her feet with a groan. She stared openmouthed at the second man who filled the doorway. He was huge.

"What the hell?"

She took advantage of the big man's confusion to give him a hard shove. As he fell back through the doorway, she leapt off the chair and darted past him. Unfortunately, he reached out at the last moment and caught her skirt. It tore at the waist but didn't pull free. He began to rein her in like a lassoed heifer.

"You did me a favor, *chiquita,* getting rid of Tex like that. Now I have you all to myself."

Lindsey clawed and kicked, but to no avail. He snagged an arm around her waist and pulled her tight against his chest.

"Let me go!" she cried.

He shook his shaggy-haired head. "Not so fast, *niña.* I like you right where you are."

She kicked him in the shin, which was when it dawned on her she was barefoot. She must have lost her high heels sometime during the kidnapping. The blow surely hurt her worse than her assailant, because she yelped in pain, while he just laughed.

She caught sight of the third man—the one who must be Burr—watching her, his fierce, hooded eyes filled with...loathing? She couldn't take her eyes off him, even as Epifanio pulled her body tight against his.

Burr's lips were pressed flat in disgust, distorting the shape of his mouth. His chin had a slight crease down the center of it and jutted as though seeking a confrontation. A diamond sparkled in one earlobe, and she saw a tattoo on his arm below the folded-up sleeve of a black T-shirt, although she couldn't make out what the tattoo was. He had a day's growth of black beard that did nothing to hide the angular planes of his face. His cheekbones were high and wide, and his nose was crooked from having been broken, from the look of it, more than once.

The pull of tearing fabric brought her attention back to the Mexican. She bucked violently to free herself from his grasp.

He ripped the bodice of her gown, exposing the white merry widow beneath it. "Fight me, bitch," he said in a low, rusty-hinge voice. "I like it when a woman fights."

Lindsey didn't disappoint him. Furious and frightened, her fingernails clawed down the side of Epifanio's face, leaving four distinct bloody scratches. She grasped his hair and yanked hard, then reeled when he slapped her across the face with his open hand, drawing blood where her teeth cut her lip.

Lindsey got a quick glance at what appeared to be a coiled black snake tattooed on Burr's arm as he grabbed Epifanio and spun him around. She felt herself pulled free of Epifanio's grasp and flung past him. She hit the wall hard and, momentarily stunned, slid down in a heap.

"I told you to leave her alone."

Dazed, she watched Burr confront Epifanio. He was easily as tall as the Mexican, but lean where the other man was barrel-shaped. His hair was as shiny black as a raven's wing and clubbed into a tail at his nape. He wore tight black jeans and black cowboy boots.

Burr was all sinew and bone. And clearly dangerous. His spread-legged stance was challenging, his balled fists intimidating. A muscle worked where his jaw was clenched. His eyes were a brown so deep it was almost black. There was no compassion in those beautiful dark eyes, just cold-blooded menace.

"Stay out of this, Burr," Epifanio warned. "The woman is mine."

"She belongs to Hector. He'll have your hide if

you keep up with what you're doing. Let her be, Epifanio.''

Epifanio's eyes narrowed. His lips flattened. "Get outta my way, Burr."

Burr didn't move an inch.

A switchblade appeared in Epifanio's hand. Lindsey flinched when she heard the *snick* as he flipped the blade from its sheath.

"Move outta my way, Burr."

Burr shook his head, a slight, almost imperceptible movement.

Epifanio lunged with the knife, intent on catching Burr by surprise. Burr caught the wrist of the hand that held the switchblade just as it reached his body, turning it aside so the knife skimmed across his chest instead of plunging into it. Lindsey gasped when she saw the streak of red left by the blade.

It dawned on Lindsey that she could escape while the two men were locked in mortal combat. She inched backward toward the door but found it impossible to take her eyes from the drama unfolding before her. It seemed unlikely that Burr would win. He was outmatched in size and strength by the other man. Given that scenario, it was imperative that she escape if she could.

She scrambled toward the door on her hands and knees, forcing herself to ignore the fact that Burr was probably going to die for coming to her rescue. He was a villain, just like the others. If Epifanio didn't kill him, he was going to spend the rest of his life in prison for kidnapping her.

Lindsey pulled herself upright using the doorknob.

She had opened the door a mere inch when someone grabbed her, and a flat male palm forced the door shut.

She made a guttural sound deep in her throat that was part outrage, part fear. She turned with her fingers arched into claws aimed at her captor's face, then realized it was Burr who had hold of her. She searched quickly for Epifanio and saw him lying on the floor, the switchblade imbedded in his chest.

Her hand froze in midair, and her stomach revolted at the sight of the dead man. Her eyes shot to Burr's face, which gave no evidence of any feeling whatsoever—neither revulsion nor remorse—for what he had done.

She swallowed back the bile burning her throat. "Is he dead?"

"Yes."

"What are you going to do with me?"

"The hell if I know," he muttered viciously. "We'd damn well better get out of here. Keep your mouth shut when we're in the hall." He opened the door and started to drag her through it.

Lindsey was too terrified to cooperate with her savior—an unshaven man in a black T-shirt and jeans, a man with a pierced ear and a ponytail and a snake tattoo, simply didn't fit her image of a knight in shining armor. "Let me go," she pleaded. "I won't tell them anything about you."

"Look, Blue Eyes—" As Burr spoke, there was a shout from the other room.

It was Tex.

"Hey! Where the hell do you think you're going?"

Tex took one look at Epifanio's body, and a gun appeared in his hand from a holster that had apparently been hidden inside his denim jacket. He aimed it in Burr's—and therefore Lindsey's—direction.

"You sonofabitch!" he hissed.

Lindsey squeezed her eyes shut against the sight of the deadly gun bore, waiting for the sound of shots. But there was only one deafening blast, close to her ear. Her eyes flashed open.

Tex lay in the doorway, a pool of blood spreading on the beige carpet around his body.

She turned to stare, horrified, at Burr, who was holding a .38 snub-nosed revolver in his hand. While she watched, he returned the small, deadly weapon to his boot.

Lindsey had been in such a constant state of terror for the past few minutes that her body quivered from excess adrenaline. She felt dizzy, and she wanted desperately to give in to the darkness that threatened to overwhelm her. She wanted even more to live. And she knew that if she fainted now, she might never see daylight again. Her eyes sought out Burr's, wondering what the chances were that he would let her go.

"You're in shock," he said matter-of-factly. He manhandled her over to the couch, forced her to sit, and shoved her head down between her knees. When she tried to rise, he ordered, "Stay there!"

He peered out into the hall, looking to see if anyone was curious or stupid enough to personally investigate the shot. "We don't have much time. Someone has probably called the authorities about that gunshot."

Lindsey closed her eyes to avoid seeing the two

bodies and breathed deeply, trying to regain her equi-librium. She heard Burr pacing the carpet and mut-tering to himself. He picked up the phone receiver and dropped it back into the cradle.

"Damn! Damn it to hell!"

She sat up and stared at the furious man standing spread-legged across from her with his hands on his hips.

"I guess I don't have any choice," he said. "Come on, let's go."

"Go where?" Lindsey demanded in her most im-perious voice.

"Look, Blue Eyes. When I say 'jump' you say 'how high?' Have you got that?" He grabbed a black leather jacket off one of the chairs and slipped his arms into it.

"If you let me go," Lindsey said, "I'll tell my father you saved me from those two men."

"Hell, if I let you go, Hector will just snatch you back up again. Or shoot you or your father or some other member of your family. He means business. You don't have any choice. You're coming with me."

"Where?"

"Damn it, just do what you're told!" He grabbed her arm and yanked her up off the couch.

Lindsey tried to jerk herself free, but ended up nearly wrenching her arm from the socket. She saw the direction Burr's eyes took as she slammed into him and looked down to see what he found so fas-cinating. Which was when she realized the extent of the damage to her bodice. The merry widow was far more concealing than many bathing suits she had worn, but it was an undergarment. It did its job well, forcing her generous breasts upward so that a great deal of flesh was mounded above the two white cups.

Burr swore. "You're not going anywhere like that without attracting more attention than I want." He pulled off his jacket and handed it to her. "Put that on."

She looked down the full-length taffeta skirt all the way to where her toes curled into the thick carpet. "I don't think your jacket is going to completely solve the problem." It was warm, though, and smelled, surprisingly, of a very male after-shave.

Burr pursed his lips as he observed her bare feet. "I suppose you're right. Guess we'll have to use the stairs down to the garage in the basement."

She started to take the jacket off, and he said curtly, "Keep it."

He didn't give her a chance to protest, just grabbed her hand and headed for the door. He stopped at the portal and turned to her. "If you scream, I'll have to knock you out. Do you understand?"

Lindsey nodded. She had no doubt he would do as he promised. Her mind was racing, trying to think of some way she could escape him. But no one appeared in the stairwell, and she knew he would catch her if she tried to flee. They had nearly reached the garage in the basement. Lindsey knew she was running out of time. She had to take the chance that someone would hear her and come to her rescue.

She took a deep breath and screamed.

"Damn you, lady! I warned you!"

Lindsey saw the fist coming, felt her teeth snap

when flesh connected with flesh, felt her legs begin to crumple under her. She was stunned, but not unconscious, so she heard Burr swear again as he caught her in his arms, threw her over his shoulder in a fireman's carry, and moved stealthily into the garage.

Chapter Two

Burr was furious at the way things had turned out. This wasn't supposed to have happened. He had hoped to let the situation play out naturally. But Tex and Epifanio had gotten the bright idea to rape the governor's daughter. He couldn't let that happen, so he had interfered.

And blown eighteen months of undercover work as a member of the Texas Mafia.

He damned all spoiled little rich girls, like Miss Lindsey Major, who believed they were immune to the rules that applied to everybody else, who considered themselves too far above the vermin that roamed the dark alleys of the world to ever be threatened by them. She had been told that Hector Martinez was planning something. Burr had risked a great deal to make the anonymous phone call to the governor's mansion himself. She had answered the phone, so he knew she had been made aware of the danger. And damned if she hadn't ignored his warning and gone out to that charity ball after all!

She had cavalierly dismissed the security man at the end of the walk, instead of having him escort her to the front door of the mansion—where she had been snatched and dragged back into the concealing forsythia bushes before she could get inside.

But he had to admire her spunk. No tears from Miss Lindsey Major, just clawed fists and fight. Unfortunately, she had complicated things by screaming when he had warned her to be quiet. God only knew what repercussions there would be when word got out that he had hit her.

Hell, he hadn't wanted to take the job in the first place, but the captain of the Rangers had convinced him that someone had to do it. The last Texas Ranger they had sent undercover, Burr's best friend, Lieutenant Larry Williams, had been found dead in his car trunk. Burr was a natural to take Larry's place, the captain had said, because he had grown up in the gangs in Houston along with Larry, and he knew the rackets. He had the snake tattoo from his youth and understood the lingo. A pierced ear and long hair and a black leather jacket had completed his disguise. No one with the Texas Mafia had suspected Burr Covington was actually a lieutenant in the Texas Rangers.

He had been really close to nailing Hector Martinez for the murder of his friend, but all that effort was down the john now. It was some comfort to know he would be able to convict Hector of kidnapping the governor's daughter. But they would have to catch Hector first, and that was going to be more difficult than it sounded. Hector had more underground hiding places than a rattlesnake.

Burr wasn't sure what to do now. He had been hoping against hope that he could continue his role undercover. But after what he had done to Epifanio and Tex, and with the governor's daughter in his custody, there wasn't much chance of that. He needed to get in touch with Captain Rogers and find out what he was supposed to do with the woman. With any luck, it would be a simple matter of tucking her away somewhere safe until they either caught Hector or the Turk's death sentence was carried out.

Burr set the governor's daughter down on the passenger side of a black Jaguar with black leather seats. The car happened to be his own, but it fit the image he had been portraying, so he had used it. He saw the woman was regaining consciousness, so he gave her cheek a little slap.

"Wake up," he said. "We need to talk."

He might as well tell her who he was, Burr figured. That way she was more liable to cooperate. Although, even that wasn't a guarantee. A woman used to ordering people around, a woman used to having her own way, wasn't going to like taking orders. Only, Burr was determined to stay in control of the situation, even if she was the governor's daughter and had the damnedest blue eyes he had ever seen. Not to mention a few other hard-to-ignore assets.

His gaze slid to the opening in his jacket, where her breasts rose as she heaved in a deep breath and let it out in a shuddering sigh. He had an uncontrollable urge—which he carefully controlled—to put his mouth against her flesh to see if it was as delectable as it looked.

He heard her gasp and lifted his gaze to meet hers. Damn, but her eyes were beautiful! They were wide-set and heavily lashed and large enough for a man to get lost in. He could see why they said she had the bluest eyes in Texas. Except, they weren't blue, really. More a sort of lilac color. But definitely unique and absolutely dazzling.

Now he noticed that the rest of her features were rather ordinary. Her nose was small and straight, her mouth wide and full. Her chin jutted slightly, but he figured that was probably because she made a habit of leading with it. She was always going to attract male attention with her lush figure, and her mane of golden hair was indeed a crowning glory.

It was said she used those eyes of hers to put a man on his knees and get her own way. Well, those baby blues weren't going to work on him.

All the same, he felt a jolt of guilty shame when she accused him of wrongdoing with her eyes and followed that with the outraged statement, "You hit me!"

With an effort, he managed a shrug. "It was your own damn fault. I warned you not to scream."

He watched as she pulled the jacket closed. So. She had caught him looking at her. She must be wondering what his intentions were. Hell, he wouldn't mind having her under him in bed. What man wouldn't? But he knew better than to think he could have what he wanted. She was the governor's daughter. He was a man who had grown up on the wrong side of the tracks.

He bent down on one knee beside the open door and realized with an inward sigh that she had brought him to his knees, after all. "Look, Blue Eyes—Miss Major—we have to talk."

She swallowed hard but said nothing.

He was uncomfortable kneeling beside the door, and there was always the chance she would get it into her head to scream again. He stood and closed the car door and started around the front of the Jaguar to the driver's side.

Before he had gotten halfway around the car, she shoved open her door and ran, screaming at the top of her lungs.

Burr caught her before she had gone twenty feet, tackling her like a football player, the two of them rolling over and over until they were stopped by a concrete abutment in a dark corner of the garage. He came to rest lying on top of her, uncomfortably aware of the feminine shape beneath him. His body reacted instantly, instinctively.

Burr was embarrassed and unable to stop the slow flush that climbed his throat. His body had responded like some randy teenager's to the feel of her flesh between his thighs, rather than like the rational, professional, thirty-six-year-old Texas Ranger he was. Hell, he was probably going to have to answer to the captain for that, too.

Lindsey recognized the hardness pressing against her abdomen and felt a renewed terror at her predicament. Worse, Burr's weight kept her from taking a breath, which she desperately needed since the fall had knocked the wind from her.

She knew frustration when she saw it. Her father rarely lost his temper, though he could become dangerously angry. Burr's dark eyes burned now with that same controlled fury.

"Damn you. I ought to…" He didn't finish his threat. His eyes searched the garage, looking for whoever might have heard her scream.

Her mouth worked as she gasped, "Please… Please. I…can't breathe."

He eased his weight onto his arms, but held her captive with his lower body—his aroused lower body. "That was a stupid thing to do, Blue Eyes."

She noticed he had given up the deferential *Miss Major.*

She felt a surge of hope when she saw a couple come out of the elevator and start toward their car.

"Don't make a sound," Burr hissed in her ear.

Lindsey opened her mouth to scream.

And Burr covered it with his.

There was nothing sensuous about his kiss. It was brutal, intended to keep her silent until the couple was gone. She bucked with all her strength at the same time she tried to bite him.

His mouth flattened, but he didn't otherwise respond to the pain she knew she must be causing him with her teeth. His hips pressed her down, so she felt the roughness of the concrete against her legs and back where her gown was rucked up.

She heard a car starting and the squeal of rubber on cement as it drove away. She closed her eyes so Burr wouldn't see the defeat she felt. A moment later he caught both her hands in one of his, while his other hand replaced his mouth to silence her.

"Look at me," he demanded. He used his hold on her to force her face toward him when she didn't respond and repeated, "Look at me!"

Lindsey opened her eyes and looked at him defiantly.

"In a moment I'm going to let you go. If you scream, I will knock you out—all the way out. Blink those pretty blue eyes of yours if you understand."

She blinked her eyes once, slowly.

He removed his hand, then stared at her, daring her to scream.

Burr watched in consternation as tears welled in the bluest eyes in Texas. They made her eyes luminescent and, he decided, even more attractive. He was aroused again—or still. And she was obviously terrified of him because of it. He quickly levered himself off of her and reached down to help her up. She refused his hand, stumbling to her feet.

Burr was just about to start explaining things when she ran again. He quickly caught her, shoving her up against the concrete wall. He stapled her hands flat on either side of her head against the rough surface and snapped, "Damn it, I'm a Texas Ranger! I've been working undercover. You're safe. Do you hear me? You're safe!"

"A Texas Ranger?"

Burr nodded curtly.

He felt her whole body relax against him. Then the tears came in earnest. It was obvious she was fighting them, and he debated whether he ought to try to comfort her. But that sort of thing could be easily misconstrued, and he already had enough to answer to for the captain for.

The heartrending sound of a broken sob moved him to put his arms around her and, once he had done that, it seemed the most natural thing in the world to pull her into his embrace and murmur calming words in her ear. His body once again reacted in a totally male way to her femaleness.

Burr had never had much use for prima donnas, and Lindsey Major certainly qualified as one. Unfortunately his body didn't know a thing about her personality; it was reacting strictly to the primeval need of male for female. He tightened his hold, feeling the swell of her breasts against his muscular chest.

Lindsey had thrown her arms around the Texas Ranger in relief, and they caught in the ponytail at his nape, which was surprisingly silky. She trembled at the feel of Burr's lips, soft and soothing against her forehead as he crooned words of comfort. And she was aware, again, of the fact that he was attracted to her in a way that was totally inappropriate to the situation.

Now that she was no longer in terror for her life, however, she realized with no little distress that his arousal had sparked an answering response from her. It was easiest to attribute her reaction to the Ranger as simple relief that he wasn't one of the bad guys. It couldn't possibly be more than that. She didn't know this man and, judging from the looks of him, he wasn't someone she would ever want to know. It would be best to defuse the situation as quickly as possible.

"You can let me go now," she said.

"What?" Burr had been so caught up in the pleasure of what he was doing that he was slow to notice the governor's daughter withdrawing from his embrace.

He met her gaze and saw the tears were gone, replaced by an icy look of disdain. The governor's daughter—a woman the newspapers had recently labeled an elusive ice princess because she was never seen twice with the same male escort—was back.

Burr stepped away, grabbed Lindsey's arm and, without looking back, dragged her toward his car.

Naturally she resisted. "Where are you taking me?"

Burr raised a brow at her commanding tone of voice. "Somewhere you'll be safe."

"I demand that you take me home."

"I'm afraid that isn't possible right now."

She dug in her heels, and he was forced to stop or hurt her. He didn't want to be accused of using unnecessary force.

"I insist you let me call my father right now and tell him I'm all right."

"Not here." Anticipating her argument, he explained, "There's still a chance one of Hector's goons may show up."

She hesitated, evaluating what he had said. "All right, I'll go with you. But we stop as soon as it's safe, and I call my father. Agreed?"

"Agreed." Of course, her idea of when it might be safe to stop and his probably differed. But Burr didn't think this was the time to bring that up.

The Jaguar was the kind of car Lindsey expected a man like Burr to own. Racy. Fast. Dark. Dangerous. She wondered if he had been given the car as part of his cover and realized she was having trouble making the leap from "bad guy" to "good guy" where he was concerned. Burr simply didn't look the part of guardian angel.

Burr opened the passenger door, shoved Lindsey in less carefully this time, and slammed it behind her. He slid over the hood and got in on the other side. The engine started with a roar that became a purr as he pulled out of the garage. He slipped from the city street onto I-35 and accelerated.

Lindsey blinked her eyes against the bright sunlight. The instant she realized Burr had gotten onto the interstate, her alarm returned. "Where are you going?"

"I told you, somewhere Hector can't find you."

Her eyes widened. "You never intended to let me make a phone call, did you?" She reached for the door handle.

"Don't even think about jumping out," he said. "You'd end up seriously injured or dead. Trust me."

"*Trust* you? First you hit me, then you fall on me like a beast in rut and manhandle me like I was some criminal, and now you're driving me God knows where and threatening me with dire consequences if I try to leave your august presence! Give me one good reason why I should trust you."

"I saved your life."

There was a moment of silence. "Well, there is that," she conceded ruefully.

"Look, I can't take you anywhere near the governor's mansion until I talk to my captain. Hector may have someone watching the place. I don't want to be seen returning you home. In fact, I've got to find someplace to hide us both.''

''Why do you have to hide?'' Her eyes went wide with a sudden horrible thought. ''You weren't lying about being a Ranger, were you?''

His lips curled in a bitter smile. ''No, I'm a Ranger, all right. But there's a slight problem nobody counted on.''

''What's that?''

''Hector is liable to be a bit perturbed when he finds out I killed his brother.''

''His brother?''

''Epifanio.''

''Oh, no!''

Lindsey bit her lip worriedly as Burr exited west onto U.S. 290 heading toward Fredericksburg and the hill country. A long, poignant silence developed as she watched the miles fly by. Her glance slid to the man driving the Jaguar. Maybe she simply hadn't given him the right incentive to take her home.

''I'm sure my father would reward you generously—with a great deal of money—if you would just take me home.''

''Do you think you're worth it?''

She arched an aristocratic brow. ''What do you mean?''

''I know for a fact you were warned not to go out last night. Why did you?''

''That's none of your business.''

''You made it my business when you got yourself kidnapped.''

''I had promised to attend the ball. I had to go.''

"So you were just doing what spoiled little rich girls do, is that it?"

"Spoiled—" Lindsey bit back her retort. She wasn't going to argue with a man wearing a ponytail and a diamond earring. "You know nothing about me."

"I know what I read in the papers."

Lindsey laughed. "I suspected you were a fool. Now I've got proof."

He glanced sharply at her.

"Anyone who believes what he reads in the papers—"

"Is a fool?" he interrupted. "But then, I've had a chance to judge you for myself now. At least one thing they said is true. You've got the bluest eyes I've ever seen. And from the looks of you, I'm inclined to believe there's some truth in the rest of what I've read."

"You mean, that I'm spoiled rotten, the 'very much indulged' daughter of a very powerful man?" Lindsey said, her voice rife with indignation as she quoted a recent society news article.

"If the panty hose fit…"

He took his eyes off the road long enough to give her a thorough perusal with eyes that held their share of disapproval and disdain.

Lindsey gave him a withering look of scorn. "Appearances can be deceiving."

He snorted. "You can say that again."

She noticed with some alarm that he had turned off the highway onto a winding dirt road that was shaded by live oaks. "Where are we going?"

"Someplace private where I can use the phone."

"Remember, I want to talk to my father."

He brought the Jaguar to a stop in front of a small wooden cabin with a roofed porch and a stone chimney. The cabin was unpainted, and the split wood had been aged by wind and weather. There was a picture window in front, with a door to one side of it.

"Get inside," he said.

Lindsey sat where she was.

"Go on," he said. "There's no one here but us."

Lindsey stayed where she was. "What is this place?"

Burr exited the car, slid over the hood and opened her door. "Are you coming out of there on your own, or am I going to have to drag you out?"

Lindsey dipped a bare foot out of the car. She winced when she encountered the small, sharp stones on the drive. Before she had taken two painful steps, Burr swept her up into his arms. She instinctively grabbed his shoulders. The muscles beneath the T-shirt were rock hard. Her eyes met his, questioning.

"You don't weigh as much as I thought you would."

She flushed at the insult buried in the compliment. She was five-ten in her stocking feet, and nobody had ever accused her of being skinny. Fortunately, he was easily six inches taller. He carried her up to the porch and set her down.

She didn't thank him. After all, it wasn't her fault she didn't have any shoes.

Burr opened the door and gave her a nudge inside. Lindsey lifted her chin and, once she regained her balance, walked past him as regally as a queen. She thought she heard him grunt in disgust, but refused to give him the satisfaction of a response.

She looked around the cabin, which was sparingly furnished. There was an old leather couch and a raw-hide-covered chair in front of the stone fireplace. The hardwood floor was polished to a high sheen, but there were no rugs of any kind on it. Nor were there curtains on any of the windows.

She could see the kitchen from the living room. It contained a small wooden table and two ladderback chairs. She suspected the other doorway led to the bedroom and bath. There wasn't room for much else.

She turned to face Burr with her hands folded in front of her. "Now what?"

"Now I have to make some calls."

Lindsey looked around for a phone, but didn't see one.

"Not here," he said. "I have to go into town."

"What am I supposed to do while you're gone?"

"Wait here for me."

Lindsey swallowed her outrage and managed to say in a reasonable voice, "Why can't I go with you?"

"I can't take the chance you'll draw attention with those blue eyes of yours. You'll be safer here."

"I can always wear sunglasses," she snapped.

"I don't have a pair handy. Do you?"

Obviously she didn't.

"You'll be safer here," he said.

"Safer?" she asked in a sharp voice. "What if one of Hector's men finds me here? I'm totally defense-less!"

GET 2

HOW TO GET YOUR 2 FREE BOOKS AND FREE GIFT!

1. Peel off the MIRA sticker on the front cover. Place it in the space provided at right. This automatically entitles you to receive two free books and an exciting surprise gift.

2. Send back this card and you'll get 2 "The Best of the Best™" novels. These books have a combined cover price of $11.98 or more in the U.S. and $13.98 or more in Canada, but they are yours to keep absolutely FREE!

3. There's no catch. You're under no obligation to buy anything. We charge nothing — ZERO — for your first shipment. And you don't have to make any minimum number of purchases — not even one!

4. We call this line "The Best of the Best" because each month you'll receive the best books by some of today's most popular authors. These authors show up time and time again on all the major bestseller lists and their books sell out as soon as they hit the stores. You'll like the convenience of getting them delivered to your home at our special discount prices . . . and you'll love your *Heart to Heart* subscriber newsletter featuring author news, horoscopes, recipes, book reviews and much more!

SPECIAL FREE GIFT!

We'll send you a fabulous surprise gift, absolutely FREE, simply for accepting our no-risk offer!

5. We hope that after receiving your free books you'll want to remain a subscriber. But the choice is yours — to continue or cancel, anytime at all! So why not take us up on our invitation, with no risk of any kind. You'll be glad you did!

6. And remember...we'll send you a surprise gift ABSOLUTELY FREE just for giving "The Best of the Best" a try.

Visit us online at
www.mirabooks.com

® and TM are trademarks of Harlequin Enterprises Limited.

BOOKS FREE!

The Best of the Best™ — Here's How it Works:

Burr snorted. "I wouldn't say that. You didn't do so badly at the hotel."

"You know what I mean," she said with asperity. "I know what Hector had planned for me. I heard you talking through the door." She paused and admitted, "I'm scared."

Burr's eyes narrowed. He seemed to debate a moment before he spoke. "You've got nothing to fear if you stay here."

Lindsey looked at him, really looked at him. At the long hair. The earring. The twice-broken nose. The snake tattoo. "I repeat, I don't see anything that leads me to believe I can trust you to have my best interests at heart."

"As someone recently told me, appearances can be deceiving."

"I won't stay here alone," she said. "The moment you're gone, I'll walk back to the road."

"I'm sorry to hear that."

He moved amazingly fast, catching her arms and dragging them behind her. He found rope in the kitchen and tied her hands. He wasn't precisely rough, but he yanked the clothesline cord tight around her wrists. He pushed her toward the open doorway that led to what turned out to be, as she had suspected, the bedroom.

He picked her up and dumped her on the bed before tying her ankles together. "You should do all right here until I come back."

"How long is that going to be?" She felt humiliated and indignant, and both of those emotions were apparent in her voice.

"Not long enough for you to work yourself free of those ropes," he said, as though reading her mind. "Just lie still and be good. I'll bring you back something to eat."

Lindsey suddenly realized she was famished. It had been almost twenty-four hours since her last meal. But she refused to be mollified by the bone he had thrown her. "My father will have your badge when he hears about how you've treated me. You'll be writing parking tickets for the rest of your life!"

"I'm sorry to have to do this," he said as he tied a pillowcase around her mouth. "I don't think there's anybody around to hear you if you scream, but I can't take the chance."

Then he was gone. She heard stones scattering as he left the driveway. She immediately tested her bonds, but they didn't give. She began looking around the room to see what she might use to cut herself free. Then it dawned on her that he hadn't tied her to the bed. There was nothing to keep her from just getting up and hopping away.

Burr was worried. He wondered whether it might not have been smarter to take the governor's daughter home, after all. But he knew that wouldn't have solved anything. Hector would just make some attempt on some other member of the family. No, this had to be solved while Hector still thought someone on his side had the woman.

Burr was also angry with himself for not finding some other way to rescue "the bluest eyes in Texas" without having to kill Hector's brother. But he hadn't been given a choice. At least he had the girl—the woman, he corrected himself—to bargain with. And what a woman!

Lindsey Major was the kind of woman he had always dreamed about, whenever he let himself dream. She was tall, with lush curves and soft skin. He knew about the soft skin because he'd had to touch her to tie her up. And he knew about the curves because he had picked her up and held her in his arms.

Burr felt his body respond to the memory of how she had felt with her warm breasts nestled against his chest. He cursed under his breath. He might as well desire some image on a movie screen. He had about the same chance of intimacy with the governor's blue-eyed daughter.

He found a phone booth in the small town closest to the cabin. The town consisted of a gas station and a general store, which also contained a post office. People stopped here for gas or to get a soda on their way to hunt in the hill country, or on their way to go floating down the many streams in the area on an inflated inner tube. He hadn't come here once in the eighteen months he had worked for Hector, and he was pretty sure there was no way Hector could trace him here.

He called the governor's mansion, knowing that was where the captain would be. It took a while for someone to acknowledge who he was and to get the captain on the phone.

"I've been compromised," Burr said.

"Damn!" A pause and then, "Is she safe?"

"I've got her."

"Where?"

"At my cabin in the hill country."

"What happened?"

"I had to kill Hector's brother."

"Come on in, Burr. The game's up."

Burr shook his head, then realized Captain Rogers couldn't see him. "No, Captain. I haven't spent the past eighteen months undercover with these bastards to have it all go down the drain now. I think I can still get Hector. But I need to do something with the governor's daughter. Is there someplace I can drop her off?"

There was a long pause, and Burr heard Captain Rogers discussing the situation with those around him.

"You there, Burr?"

"Yes, sir."

"I want you to call Hector and tell him you're willing to deal for the governor's daughter." Frank continued speaking, telling Burr the details of the plan he had worked out with the other law enforcement officials who had responded to the governor's call for assistance.

When Frank had finished, Burr said, "I don't like it. I could manage better without the woman."

"She's safe with you. We'll take care of Hector."

"Hector's not going to deal unless he sees me in person," Burr said.

"You call him. Offer him the deal. Then sit tight with Miss Major."

"I think Miss Major would be happier if she went home."

"That's not an option, Burr."

"But, sir—"

"Don't waste your breath arguing. The decision has been made. Miss Major stays with you."

Burr heard someone ask for the phone.

"This is Governor Major. Who am I speaking to?"

"This is Ranger Lieutenant Covington," Burr replied.

"How is my daughter?" the governor asked. "Is she all right?"

Burr heard the emotion in the governor's voice. *He's going to have my head, all right. Just like she said.* "She's fine, Governor."

"She's not hurt?"

"No, sir. She's just as beautiful as the newspapers say. And just as contrary." Burr swore under his breath. *Why did I say that? I'm going to get my tail kicked all the way back to Austin for insubordination.*

He heard the governor chuckle. "That's my girl, all right." He gave a patent sigh of relief. "Thank you, Lieutenant Covington. Take care of her for me."

"Yes, sir. I will, sir."

"You heard the governor, Burr," the captain said. "I'll get back to you when we've taken care of Hector. Until then, you take care of Miss Major."

"Yes, sir." Burr waited for a click, then slammed the phone onto the hook. A moment later he picked it up again and began to dial.

When Hector came on the line, Burr pricked him by asking, "Did you lose something?"

"Where is she?" Hector demanded.

"I've got her."

"What happened?"

Burr said nothing.

"I asked you what happened."

"They gave me no choice."

"The girl belongs to me. I want her."

"I want to make a deal, Hector."

"You bring her to me now, and I might let you live," Hector said. "Otherwise, I'll hunt you down. And kill you and the girl both."

Burr quickly gave Hector the terms Captain Rogers had outlined. When Hector arrived at the rendezvous site, there would be law enforcement officials of all kinds waiting to apprehend him.

"I'll keep the girl as insurance," Burr said. "You'll get her when you show up with the money."

"You're a dead man, Burr," Hector said.

"If you don't get the girl back, you can't negotiate with the governor for the Turk's life," Burr reminded him.

Burr hung up the phone on Hector's threat to kill him slowly when he caught up to him. After a stop to buy supplies, he was careful not to be seen leaving town and watched to make sure he wasn't being followed when he turned onto the dirt road that led to the cabin.

It was time he had a talk with the governor's daughter. He went directly to the bedroom where he had left her.

She was gone.

Chapter Three

If she had possessed a decent pair of shoes, Lindsey thought, she could have made it to the main road. But the men's cowboy boots she had found in the closet of the cabin weren't doing the job, even with two extra pairs of socks.

She hid behind a tree when she saw the Jaguar returning along the dusty road. Burr would know in a moment or two that she was gone, and he would come looking for her. There was no sense running. Not in these damned boots. But she wasn't sure she wanted to give up, either. Being in Burr's custody hadn't exactly been a picnic so far.

She rubbed her shoulder where she had bruised herself falling out of the high, four-poster bed, and ran a gentle finger over the cuts at her wrists where she had used a knife from the kitchen to free herself. It had been stupid to try to escape. In all probability, her father had demanded her return, and Burr had come back to set her free.

She hadn't decided yet whether she was going to complain about what Burr had done to her. He was responsible for more than a few of the bruises she now bore. She moved her jaw cautiously. It was swollen and sore, but she was pretty sure he hadn't hit her as hard as he could have.

"Have a nice walk?"

Lindsey stiffened at the sarcasm in Burr's voice. She turned slowly to face him, gritting her teeth when she saw the amusement in his eyes at the outfit she was wearing.

"You look like a little girl dressed up in her father's clothes."

Lindsey looked down at the oversize orange University of Texas sweatshirt, men's jeans, and boots she was wearing. The jeans were held up with some of the rope that had been used to tie her hands. "This was all I could find."

"If you'd just been a little patient, I would have solved the problem for you. I bought some things for you in town."

"I won't need them, because you're going to be taking me home," Lindsey said in a firm voice.

He shook his head. "I'm afraid not."

"My father—"

"I spoke to the governor personally. He agreed you'd be safer with me until Hector's been picked up."

Lindsey felt her chin begin to tremble. "How long is that going to take?"

"Until tomorrow, if we're lucky."

"And if we're not?"

"We'll worry about that when the time comes." Burr reached out a hand and traced the bruise on her jaw. "I'm sorry about that."

Lindsey jerked her head away. "You've got a lot more than that to be sorry for!"

His eyes grew cold. "I was doing my job the best way I knew how. If you had paid attention to the warnings you were given—"

"I had no warning about anything like this!"

"You were told Hector was making plans."

Lindsey bit her lip. "I didn't think—"

"Your kind never does," Burr interrupted.

Lindsey's face flamed with anger "This isn't my fault!"

"It sure as hell isn't mine!" Burr retorted. "I spent eighteen long, lousy months undercover with the Texas Mafia, trying to get enough information to prove Hector Martinez ordered the death of a friend of mine. Thanks to you, prosecuting Hector for that crime isn't going to happen now."

There was a pause while Lindsey absorbed what he had said. "I'm sorry."

"Yeah, well, sorry doesn't cut it, Blue Eyes."

"Don't call me that!"

"I have it on good authority—the news media— that you're the lady with the bluest eyes in Texas."

"My eyes have nothing whatsoever to do with who I am."

"What you are is arrogant and uncooperative."

"How dare you—"

"You ready to walk back now?"

Lindsey stuck her chin in the air and began walking back toward the cabin. Her stride was hampered by a broken blister on her left heel.

"Something wrong with your leg?"

Lindsey heard the concern in Burr's voice, but answered haughtily, "Nothing that concerns you."

She continued her determined limp toward the cabin.

Lindsey gave a cry of surprise as Burr swung her up into his arms, shifting her until he was holding her close, with her breasts crushed against his chest. Her arms involuntarily circled his neck. She sought out his face and was surprised to find his eyes hooded, his nostrils flared. She was unnerved by the male energy vibrating from the man whose arms had closed securely around her shoulders and under her knees. Her eyes came to rest on his mouth, which was partly open, the lips full, the mouth wide.

"What do you think…" Her voice was raspy, so she cleared her throat and tried again. "What do you think you're doing, Mr.—? What *is* your last name, anyway?"

"Covington," Burr replied. "I thought I'd give you a lift back to the cabin." He had already started walking, in fact. He kept his eyes focused straight ahead.

"Did it ever occur to you that I would rather walk than be put in the position of accepting your help?"

"There are a lot of things that occur to me when I think about you." *Like how good you feel in my arms. Like how those blue eyes of yours would look if I was inside you making sweet, sweet love to you.*

Lindsey didn't bother asking Burr to explain himself. She didn't want to exacerbate the situation. She held on to his neck because that eased the weight he had to carry in his arms, not because the silky hair at his nape felt good. She snuggled closer so he wouldn't drop her, not because she liked the feel of hard muscle pressing against her breasts. And she laid her face against his throat so she wouldn't have to look at him, not because she wanted to smell the essence of him on his skin and clothes.

When they arrived at the cabin, Burr set her down on the porch and offered her an olive branch. "Look, if we're going to be stuck together for the next twenty-four hours, we may as well call a truce."

"I wasn't aware there was a war going on."

Burr snickered. "Fine, Blue Eyes. I don't mind the sniping if you don't."

"Wait!" Lindsey laid a hand on Burr's arm. She recoiled when she realized she had touched the snake tattoo.

His lips curled in a cynical smile. "Not the kind of thing you're used to, is it?"

Lindsey's eyes narrowed. "I don't understand why you're so determined to insult me. And I should mention, it isn't doing your career any good."

"Is that a threat, *Blue Eyes?*" Burr said in a low voice.

"That would be rather foolish under the circumstances," Lindsey conceded. "I am, after all, at your mercy for the next twenty-four hours. It would seem discretion is the better part of valor. Truce?" She held out her hand for Burr to shake.

Burr's hand enveloped hers, and she realized for the first time how big he was, and how strong, and that his palm and fingertips were callused as though he worked with his hands. Perhaps he did in his spare time. She knew little or nothing about him.

"You can change in the bedroom while I cook us something to eat."

Lindsey disappeared into the bedroom and shut the door behind her. She was surprised at how well the jeans fit, not to mention the tennis shoes. However, she decided she would rather walk barefoot until she could find a Band-Aid for the blister on her heel. She pulled on a T-shirt that pictured a dead armadillo on the front with the words Road Kill blazoned across it and headed back to the kitchen.

Burr was dismayed at how the jeans fit her. They outlined her legs and fanny too well. And the T-shirt was downright dangerous. She had obviously abandoned the merry widow, and he could see the soft curve of her breasts beneath the cotton. He frowned when he realized she was barefoot. The sight of her toes curling on the hardwood floor made her look as vulnerable as a child. Only she was a full-grown, red-blooded woman. And his body responded to her like a full-grown, red-blooded man.

"The shoes didn't fit?" He was amazed at how rough his voice sounded. He turned back to the stove to hide the bulge that was making his jeans uncomfortably snug.

"I was wondering if you have a Band-Aid."

At his look of confusion, she set her bare foot up on the counter beside him and showed him the blister on her heel.

"See?"

Whoever would have thought an ankle could be

such a source of erotic stimulation? Burr stared at her foot until his eyes glazed, then forced his attention back to the potatoes he was frying on the stove. "Don't have a Band-Aid. I'll get one tomorrow when I go into town."

"Guess I'll have to go barefoot until then." She put her foot back on the floor and wiggled her toes. "It feels kind of nice," she admitted. "I can't remember the last time I walked around barefoot. Oh, yes, I do," she said.

To Burr's relief, she wandered to the kitchen table and sat down. He bent over and checked the steaks in the oven broiler to hide his state of arousal.

"I was six, and my mother and father took me to Padre Island, to the beach. My mother was pregnant with Carl—he's my younger brother—and I got to race up and down the beach barefoot. I loved it."

"That was a long time ago," Burr said.

"Yes, it was. Those were some of the last carefree days my family had. Father entered politics that year. I didn't see as much of him after that. He was always on the road campaigning, first for state representative, then for congressman, and finally for governor."

Talk about Lindsey's father reminded Burr of who she was, and why he had to keep his distance. If he was lucky, he would get out of this situation with no more than a reprimand. If he let his libido get out of hand, there was no telling what the consequences would be. Only, it was damned hard to remember who she was when she was slouched back comfortably in the kitchen chair with her fingers meshed behind her head, raising the tips of her breasts against the T-shirt. Her right ankle was crossed over the opposite knee, in a naturally sexy pose.

He checked the steaks again. "These are about ready. How do you like yours?"

"Pink."

The word brought to mind all kinds of things Lieutenant Burr Covington would rather not think about. Lips. Blushing cheeks. Nipples. *Damn it, Covington, get your mind off the woman! She's out of bounds. Got it?*

"Do you have any wine?" she asked.

Burr stared at her in confusion.

"To go with the steak," she explained. "I love a dry red wine with steak."

Burr snorted. "I've got some beer."

"Lite?"

He snorted again, only this time it turned into a rumbly sort of laugh. "Hell, Blue Eyes, how about a diet cola?"

Her eyes reflected her disappointment, but she said, "I'll take it." And then, to explain herself, added, "I never learned to like beer, but the lite beers don't seem to taste as bad."

"You wouldn't have lasted long in my neighborhood," Burr muttered.

"What neighborhood is that?" Lindsey inquired.

"The wrong side of the tracks in Houston."

"Is that where you got the tattoo?"

Burr held his arm up and looked at it as though the tattoo had suddenly appeared there. "Yeah."

"May I look at it?"

He held his arm toward her. To his chagrin, she

got up from the table and came over to him. He held his breath as she traced the shape of the coiled, hooded cobra with her fingertips.

Then she looked up at him, catching him like a deer in a set of headlights with those blue eyes of hers. "Does the snake mean something special?"

"It was an initiation rite of the gang I was in as a kid." He rubbed his skin, which was suddenly covered with goose bumps, brushing her hand away in the process.

"You were in a street gang in Houston?" Her eyes went wide with astonishment.

"Yeah."

"What? I mean…how…"

"The steaks are done," Burr said. "Sit down and I'll serve up supper."

Burr knew she was curious about his past, but she could just stay that way. He had decided talking to her wasn't such a good idea after all. He managed to think of grisly things all through supper, which kept his mind off the woman across the table from him. Or mostly kept his mind off her. She ate like she was starving, not at all like a dainty debutante. She cleaned her plate with a gusto that made him wonder if she did everything—and his mind was picturing all sorts of indiscrete activities—with that sort of relish.

"That was delicious," Lindsey said when she finished.

She made no offer to wash the dishes, not that Burr had thought she would. He didn't suppose a governor's daughter got KP duty too often. He thought about just taking care of them himself, but damn it, he was tired. And he had done the cooking.

"You'll find the dish soap under the sink."

Lindsey stared at him blankly for a moment, until she realized what he was implying. "Oh."

In case she wasn't perfectly clear on what he meant, Burr said, "I cooked, you clean."

"I suppose that's fair." She rose and began clearing the table.

Burr was impressed by her willingness to do her share. Unfortunately, he was unable to sit and be waited on. His mother hadn't allowed it when he was growing up, and he couldn't make himself do it now just to spite a woman who couldn't help the fact she had been raised with a silver spoon in her mouth.

"I'll scrape the dishes," he said. "You wash and I'll dry."

"All right."

She was so careful with the dishes, he knew the job wasn't one she was familiar with. "I don't expect you have to wash dishes in the mansion too often."

"No," she said with a quick grin. "I hadn't realized how much fun it is."

"Fun?" He felt his body draw up tight as he watched the way she caressed a plate with a cloth hidden by a mound of white soapy bubbles. Then she rubbed the cloth around and around inside a coffee cup. Burr felt his cheeks heat. He had never realized washing dishes could be such a sensuous experience. He threw his towel on the counter and headed for the living room. "We can let the rest dry in the drainer. I'll light a fire. It's getting cool outside."

He knelt down in front of the stone fireplace and dropped his forehead to his knee. In twenty hours he would be free of her. He just had to hold on until then. He busied himself building a fire and soon had it crackling. When he turned around, he found Lindsey sitting cross-legged on the couch behind him.

"This is nice," she said.

Too nice, Burr thought. The fire lit up her eyes and made her skin glow with warmth. He had liked it better when she was fighting him. At least then he was being constantly reminded why getting personally involved with the governor's daughter—an ice princess and a spoiled brat, not to mention the girl with "the bluest eyes in Texas"—was a bad idea.

He sat down where he was and crossed his legs, keeping the distance of the room between them. It wasn't enough, of course. But it would have to do.

"What's it like to live in the spotlight?" he asked.

"You wouldn't like it," she replied.

He raised a brow. "Why not?"

"People who don't know a thing about you are always making judgments about you."

"No, I wouldn't like that. I suppose you believe you've been judged unfairly."

"I'm not what the newspapers say I am," she said.

"And what is that?"

"I'm not arrogant, for one thing. Or coldhearted."

Burr cocked a disbelieving brow but didn't say anything.

"It's just that I don't suffer fools gladly."

"I see."

"I don't think you do," she said in a voice that

dripped ice. "There is another side of me, a private side, that no one ever sees."

His lips curled in a mocking smile, which suggested that if she believed what she was saying—about not being arrogant or coldhearted—she didn't see herself very clearly. "I guess I haven't met that other woman yet."

"Nor will you," she said in her haughtiest voice. She rose imperiously. "I'm tired. I think I'll go to bed now." Then she turned her back on him and stalked to the bedroom, her fanny gloriously displayed in the skintight jeans.

Burr gritted his teeth. Eighteen hours. She would be gone then, and he would never have to lay eyes on her again. He stayed where he was until he was sure she had the bedroom door closed. Then he rose and settled himself on the couch, using a pillow and the afghan to make himself a bed. He lay staring at the fire for a long time before he finally fell asleep.

Meanwhile, Lindsey was finding it impossible to relax. She didn't want to turn off the lamp, but it had a high-wattage bulb that flooded the room with light. When she tried the dark, it was too frightening. Memories of her kidnapping returned, of waking up in the hotel room, and the deaths of the two villains Burr had been forced to kill. She wanted to go home, to return to the somewhat normal life she had led before all this had happened.

She kept remembering Burr's accusations about her character. If she had been disdainful of the men she met, it was because they treated her like some stone goddess, not a flesh-and-blood woman. Or they were so puffed up with their own consequence they expected her to fall gratefully at their feet. Or they were more interested in her father's political power than in her.

Burr fit none of those neat categories. He wasn't intimidated by her position, and in his arms she was anything but a woman of stone. Her father's power had failed to influence him. She found it amazing and utterly frustrating that a man she found so intriguing seemed to be doing his level best to ignore her!

Her attraction to Burr surprised her more than a little. After all, he was a gang member from Houston who had somehow become a Texas Ranger. And he certainly looked the part.

Appearances.

Lindsey, who had spent her life being judged by her looks, was appalled to realize she had been equally judgmental of Burr's outward trappings. There must be more to him than what showed on the surface. Otherwise, why had she been so drawn to him?

Maybe she found Burr so fascinating because he was different, because he came from the wrong side of the tracks, because he was dangerous. Burr possessed a different kind of power than her father wielded, but there was no doubt Burr Covington was a powerful man. And one who was far more likely to get himself shot than any politician or businessman or financier she could have chosen to fall in love with. And yet, she had been willing to give in to the powerful attraction she felt toward him.

He had made it clear he wasn't interested.

That was another totally new experience for Lindsey Major, debutante and governor's daughter. Normally, men fawned on her and begged for her favor. She refused them; they didn't refuse her. She felt humbled, humiliated, and hurt by the Ranger's rejection of her.

Those feelings lasted about as long as it took Lindsey to acknowledge them. They were replaced almost instantaneously by annoyance and determination. She had spent a lifetime using her famous eyes to cajole, entreat and demand what she wanted and rarely failed to get her own way. She didn't want Burr Covington, but she did want a little revenge to assuage her ego. It would be a simple matter to get him to admit he wanted her and then refuse his advances.

Lindsey figured she had about seventeen hours to bring Burr Covington to his knees.

Chapter Four

Lindsey woke to a steady thudding sound, which she finally recognized as an ax striking wood. She got out of bed, crossed to the curtainless window and looked out onto the backyard of the cabin.

Burr was dressed in nothing but a pair of worn jeans, and goose bumps rose on her arms at the sight of him. He had shaved, and she was surprised to see that he looked almost handsome. The broken nose gave his face character, she decided. His hair, free of the ponytail, was plastered to his forehead by sweat and hung in damp curls on his bare shoulders.

He had been working hard enough splitting logs that his muscular torso glistened. Her gaze was drawn to a crystal drop of liquid as it rolled downward across a washboard belly toward his navel. She noticed the scabbed-over cut near his ribs where Epifanio had slashed him with his knife. It wasn't the only mark on his body. There was also a scar near his collarbone that looked suspiciously like a healed bullet wound. She wondered whether he had gotten it as a kid in a Houston gang, or during his duties as a Texas Ranger.

As she watched, he paused and wiped his forehead

with a bandanna he pulled from a rear pocket of his jeans.

And noticed her staring at him from the window.

She leapt back out of sight, then realized that was foolish, since he had already seen her. She took a deep breath, shoved the window open and leaned out, unaware that the V-necked T-shirt she was wearing gave Burr a revealing glimpse of female pulchritude. "Good morning," she called.

"There's coffee and cereal in the kitchen," Burr replied curtly. He began swinging the ax again.

She had been dismissed.

Whatever second thoughts Lindsey might have harbored about her plan to bring Burr Covington to his knees flew out the window along with a fly that had been buzzing by her ear. So he thought he could ignore her, did he?

You're being childish about this, Lindsey.

Am I?

The man is only trying to do his job.

That Ranger has insulted me for the last time.

He doesn't strike me as the kind of man who'd ever kowtow to a woman.

Just wait. I haven't been labeled the girl with the bluest eyes in Texas for the past seven years without learning a few things about how to manipulate the male of the species.

Lindsey stripped off the overlarge T-shirt she had slept in and took a quick shower. Then she put on the T-shirt, jeans and tennis shoes Burr had bought for her in town, using some tissues to cushion the blister on her heel.

She didn't normally have more than toast and coffee for breakfast, but the colorful box of sugar-coated kids' cereal on the table looked tempting. She poured herself a bowl, doused it with milk, then surprised herself by eating ravenously. Maybe being kidnapped had given her an appetite. As she munched the last few bites of cereal, Lindsey pondered how she could best seduce the Ranger.

Now you're going to seduce *him?*

How else am I going to lay him low?

How about an intellectual argument?

Somehow that wouldn't be the same.

It sure sounds safer than bearding the lion in his den.

He may look like a lion, but by the time I'm through with him, he'll be following me around like Mary's little lamb.

It dawned on Lindsey that while she had gathered a large male following over the years, she had done nothing purposely to garner their attention, other than having blue eyes, of course. Unfortunately, Burr hadn't fallen under her spell. For the first time, she was going to have to do something other than flutter her eyelashes to attract a man. Since everything else about her was rather ordinary, she wasn't sure exactly what she was going to use for bait. Maybe having an intellectual discussion with Burr wasn't such a bad idea after all.

Burr was immediately aware of Lindsey when she

headed out the back door toward him. She had a graceful walk without the limp. Her hair was tied up in a ponytail that made her look a lot younger and more approachable. She wasn't wearing any makeup, either. She looked about twenty and as innocent as a lamb. However, he knew that wasn't possible. A woman like Lindsey Major was sure to have put a few notches in her bedpost. Not that it was any of his business. Besides, having been around more than a little himself, he was in no position to be throwing stones at glass houses.

"Is there anything I can do to help?" Lindsey asked when she reached Burr's side.

"I need to haul some of this wood inside, but otherwise, I'm done here."

"I'd be glad to help with that, but do you suppose we could go for a walk first?"

Burr's gaze shot to her feet. "Are you going to be all right in those shoes?"

"If not, I'll just take them off and go barefoot."

Burr noticed Lindsey was looking everywhere but at him. He set down the ax and mopped his chest and back and under his arms with the T-shirt he had taken off when he had started working.

An enchanting flush rose on Lindsey's face.

Surely this isn't the first time she's seen a man working without a shirt! Burr thought. But she was clearly affected by the sight of him, so he stuck his arms in the plaid Western shirt with folded-up sleeves that had come off at the same time as the T-shirt and buttoned a couple of the buttons.

"I'm ready when you are," he said.

She gave him a gamine smile and headed off toward a cluster of pecan trees in the distance that surrounded a pond deep enough to swim in. He followed after her, wondering why she was being so friendly all of a sudden. He didn't think she had changed her opinion of him overnight, so he was naturally suspicious of her intentions.

He kept his eyes on her, which was easy, considering how her fanny moved in the tight-fitting jeans. There was a sexy little sway to her walk that was as enticing as any perfume he had ever smelled. He realized that if she had walked off a cliff, he probably would have followed her over the edge. The sunshine did something magical to her hair, revealing a dozen different shades from red-gold to golden chestnut. He saw the pleasure on her face as she closed her eyes and tilted her head back, basking in the sunlight.

Burr felt his body responding to the woman in front of him. More disturbing, however, was the way his mind recorded all the sensual data about her. As a Ranger, he was used to making snap judgments about people based on their actions. The way she walked told him she liked being a woman, and that she had a great deal of self-confidence. The sun-streaked hair told him she spent a lot of time outdoors, and that she probably had an expensive hairdresser. And the way she turned her face up to the sun told him she was a sensual person, ready to greet with open arms whatever life had to offer.

He tried to make that evaluation of Lindsey Major

mesh with what he had read about her and what he had experienced so far in her company. The pictures didn't match.

"Penny for your thoughts?"

Burr hadn't even realized Lindsey had stopped. She was facing him with her hands on her hips. He took one look at the beautiful woman in front of him and said, "Why aren't you married?"

"I don't think that's any of your business."

"I suppose not. I just wondered why a beautiful woman like you hasn't found herself a husband and settled down to raise a family."

"I've already got a family."

Burr frowned. "I don't understand."

Lindsey turned and started walking toward the trees again, and Burr fell into stride beside her.

"Since the Turk killed my mother five years ago, I've been responsible for raising my younger brother, Carl, and my sister, Stella."

"Seems to me your father ought to be doing that."

She turned and gave him a bittersweet smile. "He doesn't have the time. He's a public servant who takes his duties seriously. I also act as my father's hostess at dinners. You can see why I don't have time to go hunting for a husband."

"I wouldn't think you'd have to go hunting," Burr said frankly.

Lindsey glanced sideways at Burr, and his heart jumped. Her eyes seemed to invite all kinds of things he knew she couldn't possibly intend. Her next words suggested she meant everything her sultry gaze had conveyed.

"I haven't met anyone I was interested in getting to know." She paused. "Until you."

Burr stopped in his tracks. He was used to keeping his feelings to himself, but it took a great deal of effort to keep the astonishment—not to mention the suspicion—off his face. "I find that a little hard to believe."

"You're…different."

Burr smirked. "I see. Is it the broken nose or the tattoo you find so fascinating?"

"That's not fair!" Lindsey retorted.

The heat in her face told him he had hit the nail on the head.

"I'm sure there's more to you than your appearance suggests," she said, compounding her error.

Burr laughed out loud.

"I was trying to *compliment* you!"

"I don't think I've ever been damned so well by such faint praise."

"What I meant is that I don't think I've seen the real Burr Covington yet, and I'm curious what's behind the 'bad boy' facade."

"What you see is what you get."

She shook her head, sending her ponytail swinging in the breeze. "I'm convinced there's more to you than meets the eye, and I'm determined to get to know the real Burr Covington before the day ends."

"What's the sense of that?" Burr asked. "After I

return you to your father this afternoon, we'll never see each other again.''

''It doesn't have to be that way,'' Lindsey said in a quiet voice.

Burr's lips curled in a cynical smile. ''What kind of rig are you running, Blue Eyes? What is it you want from me?''

She looked at him with those stunning eyes, and he felt his heart skip a beat. He hadn't expected to be as vulnerable as the rest of the pack that worshipped the bluest eyes in Texas. But he found himself wondering what it would be like to wake up to those eyes every morning for the rest of his life. He shook his head to break free of her spell.

''Well?'' he demanded. ''What is it you want?''

''I'm attracted to you,'' she blurted. ''I thought—''

''Oh, no, you don't. I am not, I repeat, *not* getting involved with the governor's daughter. I'm supposed to be guarding you, for Christ's sake!''

He didn't know quite how it happened, but she took the few steps to reach him and laid her hands on his chest and looked up at him, her lips parted.

''I want you to kiss me,'' she said in a husky voice.

Burr's hands clamped down on Lindsey's arms so hard they were liable to be bruised when he let go. But, hell, better that than the other alternative, which was to kiss the woman—which he had to admit had crossed his mind as a potentially pleasant experience—and damn the consequences.

''We are *not* going to do this.''

''Why not?''

"Because you are who you are, and I am who I am."

"That's not a very good reason to deny ourselves."

"Then I'll give you a few more. I grew up in a gang in Houston—you grew up as Texas royalty. I live life in the trenches—you amble along up top. And this situation is only temporary. You wouldn't look twice at me if we weren't stuck here together."

Her eyes flashed, and she stabbed a forefinger against his chest. "Hogwash. The only thing that matters is whether or not you're as attracted to me as I am to you. Are you?"

He let her go and forked a hand through his hair in agitation. "All right, I'm attracted to you! Is that what you wanted to hear?"

She grinned from ear to ear. "It's a start."

"Just remember you asked for this."

Burr captured her in his arms and lowered his mouth to hers. He felt her catch fire when he put his tongue in her mouth to taste her, but he didn't stop there. He had wanted to hold her breasts since he had first caught sight of them. He shoved his hand up under her T-shirt and palmed her flesh. She made a sound of protest before arching into his hand. He used his other hand to hold her close while he rubbed himself against her with a body that was stone hard. When he let her go at last, there was a stunned look on her face.

He took a step back and let out a shuddering breath. "Is that what you were after, Blue Eyes? Be sure it's what you want before you start playing games with me again." He didn't recognize his voice. It was harsh and grated like a rusty gate.

"I wasn't...I didn't mean..." Her denials fell flat because she had goaded him, and she had meant to provoke exactly the response she had gotten. Only the encounter had been far more devastating for her than she had imagined. She felt shattered. Overwhelmed. Aroused. And afraid to act on what she was feeling for fear of the consequences.

"Now you know the real difference between the two of us. I'm not into playing games, Blue Eyes."

"And you think I am?"

"Aren't you?"

"I wasn't thinking about the differences between us when you were kissing me."

"That's good, because when I look at you I see a woman I want to get so deep inside I can't see daylight, a woman I want underneath me panting and scratching and as eager for me as I am for her. How about it, Blue Eyes? You ready for that?"

Burr watched Lindsey's jaw drop. Then she whirled and fled back to the cabin as fast as her legs could carry her.

You're a damn fool, Covington. She was asking for it. You should have given it to her. Why did you scare her off?

She doesn't know what she's getting into. I would be taking advantage of her at a vulnerable time.

She came on to you.

She's a woman who doesn't know what the hell she wants.

You had your chance to make love to her and you blew it.

Yeah. Sometimes those are the breaks.

Acknowledging his folly didn't make Burr feel any better. He headed toward the pond situated among the pecan trees. He needed a dip to cool off. He couldn't remember a time when he had been so turned on by a woman. Why the hell did it have to be her? They had nothing in common. There was absolutely no future for the two of them. He simply wasn't the kind of man who chased after windmills.

Lindsey had been shocked and not a little shaken by Burr's prompt and devastating response to her sexual invitation. She was used to a more civilized male creature, one who would ask permission and accept limits. Burr had given her fair warning and then taken what he wanted from her.

Not that she had protested much...or at all. In fact, she had quickly found herself a willing participant in anything and everything he'd had in mind to offer her. And she had to admit there was every bit as much give as there was take in what he had done.

So why did you run, Lindsey?

The answer to that was simple. She had been frightened by the powerful feelings Burr incited. She had no explanation for her attraction to the Ranger. She only knew she wanted to feel his arms around her, wanted to put her arms around him and hold him close. She was as appalled as she was astounded that she could be so attracted to a man like him. He didn't mince words; he didn't play games. He had a tattoo, for heaven's sake! But his need for her, his intense desire, was a strong aphrodisiac.

She had thought she could tease the lion and escape unharmed. But this beast had sharp teeth and dangerous claws that could drag her down and destroy her if she let him.

She remembered the avid look in Burr's eyes as his hand had cupped her breast. It was impossible to forget the taste of him, the rough feel of his tongue as he probed her mouth, the way his teeth caught her lower lip, and how her body had drawn up tight as he sucked on it. Her hips had met his thrusts and sought more of the delicious feelings as he brushed against her through two layers of soft denim.

Lindsey had fooled around in high school, done a little petting, but she had never gone "all the way." Somehow, the things her mother had told her about saving herself for marriage had made sense. Since she had expected to meet her future husband in college, that hadn't seemed like such a long time to wait.

Then her mother had been killed, and her life had been turned upside down. For the past five years she had lived as celibate as a nun. Perhaps it was those years of deprivation that had caused her to respond so wildly to Burr. Or maybe grown-up hormones were more powerful than the teenage ones. All she knew was that what she had felt with Burr far surpassed anything she had ever experienced in the past.

Lindsey felt confused and still half aroused and wasn't sure what her next move ought to be. Maybe the smart move was to make no move at all. She would let Burr set the tone for the rest of the day. Much as it irked her to concede any battle, she knew when she was outgunned. It would be better to retreat while she still could.

She spent the next hour carting firewood into the house and wondering where Burr was. When he returned, she realized he must have gone swimming. His hair was slicked back and his skin was pearled with drops of water. She had a fierce urge to taste his skin, to lick up those crystal drops. She forced herself to stay where she was.

"You took a swim."

"Yeah."

They stared at each other for a moment without speaking. Then Burr said, "It's time for me to call in. If we're lucky, Hector's been picked up, and you can go home."

Lindsey was torn between wanting to go home and wanting more time with Burr. She had been attracted to him because he was so different from the men she usually met. She felt certain that if she didn't discover the man behind the mask before Burr Covington, Texas Ranger, dropped her off in front of the governor's mansion and said goodbye, she never would. Lindsey found that a very painful thought.

"You won't get any crazy ideas while I'm gone, like walking to the road, will you?" Burr said.

"No. I'll wait here."

"I shouldn't be more than an hour. You'll be safe here." He reached out a hand and tucked an errant curl behind her ear. The instant he realized what he had done, Burr withdrew his hand. A moment later he captured her head between his hands and kissed her hard on the mouth. "Be here when I get back."

"I will."

Chapter Five

Lindsey stepped out onto the porch as Burr shut off the Jaguar's engine. "What's the news?"

Burr joined her on the porch, his face solemn. "Hector escaped the trap that was set for him. The captain thinks he may have left the country for South America."

"Now what?"

"The captain says we stay here," Burr said flatly.

"How long?"

"Until the Turk's sentence is carried out."

"That's four days!"

"I know."

Lindsey was amazed that she didn't feel more disappointed. In fact, what she felt was elated. She had four more days to find out everything there was to know about Burr Covington. Four more days to figure out the source of the riotous feelings that had bombarded her when Burr had so solemnly announced they were stuck together for a while longer.

To her consternation, Burr completely avoided her the rest of the day, which wasn't easy, since they both had to eat and sleep in the cabin. Somehow, he arranged it so she ate before he did and retired to bed before he returned from taking a late evening walk.

Lindsey lay in bed chewing on a fingernail. Maybe Burr had the right idea. Maybe it was better if they didn't get to know each other. She tried to imagine introducing Burr to her father as someone she cared about and had a pretty good idea what he would say: she was suffering from some kind of kidnapping syndrome and had fallen for the man who had rescued her from the bad guys.

Lindsey admitted she had something like an adolescent crush on Burr. She refused to dignify her desire to have him kiss her and hold her in his arms with any other label. How could it be more than infatuation? She had only known the man for forty-eight hours. She wasn't even sure she liked him. But there was no doubt she was physically attracted to him.

It occurred to her that perhaps the best way to get over her physical attraction to Burr was to find out what kind of man he really was. Personality flaws were bound to show up that would make him repugnant to her as a lover. Her crush would die a quick death under the weight of his unattractive character traits.

However, her plan required her to spend time in Burr Covington's company, discovering the unattractive man behind the fascinating "bad boy" facade. Which meant she had to find a way to keep Burr from disappearing before she had a chance to ask him a few questions. She decided to rise early the next morning and make a breakfast he wouldn't be able to resist sharing.

The smell of frying bacon woke Burr.

"Breakfast is ready!" Lindsey called from the kitchen. "Come and get it!"

Burr wasn't a morning person. His mind didn't start functioning until he had washed the cobwebs out with a shower, and he needed several cups of coffee before he could face the day. He met the call to come directly to the breakfast table with wariness. He needed his wits about him to deal with Lindsey Major.

He had managed to avoid any contact with the governor's daughter the previous day, but if he was any judge of the situation, he wasn't going to be allowed to repeat his disappearing act. He rubbed a weary hand across his bristly jaw. He hadn't gotten much sleep because he had spent the night dreaming in lurid detail of what it would be like to make love to her.

He struggled upright, shoving the afghan off his bare legs. He pressed his palms against eyelids he would have sworn were endowed with spikes the way they scraped against his eyeballs. Maybe if he got up on the wrong side of the bed—make that couch—and let Miss Major see him at his worst, it would discourage her.

Burr felt a grin struggling to break free. If Miss Major wanted him, she was going to get him. Warts and all.

He pulled on his jeans and zipped them, but didn't bother buttoning them. They caught on his hipbones.

He headed for the kitchen barefoot, scratching his naked chest, his hair stuck up every whichaway and a dark stubble on his cheeks and chin.

When he reached the kitchen doorway he grabbed hold of the molding above his head and held on, letting his body sag slightly forward. "Got any coffee?"

Lindsey turned toward him, and he nearly laughed out loud at the look on her face. Her features ran the gamut between disappointment and delight. Clearly she was glad he had joined her for breakfast. Equally clearly, she hadn't seen a man in his condition at the breakfast table.

He let go of the molding and took the three steps necessary to sit at the table, which had been adorned with china and silverware—his mismatched plates, chipped cups and stainless-steel flatware—in a way that would have pleased Miss Manners. He leaned his head on his hand and blatantly stared at Lindsey while she filled his coffee cup. "Thanks."

"How would you like your eggs?" she asked.

"Over easy."

She cracked a couple of eggs into the pan she had used to cook the bacon. He noticed she watched the eggs as though they might run away and ignored his presence in the room.

"This is a nice surprise," he said.

She looked over her shoulder at him somewhat nervously. "I thought this might be a way to repay you in some small measure for all you've done for me."

Burr grunted. "You don't owe me anything. I'm just doing my job."

"It may not seem like much to you, but I can't help thinking what might have happened to me at the hotel if you hadn't been there."

He saw her hands were trembling but resisted the urge to get up and go comfort her. Black knights didn't comfort ladies fair. He watched her visibly calm herself.

"I thought maybe we could walk down to the pond after breakfast," she said.

Burr knew why he wanted to spend time with her. What made no sense was why she apparently wanted to spend time with him. He had already warned her what would happen if she exhibited an interest in his attentions. She was damn well going to get them! Well, she was a big girl, and she knew the consequences of playing with fire. He figured he might as well enjoy her company while he could. It was a choice he might not have made if he hadn't still been fuzzy with sleep.

Almost a full minute after Lindsey had asked him to go walking with her to the pond, he replied, "Yeah, I'll go with you." After all, he was supposed to be keeping an eye on her.

"Do you suppose it would be all right if I went for a swim?"

Burr had just taken a gulp of hot coffee, and he choked and sputtered as a vivid picture rose before him of what Lindsey would look like with water dripping off her naked body. He felt his groin tighten with anticipation. "Sure. Why not?"

Burr was surprised when Lindsey set a plate of

eggs, bacon and toast in front of him that were cooked to perfection. He gave her a look of admiration.

"I took some classes in French cooking. We practiced a lot with eggs," she explained as she joined him on the other side of the table with a plate of her own.

They ate in uncomfortable silence, which Lindsey finally broke when she said, "I was wondering how someone who belonged to a street gang ended up as a Texas Ranger."

Burr hadn't told the story to very many people. Maybe if Lindsey knew the truth about him, she would back off and leave him alone. Maybe a dose of reality would cure what ailed her.

"My father died when I was two," he began. "My mother went to work as a waitress in a truck stop outside Houston. She didn't have any family, so she brought me with her to work and kept me behind the counter. I sort of grew up there."

"In a truck stop?"

Burr's lips curved at the look of horror and disbelief on Lindsey's face. It was just dawning on her that they came from two different worlds.

"It wasn't such a bad place. The truckers sort of adopted me, but none of them ever stayed around very long, so I never got attached to any of them. The problems started when I turned fifteen. The Cobras— that was the gang I eventually joined—all showed up one day at the truck stop. I was fascinated by them. They talked hip and looked cool. Most of all, they were a family.

"At the time, I needed to belong. So I joined up. I had to do a lot of things, initiation rites, before I could be a part of the gang. It was mostly petty thievery, vandalism, that sort of thing. And they beat you up to see if you could take it."

"That's terrible!"

Burr shrugged. "That part wasn't any fun. But afterward I was one of them, so it seemed worth it. Once I was in, I got the tattoo." He brushed his fingertips absently against the coiled black snake.

"There's no telling what might have happened to me if my mother hadn't married a Houston cop." He smiled in remembrance. "Joe Bertram came into the truck stop to investigate the theft of some video equipment—which I had stolen. The minute he and my mom laid eyes on each other they fell in love. I've never seen anything like it.

"Joe became my stepfather a month later. You could say my life of crime came to a rather abrupt end. He laid down the law and made me toe the line. He forced me to quit the Cobras. When I look back on it now, I can see he was a pretty terrific guy. At the time, I hated his guts.

"The long and the short of it is, the week after I graduated from the University of Texas at Austin with a degree in business, he was killed in the line of duty."

He paused and swallowed hard.

"I didn't even know I loved him till I heard the news." Burr turned away so she wouldn't see the tears that stung his eyes. "I felt cheated that I had lost him just when I was starting to appreciate him. And I felt bad that I hadn't ever thanked him. I figured one way I could repay him for all he'd done for me was to become a cop myself.

"Fortunately, the Rangers provide a natural stomping ground for renegades and loners like me. I put in my time as a cop and applied for the Rangers as soon as I was eligible." He spread his hands wide. "Here I am."

Burr had spent his life trying to make up to his stepfather for the trouble he had given him. In all these years he had never forgiven himself for the hateful things he had said to the man who had given him such tough love, even though his mother had assured him that his stepfather had forgiven him—had known his stepson cared for him—long before his death.

"Where's your mother now?" Lindsey asked.

"She died two years ago."

"So you're all alone?"

"I don't have any family left, if that's what you're asking."

"Why haven't you married?"

"I suppose I never found the right woman."

"What would she be like?"

"I haven't really thought about it. There's no such thing as perfection, so I guess I'd settle for a woman I loved who loved me back."

"Sounds pretty simple."

"Not many women want to be married to a law enforcement officer."

Lindsey nodded. "I suppose they don't want to wind up widows. I can understand that."

"And agree with the sentiment?"

"I lost my mother to violence. I live every day with the fear that an assassin will kill my father. So, no, I don't think I've ever imagined myself marrying a man whose life would constantly be on the line."

Burr rarely pondered his mortality. He couldn't afford to because it might distract him from the job he had to do. But he couldn't deny he was involved in a dangerous profession, and he couldn't blame a woman who considered that risk when choosing a husband. Even if it put him squarely out of the running.

While they were talking, Burr had finished the food in front of him and drunk a second cup of coffee. When Lindsey started clearing the table, he rose and took his plate from her. "You cooked, I clean, remember?"

She gave him a quick look from lowered lashes before saying, "I'll go change into something I can swim in."

Burr wondered what she would find to serve as a swimsuit and was rewarded when she arrived back in the kitchen a few minutes later with a sight that made his whole body go taut.

Her face looked fresh and innocent as she glanced quickly up at him from blue eyes masked by dark, lush lashes. Her mouth was slightly parted, and he could see her breasts rise and fall in a T-shirt that made it plain she wasn't wearing a bra. Her hair was a silky mane of gold that spilled over her shoulders and begged for a man's hands to grasp handfuls of it to pull her close. The T-shirt was tied in a knot above a pair of his cut-off jeans that revealed the length of her tanned, shapely legs.

It was an outfit designed to drive a man's imagination wild. Burr turned toward the sink so she wouldn't see that his body had promptly responded to the sexual invitation she had unconsciously thrown out.

"I'll be finished here in a minute and we can go," Burr said in a voice that was surprisingly husky.

"I'll wait for you on the porch."

Burr was grateful for the respite to get his libido back under control.

Whoa, boy! That sexy little siren is the governor's daughter!

She's also a very desirable woman.

Who's off limits!

Why?

You know damn well why! She wouldn't look at you twice if the circumstances were other than what they are. What kind of future could the two of you have together?

So what's wrong with a little fling?

With the governor's daughter? Get a grip, man. Think of the consequences!

Burr tried to imagine the possible consequences of slaking his lust with Lindsey Major. The mind boggled. Better to grit his teeth and bear the pain of un-

satisfied passion. In the long run that was the smart move.

His resolve lasted until Lindsey came up from her first dip in the creek in the wet T-shirt. Her nipples had peaked from the cold, and he was treated to a sight that made idiots of adolescent males at beach parties. Burr told himself he was an intelligent grown man who knew better than to succumb to such riveting sights.

When Lindsey called, "Why don't you join me?" he responded with a muttered oath and stood his ground.

"I promise the water isn't too cold," she teased.

Maybe that was what he needed, Burr thought, a dip in some cold water. He yanked off his black T-shirt and sat down to remove his boots and socks. Then, still wearing his jeans, he strode into the icy water.

He wasn't consciously heading for Lindsey at first. Not until she began to back away from him. She should have known better than to run. A hunter could never resist the chase.

He saw the teasing smile on her face begin to fade as she realized he was coming for her.

"Burr…Burr…"

When she turned and raced for the bank, he ran after her. He caught her in the grassy verge and pulled her down. They rolled several times before he pinned her beneath him.

She didn't fight, but lay panting, her eyes wide, her body pliant. She slicked her tongue over her lips, leaving them wet. Her gaze met his, and he waited for a sign that she wanted to be freed. It didn't come.

He lowered his mouth to hers, tasting the dampness, and heard her moan low in her throat. He pressed his hips down and felt her arch upward to meet him. This time he groaned.

"Lindsey, if you don't want this, say so now."

"I want you, Burr. Please, don't stop."

He had the wet T-shirt and shorts off her moments later and shimmied out of his wet jeans a moment after that. He settled himself between her thighs and then raised himself up on his elbows to look at her.

"You're so beautiful!" He watched the flush steal up her throat to stain her cheeks. Her eyes were closed, the lashes a fan of coal across rose-petal skin. "Look at me, Lindsey."

Lindsey had closed her eyes on purpose, not wanting Burr to focus on them because she had been judged for so long by their uniqueness. She wanted to be appreciated for who she was inside, not because she had the bluest eyes in Texas. She raised her lids slowly, first to a slit, then wider as she saw the admiration and approval in his tender gaze.

He brushed his thumb across her cheek and then slid it across her parted lips. She dipped her tongue out to taste him and heard his hiss of pleasure. His dark eyes seemed to bore into her, seeking the person within. She willed him to see her as she was—innocent, needing him, wanting him, not quite frightened, but anxious about the unknown.

They didn't speak again. At least not with words.

He caressed her skin as though it were the most fragile silk, and finally lowered his mouth to suckle her breast as his hands explored her body.

Lindsey bit her lip to keep from crying out, but couldn't suppress the guttural sounds that escaped her throat. She had never imagined it could be like this, never imagined the powerful response her body could have to the touch of a callused male hand. His mouth kept moving over her, up to her throat, then to her ear, inciting pleasure wherever it roamed. She felt a shiver of desire when his teeth nipped her shoulder, and sought out his skin with her mouth to return the pleasure.

"Your skin is so soft," he mused. "And your hair." His hand tightened around a fistful of the silky stuff and pulled her head back to expose her throat for his kisses.

Lindsey was overwhelmed with feelings. She responded with the desperation she felt, tunneling her hands into Burr's hair and grasping hold to keep his mouth where it was as her body arched beneath his. She relished his groan of delight as she brushed against his shaft.

His invasion came swiftly and without warning. She stiffened and cried out.

Burr froze. He didn't pull away, merely lifted himself on his palms to stare into Lindsey's face. He caught the remnants of pain in her eyes. And the growing exhilaration.

"You should have told me," he said in a harsh voice.

"Would you have done this if I had?"

"Hell, no!"

"Then I'm glad I didn't say anything."

Burr let out his breath in a sigh. "I hurt you."

"The pain is gone now." She still felt stretched, and her body ached, but that was bearable. And she knew the worst was over. "Please don't stop."

Burr snorted. "I'm not about—"

She put her fingertips across his mouth to silence him and let her eyes plead for what she wanted. She raised herself enough to replace her fingertips with her mouth. Her tongue traced the crease of his lips and when he parted them, slid inside. She moaned with delight as Burr's tongue forced hers back into her mouth and claimed the honey to be found there.

His hands cupped her shoulders and pressed her back down as his body began to move in tandem with hers. His thrusts were slow and easy at first, but as she began to answer him, his body plunged deeper, seeking pleasure, giving it, until they were slick from sweat, until their bodies begged for air, until each cried out as he spent his seed within her.

Consequences.

It was the first thought that popped into Lindsey's head as she lay atop Burr, still gasping for air, totally enervated. They hadn't used any kind of protection. She knew better, and he must certainly be aware of the dangers of unprotected sex.

"Do you…? Have you…?"

"It's a little late for that, Blue Eyes, don't you

think?'' Burr said in a quiet voice. ''But, no, I don't have anything you can catch. And I don't expect, under the circumstances, that I'm going to catch anything from you. That leaves pregnancy. Is this the right—or wrong—time of the month?''

Lindsey's face was beet red. She kept her eyes lowered. ''I just got over... It's the wrong time of month for me to get pregnant,'' she blurted.

He pulled her close to his chest and held her there. ''Thank goodness for that, anyway.'' He was quiet for a long time before he said, ''Why me?''

''It's not what you're thinking.''

''What am I thinking?''

''That this is just a fling.''

''Isn't it?''

Lindsey was silent for a moment. Is that what Burr had thought? That she just wanted to have sex with him for the fun of it? That she didn't care for him as a person? But, honestly, what else could he think? They barely knew each other. They were strangers. The likelihood of them continuing any kind of relationship once she returned to the governor's mansion was small indeed. So why had she allowed—be honest, Lindsey—*encouraged* this to happen?

''I don't know what it is,'' Lindsey admitted. ''I think I wanted to see if I could make you want me. I didn't realize until...until you caught me that I wanted to be caught. And then...'' She shrugged. ''I'm not sorry it happened, though. I have feelings for you that are...'' *Stronger than I'm willing to admit even to myself, let alone to you.* She didn't dare speak of love. It was an absurdity under the circumstances.

"No regrets?"

She shook her head. "It had to happen sometime, and—"

Burr rolled her off of him and was on his feet an instant later. "And I was convenient," he finished in a hard voice. "Don't fool yourself into thinking I'm something I'm not. I'll always be a man more used to walking alleys than streets. There's no getting rid of my past, like there's no getting rid of the tattoo on my arm. And if it's all the same to you, Blue Eyes, I've had enough of being a convenience."

Burr was aware of a tightness in his chest. It had dawned on him that he would give anything to have a woman like Lindsey for his own, to hold and to love. He couldn't stand the thought of another man touching her, loving her. Only, he had no right to those feelings. Their situation wasn't real; it was contrived. How could he even think about proposing to the governor's daughter?

His hurt turned to anger when he realized the situation Lindsey had put him in. He was furious she hadn't told him that he would be the first man to make love to her. He sure as hell hadn't been thinking in terms of forever, as any woman who had saved her virginity as long as Lindsey had must have been. He knew, even if she didn't, that the governor's daughter wasn't going to marry a former Houston gang member, a man with a snake tattoo on his arm and an earring in his ear, even if he was a Texas Ranger.

"You should have waited for the right man to come along, Blue Eyes, instead of wasting your innocence on me."

She had hurt him, Lindsey realized, and he had snapped back with something equally hurtful. She sought some way to make amends. "I didn't mean—"

"I know what I am, Miss Major, and what I'm not. The question is, do you?"

"Now wait just a minute, Burr Covington," Lindsey said. "You can't use that snake tattoo or your broken nose to scare me off! You aren't so tough."

"Oh, yeah?"

"Yeah!" She poked him in the chest with her forefinger. "There's a fellow inside there somewhere who makes my heart beat fast, a guy who leaves me breathless. So there!"

Burr was tempted by her speech to take her back in his arms. But he already had his wet jeans on, which helped immensely to dampen his ardor and keep him from doing something that foolish. "Get dressed."

"I won't let you ignore me." Lindsey reached out and stopped him from buttoning his jeans. "I wanted *you* to make love to me, Burr. You."

Burr grabbed her wrists to keep her from touching him. His body was on fire, and he knew if he let her arguments sway him, he would be the one who got burned. If he let himself believe her, he would start thinking about a future together, and he knew better than that. "Get dressed," he repeated. "I can't leave you out here alone."

He glared at her while she tugged on her cut-offs and pulled her soggy T-shirt over her head. The flimsy cotton did nothing to hide her lush body, and he felt his loins tighten at the sight of her nipples through the thin cloth. The minute she was dressed, he grabbed her wrist. "Let's go."

"How can I make you believe that I mean what I'm saying?" Lindsey said as he dragged her along beside him.

"I should have known better than to let myself lose control like that," he muttered.

"I do care about you. I—"

He jerked her to a stop. "Don't you dare use words like that when you don't mean them! You have no idea what it means to care about anyone but yourself. You're exactly what the papers call you—a pretty pair of blue eyes without any substance behind them!"

"How do you know what I feel?" she cried. "Why are you acting like an insensitive, uncaring brute?"

"So now I'm a brute? You're the one who came after me, so what does that make you, lady? You asked for it, and I gave it to you!"

"Oh, you…you…" Lindsey was so furious and hurt, nearly blinded by the tears she was furiously blinking back, that she couldn't find an epithet bad enough to use on him.

"Who are you to be judging me," Burr demanded with a sneer, "when you don't have a life of your own? You're a substitute wife for your father, a substitute mother for your siblings. You wouldn't know how to be yourself, because there's nothing more to Lindsey Major than a pair of pretty blue eyes.''

Lindsey was appalled at how close Burr had come to describing her life and enraged that he had rejected her because of it. ''And you'll never outgrow your roots,'' she taunted back. ''You'll always be a street hood at heart.''

They stood glaring at each other. Each wanting desperately to be the kind of person the other wanted and sure they fell far short of the other's expectations.

Burr wondered what would have happened if they had met under different circumstances, when labels could have been dispensed with, when they could just have been a man and a woman meeting for the first time without the concealing masks they had both worn for so many years.

''Hey, you two, what's the problem?''

Lindsey and Burr turned to stare openmouthed at the man dressed in a ranger uniform who stood on the porch of the cabin.

Burr cleared his throat. ''Captain Rogers? What are you doing here?''

''Hector fooled us. He didn't get on that plane to South America, after all. One of our informants saw him and tipped us off. We picked him up a couple of hours ago. You can go home now, Miss Major.''

Lindsey turned stricken eyes toward Burr. ''I can go home.''

''Yes, ma'am,'' the captain continued, oblivious to the powerful undercurrents between Burr and Lindsey. "Your father's waiting for you at the mansion. I'll give you a lift there."

"I'll give her a ride," Burr said. Unspoken was the knowledge that they would finish their conversation on the way. Only, what was there left to say?

Lindsey shoved a fist against her mouth to keep a sob from escaping and raced into the cabin.

"What the hell did you do to that woman?" Captain Rogers asked.

Loved her. Burr thought. *I just loved her.*

Chapter Six

In the face of the accusations each had made against the other, both Lindsey and Burr remained silent during the first part of the drive back to Austin.

It's over too soon, Lindsey thought.

I never had an even chance with her, Burr thought.

I'm not what he thinks I am.

There's more to me than she knows.

Maybe I need to look more closely at who I am, Lindsey thought.

Maybe I ought to look at myself and see what's really there, Burr thought.

"I never realized before how thoroughly I took my mother's place after she died," Lindsey murmured, her voice barely audible. "At first, after my mother's death, my father was so desolate he couldn't function. I saw a void, and I filled it. I suppose I should have stepped back sooner, but the role was comfortable for me. I felt needed. I *was* needed. Now...I don't know. Carl and Stella are old enough to resent it when I try to parent them. And my father...I think he wouldn't have the heart to tell me he didn't need my help anymore."

"But you think he could survive now without you?"

Lindsey made a face. "He hired a new secretary last year. She's quite good at what she does."

"I see."

Lindsey was afraid Burr saw too much. "At least I'm willing to admit I need to make a change. What about you? How well do your stepfather's shoes fit, Burr?"

Burr kept his eyes on the road, refusing to meet her gaze. "You don't pull any punches, do you, Blue Eyes?" And of course she was right. It was time he figured out whether he was in this line of work for his stepfather's sake...or his own.

Burr had spent so many years giving mental lip service to the idea he was a cop to repay his stepfather, that he hadn't thought about how much he enjoyed his work. He liked being a Texas Ranger; he was good at it. And it was a satisfying job, giving him the independence his soul craved along with the opportunity to serve a noble purpose.

But was the role of Texas Ranger sufficient for the husband of a woman like Lindsey Major? He would never be rich, and his first devotion was to duty. Although he would cherish Lindsey if she were his, there would necessarily be times when his job would take him away from her. It might even kill him. He didn't want to think about how she would feel if that happened.

Lindsey snuck a peek at Burr and wondered what traits he wanted in a wife. She was beautiful, but what else did she have to offer a husband? She had a great deal of experience as an organizer and a hostess, but somehow she didn't think the wife of a Texas Ranger needed those skills. She was frightened of the danger he lived with day in and day out. Her heart caught in her throat when she admitted the perilous danger of his chosen profession.

Life with a man like Burr would never be easy. But she understood now why her mother had endured the trials and tribulations of life as a politician's wife. Loving, caring, left no choices.

Lindsey stared straight ahead as the interstate flew by, unwilling to speak again because she was afraid all the things she was feeling would pour out of her mouth. Her relationship—if you could call it that—with Burr was over before it had started. She was going back to her world. He was going back to his. Their paths wouldn't cross again, not without some effort on one or both of their parts. She was leaving it up to him to make the first move. That might be old-fashioned, but she wasn't willing to lay her heart on the line without some indication from him that he was willing to do the same.

The governor's mansion was in sight before she finally asked the question that was foremost in her mind. "Will I ever see you again?"

"What would be the point?"

Lindsey looked down at her hands, which were knotted in her lap. "I thought we started something by the river."

"If there are consequences, by all means call me."

Lindsey shot an angry look at Burr. "You know that wasn't what I meant. And I wouldn't call you now even if I were expecting triplets!"

"It wouldn't work," Burr said in a quiet voice. He glanced at her for an instant, then focused on the road in front of him. "You and me, I mean. I think in our case appearances aren't at all deceiving. You're a princess living in an ivory tower, and I'm—"

"Prince Charming. Or you could be."

Burr shook his head and laughed. "Whoever heard of Prince Charming with a snake tattooed on his arm? Can you imagine what your father would say if he saw the two of us together?"

"He wouldn't care."

Burr raised a skeptical brow, and Lindsey conceded, "At least, not after he got to know you."

"Both of us know appearances count, Blue Eyes. Think of the heyday the press would have if the two of us showed up in public together."

"What's printed in newspapers doesn't have to affect us."

"What about your friends? What will they say?"

"If they can't—or won't—accept you as you are, they won't be my friends for long."

Burr sighed. "It won't work, Blue Eyes. We're too different."

"We both want the same thing," Lindsey argued. "Someone to love...someone who'll love us back. We could have that together, Burr. Nothing else matters."

"Now I know you've been living in an ivory tower.

We wouldn't have a snowball's chance in hell of surviving the rebuke that would be leveled against us from all directions. Me for stepping out of my place, and you for stooping down from yours. Think of the headlines—Bluest Eyes In Texas To Wed Former Gang Thug, or Texas Ranger Nabs Bluest Eyes In Texas.''

"If you don't want me, just say so.''

"Wanting you has nothing to do with it! I want you like hell. I'm just trying to be realistic about the situation.''

"If your mind's made up, I don't suppose I can change it,'' Lindsey said. "But I'm stating here and now for the record that I think you're wrong. If you decide you want me bad enough to fight for me, you know where to find me.''

She was out of the car and running inside the mansion before he had a chance to stop her. Not that he would have known what to say to her if he had. She was wrong. There was no way they could have a life together. He wasn't Prince Charming. He was an ordinary man with a slightly crooked nose and a snake tattoo and a few scars he had earned along the way. When the governor's blue-eyed daughter had recovered from the trauma of being kidnapped, of being held captive by a Ranger against her will, of being made love to for the first time, she would be glad he had bowed gracefully out of her life.

Lindsey threw herself into her father's embrace and sobbed with relief as his arms tightened securely around her.

"Are you all right, Lindsey?" he asked. "Are you hurt?"

"I'm fine, Dad," she managed between gulps as she fought back her tears. "It's just...it was *awful!* There was so much blood and those two men dead, and Burr... Oh, Dad!"

"I know sweetheart. I know. You'll be fine now. Nothing bad is ever going to happen to you again. I'll see to that."

Lindsey heard the remorse in her father's voice that she had been forced to suffer through the kidnapping and his determination to protect her from harm in the future. She could feel the walls closing in on her. It was a gilded cage her father wanted her to inhabit, but it was still a cage. If the governor got his way, she would never see Burr again, that was for sure. A brilliant idea popped into Lindsey's head, and she acted on it.

"If it hadn't been for Lieutenant Covington, I would have been brutalized and blinded before I was murdered. He saved me, Dad. Isn't there something we can do for him? Some way to thank him?"

"I don't know. I'll have to think about it."

"Could we have some sort of ceremony and give him a medal? We could invite him to dinner, too, couldn't we?"

The speculative look her father gave her brought a telltale blush to Lindsey's cheeks.

"You seem to have gotten along pretty well with this Covington fellow."

"He saved my life," Lindsey repeated.

"Hmm."

Lindsey held her breath.

"All right. I'll talk to Captain Rogers and see if a commendation of some sort is appropriate."

"And we'll invite him to dinner?"

"Sure. Why not?"

Burr slipped a finger into the collar of his tuxedo shirt and tried to loosen it. He felt like a mustang running with a herd of high-priced Thoroughbreds. He was wearing black cordovan dress shoes instead of boots, and his hair had been trimmed so much it curled at his nape. There was no earring in his ear and the snake tattoo was far out of sight. Except for his broken nose, he looked like most of the other men in tuxedos who had been invited to the governor's mansion for dinner.

Only, he was a fraud. They looked comfortable in the clothes they wore. They smiled and nodded and chatted with ease. He knew the moment he opened his mouth the wrong thing was going to come out. This wasn't his milieu. He would always be more comfortable in alleys than on streets.

He had learned from the captain that this reception in his honor was all Lindsey's idea, supposedly a way to repay him for what he had done.

"I was only doing my job," Burr had protested.

The captain hadn't been willing to take no for an

answer. "You're going to dine as the governor's guest, and I don't want to hear any more argument!"

So here he was, all dressed up and fighting the bit to be somewhere else.

"Hello, stranger."

Burr turned and his breath caught in his throat. He had forgotten how beautiful she was. She was wearing a dress similar in style to the one she had been kidnapped in, only this one was black. He wondered fleetingly if she was wearing a black merry widow beneath it.

She smiled at him as though divining the direction his thoughts had taken. The look in her eyes made him want to haul her off somewhere and kiss her silly. He settled for taking the hand she extended and holding it in his own.

His thumb caressed her wrist, and he felt her pulse leap beneath his fingertips. "It's been a while," he managed to force past his constricted throat.

"Three weeks and two days."

"You've been counting?"

"Haven't you?"

He grinned. "Three weeks, two days, and eight hours."

"I've missed you." Lindsey couldn't take her eyes off Burr. The crisp white shirt contrasted against his tanned skin, and the black tux jacket emphasized his broad shoulders. He looked distinguished, but no less dangerous. For the first time in her very social life,

Lindsey was incredibly nervous. She didn't know how to act and took her cues from Burr.

Burr ignored her invitation to admit to feelings that were only trouble. The orchestra at the far end of the ballroom had just begun a waltz, so he asked, "Would you like to dance?"

"I'd love to dance."

He led her into the waltz, a dance he knew because it was popular in country bars. But the count was the same, and she was as light on her feet as he was, so they moved easily around the dance floor.

"I didn't know you could dance so well," she said.

"There are lots of things you don't know about me."

"I'd like to learn."

Burr took a deep breath and let it out. "There's no time like the present, is there? Let me introduce myself. My name is Burr Covington. I'm a Texas Ranger. I grew up in Houston, but I've been assigned to the office in Austin for the past two years."

"It's nice to meet you, Mr. Covington," Lindsey said with a shy smile.

"Please call me Burr."

"I'd be pleased to…Burr. My name is Lindsey Major. People claim I have the bluest eyes in Texas, but they're greatly mistaken. They aren't blue at all. They're—"

"Lavender," Burr finished for her. "And what have you been doing to keep yourself busy these past few weeks, Miss Major?"

"Oh, please, call me…Blue Eyes."

"Well, Blue Eyes?" Burr said, a tender smile teasing his lips.

"I've been talking to my father about going back to college. I never finished my degree in journalism, you know. I've decided to return to Baylor in the fall."

"Then you can be the one to do the writing, instead of being written about."

"That thought has crossed my mind," she said with a mischievous smile.

"I just might be transferring to that area of Texas," Burr said.

"As a Texas Ranger?"

"Yeah. One of my rewards for saving the governor's daughter was my choice of assignments. And I got a raise. So I was thinking about settling down and finding me a wife."

"Oh?"

"Would you by any chance be interested in the job?"

"Why, I think I might be willing to consider such a position. So long as you don't mind getting up every morning to the bluest eyes in Texas."

"No," Burr said as he pulled her close and lowered his mouth to hers. "I don't think I'll mind that at all."

* * * * *

WIFE IN NAME ONLY

Carolyn Zane

* * *

For my sister, Judy, with love.
Thank you for understanding.

Thanks…
Matt, my partner in chaos.
Tracey, for knowing country music.
And above all, thank you, Lord.

Dear Reader,

Wife in Name Only was my second—and to this day my favorite—Silhouette Romance novel. This is the book where Big Daddy Brubaker was hatched by my husband, Matt.

One evening I was writing and came to the point where I needed a character to play the ad agency's client. I ran through all sorts of possibilities in my mind, but none really stood out. So I went to the kitchen and found my husband foraging for food in the refrigerator. "Honey, I need a man." "You're lookin' at him." He waggled his brows. "No, I mean a fictional man." I explained my needs and he said, "A little Texan with a big heart and nine really stupid kids all named after country-and-western singers." Hmm. That idea had definite possibilities. Then Matt said, "Call him…Big Daddy. Yeah, Big Daddy Brubaker. And make him a real lover." Well, the rest is history.

So far, I've written eight Brubaker books, and there are more looming on the horizon. You'll see the challenge I had, turning these "stupid kids" into decent heroes and heroines. But, as Big Daddy would say, "It's been a hoot and a holler."

Happy reading,

Chapter One

Ted Anderson hung up the phone, leaned back in the plush leather chair that sat behind his huge desk, and surveyed with satisfaction the lavish view of downtown Portland from his penthouse suite at Anderson and Anderson. He sighed happily to himself. Judith was coming home to take his place in the ad agency. He never thought he'd see the day. If anyone had asked him a dozen years ago whether or not his gawky, outrageous daughter would ever have what it takes to step into his shoes as a principal in one of the country's leading advertising agencies, he'd have died laughing.

"Well?" Ed Anderson, Ted's best friend and partner for over thirty years tapped his pen on Ted's ink blotter to gain his attention. "What did she say?"

"Yes," Ted replied, smiling. "She said she could make it."

"Wonderful! We're all set then. How soon will she be here?" Ed crossed over to Ted's wet bar, pulled a sparkling water out of the refrigerator and settled himself comfortably on the large leather sectional couch.

"She says she needs two weeks to wrap up her work load and bring the new guy up to speed, but that's no big deal. She'll drive down from Seattle that Friday and the movers will bring her personal effects to our place on Saturday. What about Luke?"

Ed beamed at the mention of his successful son. "Today was his last day in San Francisco at JDD&K. He's taking a week off to do some traveling, so he should arrive about the same time as Judith."

"Great." Ted stood and stretched. He had aged in the past twelve or so years that they'd been handling the world-famous Dalton Industries account. At sixty-five, he was tired. Tired of the rat race, tired of the BS. Tired of the endless stress that came with sharing the responsibilities of general partner and creative director for one of the largest ad agencies in the country. Grabbing a sparkling water from the wet bar, he joined Ed on the sectional.

They'd come a long way over the years, Ted thought, eyeing Ed's graying head with fondness. And to think it all started because they had the same last name. Anderson. Lucky for them their sergeant in the Korean War had assigned KP duty alphabetically, or they might never have discovered their mutual love of advertising.

"We're a couple of lucky SOB's, Teddy, old boy." Ed toasted Ted with his water bottle. "With two such fabulously talented and professional kids to take over our business, I feel just great about us taking off for the reunion in Korea."

Ted grinned and kicked off his shoes. "Yeah, it's going to be great to see the guys again, isn't it?"

"I just hope we can all recognize each other."

"We will," Ted chuckled. "Fatter, balder, but the same basic guys. It was a great idea the girls had, to combine the reunion in Korea with a year of traveling around the world. Barbara has wanted to do that forever."

"Greta, too." Ed polished off his water and set the bottle down on the glass coffee table. "Well, now that we're retiring and the kids are taking over for us, they'll get their chance. If it was anyone but Luke, I'd worry the entire time."

Ted nodded in agreement. "I feel the same way about Judith." His daughter's creative work at Seattle's Morgan, Van Zant, Grey and Getty was renowned throughout the Northwest. Ted was glad she was moving back to Portland to work at Anderson and Anderson before she started stealing his accounts. Judith's style was trend-setting, cutting-edge stuff. At only twenty-six, she had twice the talent he'd had at her age. He was extraordinarily proud of her.

"When was the last time Judith was in town?" Ed burped comfortably.

Ted's frown was thoughtful. "Last Christmas, I think. We went to Seattle the year before. When was the last time you and Greta saw Luke?"

"Thanksgiving, two years ago. Time flies, and we've been so busy... It'll be good to see them both."

"You know, Ed, I don't think they've seen each other since Luke went into the service. About the time we landed the Dalton account."

Ed rubbed his chin. "Really? Hmm, I'll bet you're right. It's probably a good thing. As I recall, they didn't always get along that well as children."

"Ha!" Ted snorted. "That's an understatement.

Let's just say Judith's teen years left something to be desired."

Ed laughed and stood up to leave. "True. Hopefully, they've forgotten all about their little tiffs. I can't even remember what they used to fight about, but Lord almighty, you'd think the world was ending."

Nodding, Ted shoved the niggling feelings of doubt about Judith and Luke's ability to get along to the back of his mind. Maybe it wasn't fair not to warn them that they would be working together. So much for truth in advertising....

Ted stood and walked his partner to the door. "I remember. I just hope they can get along now. They were always like oil and water, for some reason. And their styles are so different now... Well, they've both grown up, we're probably worrying over nothing."

Saturday afternoon, two weeks later, Ted pulled open his front door to find Luke Anderson standing casually on his stoop. A delighted smile pushed deep creases into the corners of his eyes at the sight of his best friend's son. Luke had always held a special place in Ted's heart, and he couldn't be happier to have him and Judith taking over the agency. He just hoped the feeling would be mutual.

"Luke!" he boomed, and pulled the young man roughly into his arms, clapping him on his back. "How the hell are you?"

"Fine, Ted," Grinning, he pulled back and gripped Ted's hand in a firm handshake. "It's great to see you," he said, following Ted through the foyer and into his den.

"Likewise, kiddo." Ted gestured to a chair in front

of the desk in his home office. "Have a seat. Can I get you anything? Something to drink? Coffee? Juice? Something stronger?"

"No, no thanks, Ted. I'm fine, really." Luke settled into his chair and drew an ankle up over his knee. It seemed to Luke, as he sat soaking up the familiar atmosphere of Ted's home, that nothing had changed. Everything looked exactly as he had left it, twelve years ago. He'd missed this place more than he cared to admit.

"Judith is upstairs. She'll be joining us shortly." Ted's chair creaked and groaned as he sat down behind his desk and pulled a sheaf of papers out of his briefcase.

"Oh?" Luke's blood pressure shot up involuntarily. Maybe he'd take Ted up on that drink after all. Judith Anderson had been the bane of his existence from the day she was born till the day he had gone into the service. During his entire youth, she'd plagued him like a bad case of poison ivy. Judith was the bratty younger sister he'd never had, and never wanted. It wasn't just her goofy looks that turned him off, either. No, Judith could be the most obnoxious, temperamental girl he'd ever had the misfortune to be stuck with.

It seemed to Luke that Judith had been foisted off on him at every social function and holiday for the first eighteen years of his life. And all because of their last name. Anderson. The infamous Anderson story. How his father and Ted loved to tell it over and over again. Big deal. So they peeled potatoes together in the war. So they both had the same last name, loved the advertising business and became best friends and business partners. So what? Was that any reason to saddle him with that lunatic redhead?

Luke reached up and tried to still the muscle that jerked involuntarily in his jaw. Giving himself a mental shake, he wondered what he was thinking. That was over now. She'd gone her merry way and he'd gone his.

Ted tossed the papers on his desk and snapped his briefcase shut. "Yes, she's changing into something more comfortable, and your dad should be here soon with our corporate lawyer. Have you met her?"

Luke shook his head. "I don't think so. But Dad told me she's sharp." He grinned mischievously. "Says she's pretty easy on the eyes, too. But he told me not to tell Mom that he'd noticed."

Ted laughed. "Ed always was a Romeo. He's right, though. Built like a brick...well, you get the picture." He chuckled and winked at Luke.

The doorbell chimed, and the sound of voices drifted to them from the foyer.

"That must be them now," Ted said, cocking his ear toward the door. "I suppose it's time to get down to business."

Luke stood as the voices grew closer. "Fine with me." He'd waited twelve years for this moment, and he was anxious to get on with the proceedings.

Judith Anderson paused with Ed in the doorway in time to see Luke run his hands through his shaggy hair and brush the lint from his jacket. Some things never changed it seemed. He was still the arrogantly boyish Adonis from her past. She had no idea why Luke was able to make her heart pound today, the way it had when she was a teen. Seeing him now, for the first time in twelve years, she realized that part of the problem was that she'd been such an ugly duckling and he'd been so gorgeous—and together. Luke always had his act together. Somehow that intimidated and infuriated her. He was cool.

Cool was definitely not a word that applied to her when she was growing up. Nerd, yes, she mused. She'd been a first-class nerd. And when cool, together Luke had bothered to notice her existence, he'd bossed her around. Vivid memories of the last time she'd seen Luke flashed through her mind, and suddenly, she was fourteen years old again, the pain of her awkward youth carrying her back in time....

In a fit of rage, young Judith Anderson pulled the rolled-up socks out of her training bra and hurled them across her bedroom. The misguided missiles struck her curio cabinet and knocked her favorite porcelain doll onto the floor. She watched in horror as two large brown china eyes rolled out of the shattered face, across the floor and came to rest at her feet. Their accusing stare served only to fuel her fury. Her face was as fiery red as her wild mane of unruly hair, and running over to her desk she'd swept up an armload of books.

"Luke...Anderson...can...go...to...*hell!*"   she screamed and flung one literary work after another out the second-story window to punctuate each word. Turning savagely she glared at her dainty bedroom to discover what new havoc she could wreak. Spotting Mr. Teddy propped innocently among the frilly pillows on her canopy bed, she stalked over and snatched him up. Maniacal laughter bubbled across her lips as she heartlessly ripped the fuzzy head off his pudgy body.

"So, you think I'm strange and she's wonderful, huh?" she yelled at the headless teddy bear. "Sticks and stones may break my bones, but you don't have a head!" Mr. Teddy's head was angrily launched out the window to land on top of the pile of discarded books.

Judith was just getting warmed up. Shrieking with frustration, she blasted the frilly pile of pillows off her bed. Arms swinging, legs kicking, the blankets soon followed. Throwing herself across her bare mattress, her tantrum erupted anew.

"Why? Why?" she sobbed, pummeling the bed. "Why is he always so mean? And why," she muttered, sniffing, "do I waste my time with a stupid crush on him? He could never really care for me." She sat up abruptly and wiped the tears from her freckled cheeks. "I know why. Because I'm ugly! I'm hideous! I'm... I'm...*repulsive!*" she wailed, kicking the mattress with furious feet.

From where she sat, Judith could see her angry, contorted face reflected in the mirror. Sunlight glinted unmercifully off the braces on her teeth. Her long, gangly body looked gawky and unfeminine, even to her own eyes. And that hair. Where had that come from? No one in her family had hair quite like that. She must have inherited some recessive Brillo-pad gene, or something, she thought, touching the springy coils of rust-colored vexation. If only she had one decent attribute. One body part that she could claim as normal. Not beautiful. Just average looking would be fine with her. But no. Her large green eyes were framed by pale lashes that practically disappeared behind her tortoise-shell glasses. Even her feet were out of control. When would they stop growing? Reaching down, she pulled off one ungainly clodhopper, flung it at the mirror, and smiled with satisfaction at her shattered image.

Judith cringed at the memories that could flash through her mind in less than a second and turn her ivory complexion a molten shade of lava. Ed and Ted had been in this very room on that day, celebrating. They'd just landed one of the most prestigious accounts in the country, the amazing Dalton Industries account, and Luke had come along for a swim in her father's pond. And, of course, to pick on her.

Her skin began to prickle and her breathing became shallow. Oh, how she hated the way he could still make her feel. Taking a deep, calming breath, she followed Ed into the den.

Luke crossed the room to greet his father and his father's lawyer. After giving Ed a quick hug and a hearty handshake, he let his eyes slide over the woman standing next to his dad. Ed was a lucky son of a gun, he thought appreciatively. What was a bombshell like her doing working for these old boys?

"What time did you get in?" Ed asked eagerly, shrugging out of his overcoat.

"This morning. I've only been here a few minutes." Smiling, Luke's eyes shifted back to the woman beside Ed. He offered her his hand with a raised eyebrow at his dad. Why wasn't he introducing her? Probably wanted this one all to himself. Luke didn't blame him. Ted moved from around his desk and pecked her on the cheek. Okay, so maybe they shared her, Luke thought, taken back by their familiarity with her.

"Judith," her low, sultry voice held an amused

note as she extended her cool, slender, well-manicured hand.

What a bizarre coincidence. This gorgeous woman's name was Judith, too. But she was nothing like Judith Anderson. This Judith was hot. Sizzling. Beads of perspiration began to form on his brow.

Judith slowly dropped Luke's hand, studying his face intently as she did so. She seemed to find something humorous there, because her large, fabulous emerald eyes sparkled at him with cool, amused expectance.

This lady unnerved him. He couldn't decide if it was her cool, haughty manner or her incredibly sexy physical appearance. A wild cascade of auburn waves tumbled over her shoulders and down her slender back. High cheekbones and a patrician nose gave her the look of an exotic model. Generous lips were drawn into a lazy smile that revealed a set of teeth dentists fantasized about. This woman was almost too perfect to be real. His Judith would hate her. Where was she, anyway? Probably lurking in some corner waiting for an opportunity to pounce.

Ed took Judith's hand in his and propelled her toward Luke. "Our corporate lawyer called in sick today, so we're on our own. That's okay, because Ted and I know the contract inside and out. Having her attend this meeting was just a formality. Now that we're all here, Why don't we get started?" Ed asked the group in general, herding them over to the chairs in front of Ted's desk.

Luke felt like Wile E. Coyote after being flattened by the Road Runner. He was sure that birds and stars were swirling around his head, chirping and coo-cooing. Either he'd fallen asleep and was having a very bad dream, or this curvaceous, luscious, voluptuous creature was *Judith!* His *Judith?* Judith the obnoxious, loudmouthed, homely little girl who'd plagued his youth? Impossible!

Judith watched the play of emotion cross his handsome face with interest as the realization of her identity dawned on him. So, she'd been right. He hadn't recognized her. Yes, it was true she'd changed for the better, but the fact that he didn't even recognize her stung. The trouble was, for a second there, she knew he'd viewed her as a desirable woman. A fully grown woman. A woman who was his equal. That knowledge thrilled her. And due to some psychological twist of fate she'd never, ever be able to understand, it made her mad. The defensive hackles were up.

Luke sensed her mood change and averted his eyes from his perusal of her body.

"Sure, Dad. Good idea. Now that we're...all here." He waited until Judith crossed in front of him and watched her slinky, graceful progression to the desk. Heavens to Murgatroyd. Where had she learned to walk like *that?* She used to walk like a lumberjack. Even her clothes screamed class. Gone were the mismatched, ragtag, loose-fitting garments of her girlhood.

Judith was wearing an expensive silk designer-label suit that fit her like a surgeon's glove. The soft peach color brought out the highlights in her hair. She'd always had long, gangly legs, but now they were long, shapely legs that matched the rest of her statuesque beauty perfectly. It was amazing. Stunned, he tried to reconcile this new version of Judith Anderson with the one he had grown up with.

The last time he'd laid eyes on her, she'd been

storming away from him toward her father's house, outraged over something he'd said. Crowding his muddled brain, the past washed over him and the last twelve years faded into thin air....

The flat, round stone skipped ten times before it sank, leaving ever-widening rings of water in the pond's glassy surface. Eighteen-year-old Luke Anderson eased back on his haunches and stretched out on the lawn to eye his handiwork. Not bad. Luckily Judith stalked off when she had, or he might have tossed her into the drink after his skipper. Out of the corner of his eye, he could see a great pile of bedding sailing out the window of her second-story bedroom window. Why did her parents put up with her tantrums? *He'd* never get away with that.

Groaning, he let his head drop into the soft green grass. He was feeling a little guilty. Normally, Judith didn't push him to the point of cruelty, but this time she'd gone too far. It wasn't unusual for Judith to drive him half out of his mind with her wacky, overly dramatic personality, however today she'd pushed the wrong button.

Where did she get off calling Mitzi a bimbo? Compared to Judith, Mitzi was an angel. Closing his eyes, he smiled as thoughts of his latest girlfriend filled his mind. Mitzi was fine. So soft, so petite, so...kissable. And Judith. He snorted out loud. Judith was as kissable as a porcupine. Not that he'd ever be crazy enough to want to kiss her. No way.

Luke blinked several times as Judith settled into a chair next to him. Seeing her now, he wondered if he should rethink his no-kissing rule. No, she still had more defenses than a football team.

Once seated, Judith smiled at Ted and slid a sidelong glance at Luke. He seemed distinctly rattled. Good. He looked the same, she noted churlishly. Older, true, but just as handsome as he had been twelve years ago. No, more handsome actually. Tiny laugh lines gave his incredible hazel eyes a new warmth. His shaggy brown hair was still thick and silky looking, but in need of a good corporate cut. He appeared to be the carefree playboy of yesteryear. It was obvious that hours of hard labor in the gym had kept him fit and muscular. Where was the double chin? The bifocals? She wanted the last laugh. Damn it anyway, it would seem she'd have to forget the Polygrip-and-cane theory.

For rather than deteriorating into an over-the-hill codger, Luke had improved. Like a fine wine. Mellowed. Matured. She hated him with a passion. Sighing out loud, she wondered what she had expected. He was only thirty.

Curious, she wanted to know if Luke still had the same powerful build under his suit that he'd had when he was eighteen. Remembering their last day together, Judith tuned out the drone of Ed and Ted's excited conversation, and thought about her teens and how much she'd admired Luke's body in those days....

Too tired to throw anything else out her bedroom window, she'd slumped, exhausted, onto her window seat. Noticing Luke's activity from her perch, Judith craned her skinny neck out the window for a better look. She pushed impatiently at her long, unruly mop in order to see more clearly. What was he *doing?* Undressing?

"Wow," she murmured, watching his athletic form, as he stretched his T-shirt over his head. From her vantage point, she could clearly see the outline of his well-formed muscles as they moved under his smooth tan skin. His shaggy brown hair was tousled by the wind, giving him an easy air of masculinity. She knew his chiseled features by heart, for he was the subject of many of her dreams and fantasies. He was as good-looking as she was ugly. Judith would rather go through Chinese water torture than admit her crush on Luke. He would laugh himself sick if he even suspected it. Boys she'd liked had been cruel before, and she'd known enough pain in her short life, because of her looks, to ever put herself through that.

Instead, she played the fool around him. Plaguing him with her pranks and wild mood swings. Something about Luke made her want to lash out. To make him suffer. She would never understand why. Maybe it was because he attracted her. Then again, maybe it was because he always treated her like a pesky little kid. He never seemed to grow tired of bossing her around.

Judith's eyes had grown dreamy as she watched Luke dive off the rocky edge, skimming the water's smooth surface with ease. A spray of crystal drops flew around his head as he shook the water from his hair and easily swam to the other side of the pond. He was a Greek god. He was beautiful and she...well, she was the beast.

Judith could feel Luke's eyes practically boring a hole through her suit. Flushing uncomfortably, she tried to guess what was going through his mind. It was so hard to tell with him. But she was sure that no handsome man in his right mind would ever truly be interested in a pesky, ugly, outrageous little nerd. And just what on earth was he doing back in town anyway, she wondered, irked by the direction her thoughts had taken. Didn't he work for some huge ad agency in San Francisco now? She was sure she'd seen the last of him when he'd left home at eighteen.

Good Lord, she was stunning. Luke just couldn't get over the change. He'd been hoping to avoid her once he got back, but now… His heart was pumping blood through his body with the force of a turbine engine. Annoyed with his adolescent reaction to this stunningly beautiful woman, he dragged his eyes away from her and looked at his dad. Just what the hell was she doing here anyway? Didn't she have some hotshot job in Seattle?

Ted shuffled through the pages that were lying on his desk. ''Now that we are retiring, Ed and I had our lawyer prepare a contract that you will both need to sign.'' He slid copies across his desk for Judith and Luke.

''Both?'' Luke looked puzzled. Why would Judith need to sign his contract? Judith looked equally confused, he was pleased to note. ''Why do we both need to sign?''

Ed and Ted exchanged guilty glances.

''Because you are both taking over the general partnership and creative directorship of the agency. Luke, you will be taking over Ed's position and Judith will take over mine. You will share all the duties involved. That's how Ed and I set it up some thirty years ago for ourselves, and that's how we'd like to see it continue for the two of you. Did we neglect to mention this?'' Ted shot Ed an uneasy glance.

What? Share? Why hadn't anyone told her that Luke was in on this deal? Judith was shocked. Her father expected her to run the agency with *Luke?* She couldn't work with him! When her father had broached the idea of her taking over his position at Anderson and Anderson, she'd been thrilled. No mention of Luke had ever been made in reference to her working there.

This was not what she'd planned at all. She had big ideas for this agency and its clients, and none of them included working with Luke. She surreptitiously glanced in his direction, and saw that he looked as flabbergasted as she felt.

Fury began to burn behind her snapping green eyes. He didn't have to look so upset, she wasn't *that* bad to work with. In fact, for his information, she'd been courted by some of the best agencies in the world. She didn't have to take this job, she desperately wanted to. All her life she'd dreamed of following in her father's footsteps. Numbly, Judith sat and tried to deal with her misgivings about this new turn of events.

There was no way she'd be able to work with Luke. No more so now than when she was a teenager. They'd never been in the same room together for more than a few minutes before they drove each other nuts, and she couldn't believe that anything had changed. Not to mention the fact that she could never forgive him for the way he'd hurt her feelings so many times when she was growing up.

Damn it, she wanted this job! Why should she have to give up her dreams because of him? Quickly, Judith considered her options. She could walk away and give up her future at Anderson and Anderson to Luke, and be completely miserable for the rest of her life. Or she could stay, run the business with Luke, and be completely miserable for the rest of her life. It was a classic lose-lose situation. Plus, it didn't help matters one little bit that she still found herself as wildly attracted to him as ever. Deciding it wouldn't be prudent to cry foul at this juncture, Judith clamped her lips tightly shut.

Ed cleared his throat and scanned his copy of the contract. "Ted and I wanted to discuss the legalities with you both, to make sure that you wouldn't have any problems."

Wouldn't have any problems? Was his father kidding? Luke wondered in astonishment and squirmed uncomfortably in his chair, unable to focus on his copy of the contract. If his dad was serious about forestalling future problems, he could start by writing the redhead at his side out of the deal. Her sexy good looks didn't fool him for a second. She might appear different, but Luke was sure that underneath the cool, sophisticated façade, lay the same tempestuous tyrant of his youth. Nobody changed *that* much both inside and out. No way. He'd served his time as the victim of her lunacy. What about all the times she'd tagged along with him on errands, waiting till they were on a busy street corner, then pointing at him and yelling "Kidnapper!" He used to threaten to break her finger. Then there was the time she followed him and his old girlfriend Cecilia to the state fair. She'd been showing off and ended up throwing up corn dogs all over his shoes. Cecilia hadn't escaped so easily either, as Judith had thrown up on her designer jeans. And how could he ever forget the time she'd told his girlfriend Debbie that he used to be a woman and that he'd had an operation, and that his new parts had come from a baboon. She'd told Debbie that he had to eat a lot of bananas or they'd fall off. The poor girl had been mortified.

Maybe the rumors about her incredible creative talent were true, but that could never outweigh the antagonism that had always existed between them. Somehow, some way, he had to get out of this mess. But how?

He'd worked damn hard for this moment and reveled in the thought that someday he would carry on his father's brilliant legacy. Judith Anderson had certainly never been part of that fantasy. He was nearly shaking with indignation as he turned to look at Judith, her lips pursed, her back ramrod straight. He wanted nothing on this earth as much as he wanted this opportunity. *Damn, damn, damn,* he thought, hating her prissy demeanor. It certainly didn't make matters easier, now that she looked like some kind of sex goddess. Feeling completely disgruntled and out of sorts, he worked the muscles in his jaw, and decided that he'd hear Ed and Ted out before he aired his grievances. Luke valiantly marshaled his powers of concentration and tuned back into the conversation that had continued without him.

"Yes," Ted agreed with Ed. "Actually, I feel pretty comfortable with the contract the way it is now, but if we need to, we can make any changes later with the lawyer."

We'll need to, Judith and Luke thought, and exchanged silent, murderous glances. Well, at least they agreed on that much, they both decided, and turned their attention to Ted.

"As you know, Ed and I are pleased to be handing the business down to our talented kids, now that we are retiring." Ed nodded, emotions swelling to the surface of his proud and tenderhearted face. Ted was fairly bursting with happiness himself. "We both agree that we could look the world over and never find two more qualified, capable people to fill our shoes at Anderson and Anderson. If it weren't for you two, we'd be selling the business now, and I have to admit that would be very painful. After all these years, it's like a baby to us."

Ed smiled poignantly at the two young people seated next to him in front of Ted's desk. "It seems like only yesterday that Ted and I met, became fast friends and opened our small agency. And now—" his eyes misted and he began to choke up "—now we're handing it over to you."

"It almost seems like fate, doesn't it, Ed?" Ted was susceptible to Ed's nostalgia. "Us having the same last name and all...why, we're practically family."

Luke suffered a sudden coughing fit and Judith wondered if the reference to being related had caused it.

Ed shrugged. "As far as I'm concerned, you are my brother."

Judith shut her eyes so that no one would notice her rolling them at the ceiling. This mushy trip down memory lane was almost more than she could bear.

Ted smiled at Ed and blinked rapidly, rubbing his eyes in the pretense that something had suddenly lodged there.

Ed continued. "Next week there will be a reunion of our platoon buddies in Korea. From there, Greta and I and Ted and Barbara will spend the next year traveling around the world." He and Ted exchanged excited glances. "We're really sorry about having to fly out tomorrow, but Ted and I are on the reunion committee and there is a lot of work to do before everyone arrives next week. Don't worry about a thing, though. The staff know the answers to any questions you may have and will be happy to assist you. We know we're putting you in an awkward position, but this was a last-minute decision. The reunion came up, and we decided that it was time to turn the business over to you two and we feel sure you'll muddle through. After all, you've both been doing the same jobs for other agencies."

"That's right," Ted interjected. "We feel confident that we can go and have a great time, knowing that the business will thrive under your talented direction." Ted's smile faded and he looked seriously at his daughter. "But there is one stipulation that Ed and I wanted to cover before we sign the contracts and leave."

Ed and Luke followed Ted's gaze to Judith. *Why is everyone staring at me?* she wondered, feeling suddenly conspicuous.

"In the past..." Ted began.

Oh, no. Judith groaned inwardly. Not the past. Anything but the past.

"You two seemed to have a hard time...er... getting along." Ted was obviously flustered at having to bring up this touchy subject. "I'm sure that you are both well aware of the teamwork that goes into running an ad agency of this magnitude. I don't have to tell either one of you that it is of the utmost importance that you two are able to work closely together in this endeavor.'' He flicked an invisible bit of dust off the gleaming surface of his desk. ''Ed's and my friendship has seen us through many rocky times over the years. Without a good, trusting and loyal relationship, we'd never have made it past the first year. That's why—'' he picked up the contract and flipped to one of the last pages ''—we have included a special clause.''

Oh, no. Luke rubbed his throbbing temples. A special clause. He should have known there'd be a catch.

''If you'll turn to section thirty, halfway down the page to section four, subparagraph D, you'll notice our stipulations.''

Judith and Luke obediently turned the pages of their documents until they found the clause Ted was referring to.

Ted adjusted his lanky frame to a more comfortable position, and regarded the two young people seriously.

''You have exactly one year to show an increase, however slight, in Anderson and Anderson's business. If, after one year, you are able to accomplish this task, the agency is yours to do with as you please. You can continue to run it together, or if you prefer, one of you can sell your share to the other.''

This was interesting. Luke was suddenly attentive. Judith would never last a year working with him and she knew it. Maybe he'd end up with the whole shooting match, after all, he thought, smiling smugly to himself.

A slow, delicious thrill shivered up Judith's delicate spine. *This was like taking candy from a baby!*

For she knew all of Luke's weaknesses well, and was already planning on systematically tackling each of them over the next twelve months. He'd never last a year working with her.

"If, on the other hand," Ted continued saying, "you manage to lose business, heaven forbid, the agency will revert to Ed's and my ownership, and will be put up for sale to a third party."

Both Judith and Luke froze, mid-gloat.

Ed stood up, took a few steps and perched on the edge of Ted's desk. Both fathers faced their offspring, their expressions somber. "We are as serious as a heart attack about this, kids," Ed said solemnly. "We didn't work our entire lives to watch you two drive the agency into the ground over a bunch of petty grievances. Our future income depends on your success. You can get along like two responsible adults and enhance the business, or we sell it. It's that simple. Is that clear?"

Luke and Judith glanced stiffly at each other, then at their fathers and nodded.

"Do we have a deal?" Ted asked expectantly.

"Um," Judith mumbled.

"Hemm." Luke nodded.

"Great." Ed beamed. "Let's shake on it."

Luke's hand felt warm and strong as it squeezed her slender one in an almost threatening grip. His message came through loud and clear, and Judith tightened her grasp viciously as she sent a challenge of her own. Was that a shadow of a smile she saw flash in his hazel eyes?

Pulling on her hand, he drew her into his arms and pecked her lightly on the cheek. "Congratulations, partner." He grinned fiendishly at her discomfort.

The springtime scent of her shining auburn hair had a disquieting effect on him. Once again he was suddenly a randy teenager, hot to trot. Quickly stepping back, he released her hand and turned to face the Anderson men, in an attempt to hide from her the overwhelming physical attraction he was feeling.

Good Lord, if her irksome personality didn't kill him, his latent physical attraction to her would. Luke felt a trickle of perspiration run between his shoulder blades as he wondered what the hell he was getting himself into.

The spot where Luke's lips had touched her cheek burned as though she'd been scalded by hot water. She was now officially in business with a man who had done more to ruin her self-esteem than he would ever know. The stage was set for the revenge of her childhood wounds and Judith planned to play her part to the hilt. That is, of course, if she could get her raging pulse under control before she suffered a massive coronary and dropped dead on the spot.

Ted pulled a bottle of champagne out of an ice bucket on the credenza behind his desk and popped the cork. The bubbly wine shot out of the bottle and flowed over his hands. Laughing, Ed grabbed the glasses and held them for his friend to fill.

Passing a glass to Judith and one to Luke, Ed held up his drink in a salute to the occasion. "A toast," he said, gazing fondly at the new partners. "To Judith and Luke. May their partnership be lasting and profitable."

Well, profitable, anyway, Judith and Luke both thought to themselves, as they clinked their glasses together.

Chapter Two

"Why the hell should *you* get that office?" Judith demanded, her heels clicking furiously down the hallway after Luke's retreating back.

"Because I was here first, that's why." Luke stopped so abruptly that Judith nearly collided with him. Turning around to face her, his eyes narrowed. "If you'd been here on time, maybe you'd have a right to an opinion."

Seething, Judith took a step closer to Luke, her hand itching to slap the smug look off his handsome face.

"I have a perfectly good reason for being late, I'll have you know, so you can forget trying to make me feel like some stupid adolescent. I want that office and I want it *now!*" she shouted.

"Yes, I can see that you're all grown-up." Luke's voice dripped with sarcasm. Turning, he continued striding down the vacant hallway till he came to the men's-room door.

"You'll get that office over my dead body!" she threatened.

Luke snorted. "Don't tempt me," he warned and pushed the men's-room door shut in her livid face.

Frustrated beyond endurance, Judith pounded the door with her fists. It wasn't fair. That office had been her father's and by all rights it should be hers now. He was just doing this to get her goat. How did he do it? How did he reduce her from a cool, restrained businesswoman, to a shrieking fishwife in a matter of minutes?

The fact that she was having a bad-hair day was the least of her problems. After she spilled coffee on the new outfit she'd so carefully chosen for her first day on the job, she'd run to her room to change. And change. And change... Nothing seemed right for her first professional appearance at Anderson and Anderson. And if it did seem right, it had creases from being jammed into a packing crate with the rest of her wardrobe.

Once every article of clothing Judith owned lay strewn around the bedroom she was occupying at her parents' house, she began to panic. Finally, she settled on a cool, well-cut navy tweed business suit composed of a tailored jacket and pencil skirt, paired with a white blouse and matching navy pumps. Not what she'd planned, but it would have to do. Her hair was a mashed, limp mess from all the changes of clothes, so she pulled it back with a clip, freshened her lipstick and ran out the door. Without her keys.

Unable to get back in the front door she'd so conscientiously locked, she ran around the house looking for an open window. Of course the only open window to be found was her bedroom window—on the second floor.

Rooting a ladder out of the gardener's toolshed, Judith battled the rose and juniper bushes, her pencil skirt binding her progress most uncomfortably, until she reached her destination. Luckily, her clothes weren't much the worse for wear, but where in heaven's name were her keys?

Thirty minutes later she found them in the refrigerator, of all places, and rushed to her car. Thankfully, she started it with a roar. Throwing it into reverse, Judith gunned the engine and pulled out into the morning traffic, only to become immediately stuck behind a school bus she was sure had stopped at every corner for at least ten minutes. She'd beaten the steering wheel and screamed in frustration during the entire commute.

She had wanted so badly to be early on her first day, and now, thanks to some voodoo spell Luke had cast on her, she'd been almost an hour late. Cursing his name under her breath, she tried the knob to the men's-room door. He'd been in there long enough. Today was not the day to test her patience with his stupid mind games.

"What the hell do you think you're doing?" Luke glared at Judith, who barged through the men's-room door as he busily flapped his wet hands under the useless air dryer. Disgusted, he decided it would be quicker to give up and wipe his hands on his neatly pressed slacks.

"I could ask you the same thing," Judith bit out, following him back down the hall to the office suite he'd claimed as his own. "You can't get away from me that easily, you know."

"Yes," he returned dryly. "I recall."

Judith blushed crimson. "That's not what I mean. And stop trying to make me feel like some pesky schoolgirl who doesn't belong here."

"Then don't act like one."

"If you would just quit bossing me around for once in your life…"

"That's the trouble with you." Luke impatiently talked over her as they headed toward the agency's front desk and lobby area. "You're still the same childish brat…"

Judith ignored his interruption and continued "…and listen to me, you'd see why that office is so important to me.…"

"…that you ever were. You may look different on the outside, but believe you me…"

"You should be in Ed's office, and you know it! Doesn't the fact that it was your father's office mean anything to…"

"…you are exactly the same on the inside. Same crap, different package.…"

"…you, you selfish, overbearing bore?"

"But you can't fool me with those sexy good looks. Oh, no. No, I'm on to you, sweetheart.…"

"Where on earth did you learn to be such an ass?"

"Nope, can't kid a kidder."

"Silly me, I forgot. You were born that way.…"

Their shouting escalated, as they barreled through the large glass double entry doors, past Mrs. Soder's desk, through the main lobby area, past the coveted corner suite and object of their heated debate, and into the creative department.

"…will have that office if I have to *chain* myself to the desk!" Judith shrilled.

"Be my guest. I can work around you." Luke's cocky smirk vanished as he and Judith battled their way into a room full of shocked and staring Anderson and Anderson employees.

The uncomfortable silence was broken by Mrs. Soder. Advancing on them, arms akimbo, she began her daily nonstop barrage of chatter. "Why you must be Luke and Judith Anderson!"

Judith bristled at the way she made them sound like a married couple. First chance she got, she was looking into getting her surname legally changed.

Luke had never met anyone quite like Mrs. Soder. Her title was chief administrative assistant, but to him she looked anything but administrative. A more appropriate title would be chief sideshow freak, he mused, taking in her purple cape, purple hat, purple stockings, purple pumps, purple nails and purple lipstick. Her hair was tinted to match the day's ensemble. And her fashion sense was only the tip of the iceberg. For such a plump, motherly looking character, she had the irritating falsetto voice of a small child. A voice that she'd used nonstop since they'd entered the room.

She was busily enveloping Judith in a bosomy embrace, talking all the while to Judith's chest. "Welcome, welcome to Anderson and Anderson...so very happy to meet you, finally, my dears...yes, indeed, your fathers have told us so many good things..." she rambled in her childish trill.

Standing next to Judith, Mrs. Soder reminded Luke of a plump concord grape. Standing next to Judith, everyone looked like a plump concord grape.

Did she have any idea how beautiful she was now? Luke eyed the new and improved Judith with amazement. Much to his chagrin, he found himself reacting to her in ways he'd never thought possible with the prickly, homely, tagalong Judith. Her complete metamorphosis had him so confused and jittery he didn't recognize himself, either. He wasn't sure if he wanted to throttle her—or if he simply wanted her. The only thing that kept him from kissing her until the shoes blew off her feet was the fact that she was, and always would be, Judith the Menace.

Mrs. Soder grabbed Luke by the wrist and drew him into the silent, still gawking crowd. "This is the gang," She waved her purple nails at the small group of curious employees. One by one, she introduced Judith and Luke to their creative team.

Stu, Mike, Jeff, Elizabeth, André and Ray. Judith struggled to place names to faces. Elizabeth would be easy, as she was the only other woman, besides Mrs. Soder and herself.

Drawing himself up manfully, Luke straightened his tie and smiled at "the gang." "Good morning, everyone. I'm Luke Anderson, the new principal and creative director at Anderson and Anderson." The men ignored him, and focused their attention on the stunning beauty at his side. Irked by their wolfish, gaping grins, Luke introduced Judith. "And this is Judith."

"Hello," she breathed huskily, shooting Luke an irritated glance. "I'm Judith Anderson, the *other* principal and creative director at Anderson and Anderson." Smiling, she sauntered into the lion's den and began shaking eager hands. Luke followed her and introduced himself to Elizabeth, a petite blonde, who was as sweet as she was pretty.

"I have an open-door policy," he informed her,

and pointed back at the suite Judith wanted. "Please, feel free to come see me with any questions or concerns."

If Judith had stepped into a time machine and been zapped backward twelve years, she couldn't have felt any uglier or gawkier than she did at that moment. Suddenly, she was all feet and freckles, next to the lovely Elizabeth. Struggling to maintain her composure, she shook Elizabeth's hand, and invited her to lunch sometime soon, in the spirit of sisterhood. Elizabeth looked very pleased and graciously accepted the invitation.

Damn, Luke thought. He was losing his touch. Why hadn't he come up with that? Not to be outdone by the magnanimous Judith, he turned to address the group.

"It's a pleasure to meet you all. Speaking for myself, I look forward to working closely with each of you—" this he directed warmly at Elizabeth "—to bring Anderson and Anderson into the twenty-first century as the leader in creative advertising…"

Speaking for himself! Let him, Judith fumed and seized the opportunity to slowly back out of the room and bolt down the hall to Ted's office and stake her claim.

"I would like to hold our first get-acquainted staff meeting in my office in…" Glancing around the room for a clock, Luke noticed Judith's sudden absence, and realizing how her devious little mind worked, he sprinted out of the room in hot pursuit.

The creative team, left to wonder when they were supposed to convene for the first get-acquainted meeting, heard the sounds of their new bosses squealing and shouting at the other end of the building. These two were certainly nothing like Ed and Ted. They sat in wonder, looking at each other with open mouths.

A door slammed and Jeff shrugged. "We're not in Kansas any more, Toto," he sighed.

"Oh, no, you don't!" Luke vaulted over the desk as Judith dove for the chair.

"Watch me!" she grunted, when Luke landed in her lap. "Oh, this is ridiculous! Get off me!" she huffed, pushing at Luke's broad back with all her might. "You're squashing me!"

"Good!" he bellowed, turning to face her, his nose less than an inch from her own. "Why don't you just say 'uncle' now and get it over with? You know you'll never be able to stick it out, so why not cut your losses? Call it a day? Throw in the towel? Take a hike?" His voice roared louder with each suggestion.

"If that's the extent of your creativity, Mr. Cliché, you need me more than I thought. Get off me, you Neanderthal, before I call security!"

Luke stood and hauled her out of the chair and into his arms. "What's wrong, Judith, afraid to fight your own battles?"

Through the roiling indignation that consumed her, Judith began to experience an altogether different sensation, as she felt Luke's strong, muscular arms lift her to the other side of the chair and hold her tightly in place. Her chest, heaving with exertion and anger, drew his eyes, and she could swear she felt the connection deep in the pit of her stomach. Between his roving eyes and her degenerate mind, Judith was ready to blow a gasket.

"Not when it's a *fair fight*," she hurled at him as

he dropped into the vacant seat. "If you want this office so damn bad, then—" she flew to the heavy oak double doors as though the demons of hell were chasing her and yanked them open dramatically "—take it!" she screamed, and slamming each door with a vengeance, she exploded past a speechless Mrs. Soder, who stood with a shocked and dismayed client.

"Hold my calls," she barked and stormed into Ed's old suite, crashing the doors closed behind her.

"You look like something the cat dragged in." Elizabeth peered across the conference table at her new boss.

Judith smiled wanly and blew an errant wisp of hair out of her face. The dark circles under her eyes were caused by too many sleepless nights, and more recently, an uncharacteristic crying jag. Tossing her pencil down on a stack of files, her grin was feeble. "I'm striving for that road-kill look."

"You've hardly achieved *that*," Elizabeth remonstrated, "but you don't exactly look like the beauty queen who took over this operation just two short weeks ago."

Judith stared queerly at the petite blonde across from her for a moment, before slumping tiredly in her chair. "That's because in the past two weeks Anderson and Anderson has managed to lose three key accounts, including the prestigious and lucrative Dalton Industries account. And that doesn't even scratch the surface of the rest of the poor, innocent clients we've managed to alienate," she sighed dejectedly.

"Are you okay?"

"Not really. My poor father. I just can't face him.

He'll be devastated." Judith sniffed and wiped at her eyes with a soggy, rumpled handkerchief.

"What reason did the people at Dalton give for pulling their business?" Elizabeth's limpid eyes were pools of concern. Her future was on the line, too, and she was as terrified as Judith was about the past two weeks' sudden decline in business.

"The same reason that the Amalgacom and Holt accounts gave. Creative differences." Her short laugh was brittle. "And not between the agency and the company. Ohh, noo." Judith stood, stretched and began pacing in agitation around the conference room. "The creative differences that are souring business deals right and left are Luke's and mine."

Elizabeth sympathetically watched the boss that she'd grown so fond of in the past weeks pace unhappily around the room.

"Ha! I wouldn't be surprised if we set some sort of record. We lost the Holt account before noon on our first day. Wouldn't Daddy and Ed be proud?" She flopped into the seat next to Elizabeth and buried her head in her hands. "What am I going to do?" she moaned, desperation settling like a morbid cloak over her bent and weary shoulders.

"Well," Judith's new friend and favored employee mused, "you've got a problem. What I just can't understand is why you and Luke don't get along. You're talented, funny, sweet and beautiful. Just ask any of the guys. And Luke is great."

How great? Judith wondered, opening one miserable eye and pondering Elizabeth morosely.

Elizabeth smiled a knowing little smile. "I think if you gave yourselves half a chance, you'd discover that you like each other more than either of you thought possible.''

''No way!'' Judith tossed her auburn tresses over her fashionably padded shoulders and sat up straight. ''You don't know him like I do. We've known each other all our lives and we have *never, ever* gotten along.''

''Why not?''

''If I knew that, we wouldn't be in this mess. I don't know what it is about him that drives me so insane, Elizabeth. I'm not kidding, I never act like this around anyone but Luke Anderson. Ask anyone I used to work with in Seattle, at Morgan, Van Zant, Grey and Getty, and they will tell you that I was aloof and in control. Almost to the point of being antisocial.'' She played with a long thread that hung from her sleeve. ''I was quiet, hardworking and professional. Respected by my peers. And now—'' she blew a short, exasperated puff of air through her teeth ''—now, I'm a joke.''

''Hardly.'' Elizabeth defended her loyally. ''Stressed out, yes, but not a joke.''

''I just don't know how we're going to tell our fathers that we lost the Dalton account. I still can't believe it. They are going to be so mad....''

''But they're giving you a year to prove yourselves, right? Maybe you can get Dalton back.''

''I don't think so. Our first meeting with them will undoubtedly go down in the record books as the single most embarrassing moment in the history of advertising. I don't think Mr. Dalton was cut out to be a boxing referee.''

''Was it that bad?''

''Worse.'' Judith began gathering her files. ''I can't

get anything done here, I'm too depressed. I'll work on these tonight.'' She clutched the files to her chest.

"Need some help? I don't have any plans for this evening.''

Judith hesitated for a split second, then nodded. "Sure. Why not?'' She scribbled her address on a scrap of paper and handed it to Elizabeth. "Come by around seven. I'll make us something simple to eat while we work.''

Luke lay sprawled out on Ted's leather sectional, his tie loose and his sleeves rolled up above the elbow. He stared at the ceiling and wondered for the thousandth time what the hell he'd gotten himself into. It just kept getting worse every day. One would think that two mature adults could put aside their petty grievances and do business in a civil manner. But obviously, the one who thought that had never had to work with Judith Anderson.

Judith. Luke shut his eyes tightly as visions of his untamed, sexy business partner filled his mind. Her fiery mane gave new meaning to the term hothead....

Luke fancied himself to be an easygoing, mellow, uncomplicated kind of guy. He was always in control of his emotions. What was it then, about this wild, rampageous woman, that had him making a complete and utter fool out of himself at every turn? Gone were the glory days of Luke Anderson, professional adman, in charge of his destiny. Now, he was just some has-been, running a loser ad agency with a cross between Lucille Ball and Attila the Hun.

Luke sighed, the sigh of a man who'd been sentenced to death row. Oh, well. On the bright side, working with Judith had given him a certain compassion for homicidal maniacs.

He could tell by the lengthening shadows on the wall that it was getting late. Too late... *Or was it?* Surely he and Judith could come to some kind of understanding and pull together to clean up this mess they'd made. He was willing to meet her halfway. She had an outstanding reputation for incomparable creative work in Seattle. Her stuff had been getting a lot of national attention. Obviously, someone had been able to work with her in the past.... Well, no time like the present. If Judith wasn't in her office, he'd catch her at home.

"Luke! What a surprise!" Elizabeth took his jacket and closed Ted's front door behind him. "We were just sitting in the kitchen, making sandwiches and working on some ideas. Come on, I'll take you back."

Luke followed Elizabeth in dismay. He'd hoped to corner Judith alone, so that they could speak freely. Vent their spleens, so to speak, and then when the air was clear declare a truce and start over. As though they'd never met before.

In the kitchen, Luke found Judith busily preparing a light meal for Elizabeth and herself at the kitchen counter.

Luke was here. Startled, Judith nearly overfilled her glass with milk. What was *he* doing here? she wondered disgruntledly, her tongue turning into a wool sock inside her mouth. He was dressed casually in a colorful polo shirt, faded, form-fitting blue jeans and a pair of sneakers. His jaw was darkened slightly by the day's growth of stubble. Why did he always have to look so damned attractive?

"Hello," she greeted him, her voice remarkably calm, but that would undoubtedly change if he were to pick a fight. "What brings you here?"

"I was hoping to talk to you for a few minutes about some of the problems we've been having at work," Luke said, taking a seat next to Elizabeth at the counter, across from Judith.

He was here to pick a fight. "Are you hungry?"

"As a matter of fact, yes."

"We're just having sandwiches, but you're welcome to join us," she offered, hoping he'd say no and be on his way.

"Thanks," he said and began piling an empty plate with bread and lunch meat.

Elizabeth looked quickly back and forth between the two. "I could leave you guys alone..." Having witnessed their discussions before, she had no desire to be caught in the middle of one of their volcanic eruptions.

Not about to let her only buffer against Luke disappear, Judith hastily reassured her. "No, no. You're fine." She handed Elizabeth a plate. "Help yourself."

Judith was still wearing the light green silk suit she'd worn to the office that day, Luke noticed. He had admired the way it swished and clung to her figure as she'd stormed in and out of his office on more than one occasion. Stop it, he warned himself and turned his concentration on the food. His preoccupation with what was going on under that green silk would surely kill him.

Assembling three immense sandwiches might have kept him busy, but now he had to deal with the problem of eating them. He could feel Judith watching him in amazement as he gamely tore into sandwich number one. The kitchen was silent, except for the occasional clink of their silverware.

Glancing at Judith, Luke watched her run her tongue across her full lower lip, to catch a dollop of mustard. He took a large bite of his sandwich to stifle a groan. She seemed oblivious to the fact that she was incredibly gorgeous now. He painfully swallowed his bite, half chewed, and fought the urge to lick a tiny daub of mayonnaise off her cheek. What the hell was he thinking? This was *Judith!* Goofy, absurd Judith. And he was sitting there fantasizing about licking her face. Not to mention her toes and all the other interesting possibilities that lay in between. This was a nightmare. Ted would kill him for these lewd thoughts, if Judith didn't do so first.

Unable to stand the deafening silence another second, Elizabeth smiled brightly. "Mrs. Soder says that Blake Fletcher-Holt called you today, Judith. That's a good sign."

"He did?" Luke looked at the suddenly pink Judith suspiciously. "Why didn't you tell me?"

"Because he didn't ask for you."

"What did he want?" Luke still chafed over the fact that they'd managed to lose the important Holt account their first morning on the job.

"He…uh…wanted to meet with me." Judith stared at her sandwich in fascination.

Luke had instinctively disliked the too smooth, too cool, oily-haired young Blake Fletcher-Holt, but not enough to turn his business away. Anyone whose personalized license plates read BADASS had to be a goon. "Why didn't you tell me?"

"It didn't seem that important at the time."

"Not important? You schedule a meeting with one of our biggest accounts, and it's *not important?*"

"He didn't call to discuss his account."

"Then why did he call? Or is there something you're not telling me? If you're working with him behind my back, so help me Judith Anderson..."

"He's taking me to dinner, okay? Just a simple dinner date."

"What?" Luke was dumbfounded. "How does he know you?"

"He doesn't know me. He was there the morning you and I were fighting over your office, and he asked Mrs. Soder who I was."

Something in Luke's gut began to tingle and burn, spreading quickly throughout his body. His flesh went cool and clammy, even as he began to perspire. She had a date! With the sleazy Fletcher-Holt, no less. The thought of Judith going out with that greaseball bothered him. A lot. Although, why it bothered him so much was a mystery. Of course Judith dated men, after all, just look at her. Making a monumental effort to remain nonchalant, he cocked an interested eyebrow in her direction and said, "He seems like kind of a pompous jerk to me." *Damn.* Where had that come from? That wasn't what he meant to say.

Judith's eyes sparkled with flames of anger. "Just because he didn't ask to talk to you, doesn't mean he's a pompous jerk."

"Did I strike a nerve?" He goaded her, wishing they could back up and start this ridiculous conversation over again. He'd come here to make peace with her.

"Why you smug, arrogant, condescending, son of

a…'' Nostrils flaring, Judith slammed her sandwich down on the counter.

Startled, Elizabeth jumped. "Hey, guys…" she tried to intervene.

"Quiet, Elizabeth!" Judith snapped. "Who the hell does he think he is, calling one of our best clients names? No wonder we're losing business hand over fist, with an attitude like that!" she was practically shouting.

"You're saying I'm the reason we lost the Holt account?" Luke's expression was deadly.

"If the shoe fits!" Judith hurled at him.

"I suppose *I'm* the reason we lost the Amalgacom and Dalton accounts as well, huh?" Luke's narrowed eyes never left her face, his voice was barely controlled fury.

"Um…you guys…" Elizabeth began tentatively.

"Shut up, Elizabeth," they snapped.

"Who do you think Ed and Ted are going to believe killed that business?" He goaded Judith and leaned forward across the counter, his biceps bulging beneath his shirt.

He looked so haughty and arrogant sitting there, staring at her with his lazy hooded hazel eyes. She wanted to smack him. Instead, without thinking, she picked up her sloppy, overflowing sandwich and flung it at his chest.

"Oh, hey, that was bright," he said quietly, looking down at his mustard-soaked polo shirt.

Judith giggled nervously at the murder in his eyes, but stopped when she felt his sandwich bounce off the side of her face. Slowly, she reached up and pulled off the piece of ham that dangled over her ear and lobbed it back across the counter at him.

"You...*butthead!*" she cried, reaching for a spoon-ful of macaroni salad.

He grabbed her wrist firmly and twisted her hand so that the salad plopped over her head and oozed into her hair. "That's *Mr.* Butthead to you, you little *witch!*" he yelled, gasping as her half-filled glass of milk caught him square in the mouth. "That does it!" he bellowed, reaching across the counter and hauling a shrieking Judith up among the remnants of their meal.

"Stop it, you big jerk!" Judith howled, fighting against Luke's viselike grip. "Put me down! *Now!*" Fumbling in the macaroni salad bowl, she scooped out a handful and mashed it into his neck.

Grunting with effort, he yanked the flailing Judith into his arms and pulled her tightly against the firm wall of his solid chest. Throwing her over his shoulder, he turned to Elizabeth, who sat speechless with shock.

Raising his voice to be heard above the squealing Judith, he said "Elizabeth, please excuse us, will you? Your hostess has some...freshening up to do." With that, he turned and strode easily out of the kitchen, Judith bobbing furiously over his shoulder. Elizabeth's jaw was slack as she watched them go, fighting all the while.

"Ouch! Put me down, you gorilla!" Judith ground out, pounding on his firm behind.

"Forget it, you little hellion," he growled, "I'm not finished with you yet."

"No!" Judith spat, as Luke entered the spacious bath that connected to her parents' master-bedroom suite. He turned on the shower and tested the water's temperature. Deciding it was just right, he stepped inside and set Judith under the steamy spray.

"Stop! You'll ruin my...suit!" she sputtered, as the hot water pounded down over her head, plastering her salad-filled hair to her face.

"You should have thought of that before you decided to play football with your food," he shouted, holding her under the faucet with one hand and reaching for a bar of soap with the other.

"Quit it!" she yelped, when he began vigorously soaping her luxurious hair. "You're getting...soap... in my...contacts.... Ooowww!"

"Tough." He was beyond caring about her discomfort. Hot water pelted soothingly over her face and into her eyes, as he cradled her head to rinse the lather out of her hair. "That's better now, isn't it?" Drops of water glistened on his sensuous lips. He was grinning at her.

"You still have macaroni salad on your neck." She smiled sweetly, twisting to escape his firm grasp.

"Oh, no, you don't, sweetheart." He tightened his hold on her waist. "We're still not finished."

His smoldering eyes traveled down to where the wet silk of her light green suit clung and molded to every subtle curve of her body. Worriedly, her eyes bolted up to his face, in an effort to understand what he meant. Time seemed to stop as his smoky eyes penetrated her gaze. The sound of the shower faded into so much background noise and their ragged breathing filled her ears. He was so beautiful, she thought, his handsome face mere inches from her own. She knew she must look like hell.

The feel of Luke's strong hands burned her waist through the thin fabric of her silk suit. She spread her palms out across his chest to steady her weak knees, and lowering her eyes, she could make out the hard ridges of his flat stomach where the damp fabric of his shirt molded unmercifully to him. His wet jeans were stretched taught across corded, muscular thighs. Pushing against him, she attempted to put some space between his hard, wet body and her soft one.

Pulling her back against him and under the spray, he rested his forehead against hers so that their noses were touching and he groaned. His lips lightly brushed hers as he spoke.

"What the hell are we doing to each other?" he muttered, running his hands up her back and massaging the smooth planes he found there. "Why is it always so violent between us?" He tipped her head up and searched her face. Sparkling drops of water like small diamonds clung to her long lashes. Lifting his mouth, he pressed it tenderly to each one in turn.

Judith was sure she'd died and gone to heaven. She had waited for this moment all her life. "I don't know," she whispered, her low voice breathy. "You always just make me so mad." She looked up at him, her nose grazing the light stubble on his cheek. "Sometimes I...hate you. I don't even know why."

He smiled. "I know. Sometimes...I hate you, too."

"You're nuts. You know that, don't you?"

"Me? You're the one with the ballistic sandwich." Luke reached up and shut off the shower's faucet. They stood for a moment, simply holding one another. "We should probably get back, before Elizabeth thinks we've killed each other."

Judith looked ruefully down at her soggy suit. "Like this? You've got to be kidding."

"No, not like this." Luke echoed and rolled his

eyes. Stepping back, he reached down, stripped his shirt up over his head and slapped it over the large shower door.

Judith was horrified. And fascinated. "Like *that?*" His smooth tan torso was better now than the body of the young demigod she'd fantasized about as a teen. He exuded sinewy animal strength. No wonder he'd had no trouble hoisting her over his shoulder.

"No, not like *this.*" The creases beside his mouth deepened at the surprise…and was that innocence?…he read in her expression. He pulled off his shoes and unzipped his pants.

"What are you doing?" she gasped, backing against the tiled wall of the shower. "Put those back on!" she ordered him, clutching her arms firmly across her breasts.

Pausing, he eyed her in exasperation. "No. They're soaked. We've already made enough of a mess for one day. I'll go get us some dry things. Turn around if the sight of my underwear freaks you out."

Judith couldn't stop herself from glancing down at his damp jockey shorts. *Oh, my!* Scarlet cheeked, she spun around and faced the wall. His laughter rang in her ears.

"Don't be such a prude. Surely you've seen a naked man before." It was more of a question than a statement.

"Of course, I have," she stated tartly. She had, hadn't she? Somewhere, in art class or something. And where did he get off calling her a prude? Having the morals of an alley cat did not make one worldly in her opinion. Just because Judith had yet to find the man she could trust her heart and body to was no reason to consider her naive. She was a grown-up, sophisticated adwoman, and she'd thank this modern-day Don Juan to remember that.

"Oh?" His voice was hard. "I suppose Blake *Lecher*-Holt is only too happy to bare his pompous behind for you." He howled with laughter.

"You leave Mr. Holt's tush out of this, you...you animal." She spun around, seething at his audacity.

Luke had stepped out of the shower and fastened a towel around his hips. She watched, hypnotized by the play of his rippling muscles, as he briskly dried his body with a second towel. When he was done, he tossed it into the shower at her.

"Here." He arched a lazy eyebrow at her. "You're all wet." Roaring with laughter again, he sauntered into the bedroom in search of dry clothes.

If Elizabeth found it strange when Judith and Luke returned to the kitchen clad in matching terry-cloth robes, she made no comment. Instead, she picked up a cloth and began wiping down the counter, a knowing smile on her lips.

Chapter Three

"Ms. Anderson?" Mrs. Soder's chalkboard-and-nails trill stopped Judith on her way through the reception area. "Ms. Anderson, there is a man waiting for you in your office. I told him you were out, but he said he'd wait. I didn't know what else to do, so I let him in. I hope that's okay, but if it's not I can go in..."

"Who is he?" Judith interrupted impatiently. Getting a word in edgewise with Mrs. Soder required a crowbar.

Today, Mrs. Soder had chosen to deck herself out in the color red. Her cherry red clothing, hair tint, makeup and accessories had Judith squinting from the painful brightness.

"He says his name is Big Daddy Brubaker, although I can't imagine where a little guy like him picked up a name like that. Why, he's no bigger than my thumb!" she squeaked, and held up one scarlet thumbnail. "Do you think it's a code name or..."

"How long has he been here?" Judith cut in again.

"Maybe half an hour or forty-five minutes, but not more than…"

"Where is Luke?"

"He's still at lunch." Mrs. Soder pursed her smudged, gooey red lips together in a childish pout. "I wish he would call in because…"

"Thank you, Mrs. Soder. Please hold my calls while I meet with Mr. Brubaker. If Luke comes back…send him in."

"Yes, Ms. Anderson," Mrs. Soder shrieked.

Her eardrums throbbing, Judith made good her escape before the lady in red could think of something else to say. Entering her office, she glanced around for the mysterious Big Daddy. He was nowhere to be found. He had either grown tired of waiting or Mrs. Soder had been nipping the sauce at lunch. Sighing, she tossed her briefcase on her desk. Another piece of business down the tubes. Dinner with Blake Fletcher-Holt had been a fiasco, too. She'd spent the entire evening fighting off his slimy advances.

"Ahh. Hello, theyah," a deep voice boomed, as the swivel chair behind her desk spun around, revealing a diminutive man in a ten-gallon hat that appeared to have swallowed his head.

"Hello," Judith answered tentatively, startled by the strange apparition seated with much authority before her. "May I help you?"

"Why, yes, ya may, honey pie!" Big Daddy boomed and leapt out of the chair to enthusiastically attack Judith's hand. "I'm Big Daddy Brubaker, from the Lone Star State, and y'all must be…"

"Judith Anderson, one of the two principals, here at Anderson and Anderson."

"Of course! So I've heard. The name Luke doesn't suit ya at all! Judith is much bettah. Pretty name for a pretty woman. Just like the movie. But, then, y'all must heah that all the time." His eyes were two shiny black raisins, surrounded by rumpled layers of leathery skin. His jacket was cut in a Western style, complete with fringe, and even though he wore high-heeled cowboy boots, the top of his hat barely reached Judith's shoulder.

Not altogether sure why, something about Big Daddy Brubaker appealed to Judith. His Southern drawl was charming as were the deep cracks that years of smiling had etched around his eyes and mouth. But more than that, Big Daddy wore his tender heart like a badge for all the world to see. He exuded an aura of gentleness that drew Judith like a magnet.

"Let's have a seat," Judith suggested and gestured to a group of comfortable chairs near her window.

"Now, theah's an idea, little gal." Big Daddy's loud voice filled the room.

Little gal? Judith smiled to herself. "What can I do for you, Mr. Brubaker?"

"Big Daddy. Call me Big Daddy," he ordered. "Everyone does."

"All right, then, er…Big Daddy."

Big Daddy unbuttoned his coat and pulled a tiny booted foot up over his knee. A large smile wreathed his hawklike face. "Well, now, I got a little problem and I've heard good things about y'all Andersons up heah in Ory-gone. Heck of a campaign ya put together for old man Dalton. Heh-heh-heh. Yup. Loved that!"

Judith chewed her lower lip nervously. She'd better set him straight about the Dalton mess now. He'd find out soon enough, anyway. "Well, actually, I didn't have much to do with that campaign. In fact..."

"Beautiful and modest!" Big Daddy slapped his knee in delight. "That's just what I'm looking for. Ya see, I've got a unique set of circumstances that will require a unique ad agency."

"Oh?" Judith swallowed. She guessed they were about as unique as you could get.

"Yup. Had a little oil spill. Some crazy son of a gun...pardon my French—" he tipped his hat at her in apology "—drove one of my tankers too close to the shore. The good name of Brubaker Oil has suffered ever since."

"Yes, I remember reading about that. I'm sorry," Judith murmured.

"Why, thank you. Any-who, I need an ad agency that can put Brubaker Oil back in the good graces of the American public." Big Daddy pushed his huge hat back on his head and beamed at Judith. "And I think y'all Andersons are just the people to take the challenge. I'm very impressed with youah style. Your stuff is light-years ahead of the crap, pardon my French, that my last ad agency tried to pass off on me." His brows knitted together pensively. "I finally had to cut those yahoos loose. All they ever did was bicker and fight. Like to have driven me crazy."

Uh-oh. Judith's heart sank. Luke wasn't here, so at least they could avoid another embarrassing scene in front of a potential client. "That's too bad," she said as a light knock sounded at her door. *Uh-oh.* Luke was here.

"Mrs. Soder says you asked for me?" Glancing from Judith to Big Daddy, Luke entered the room and strode over to where the small man stood up to greet him. The fringe on Big Daddy's jacket danced as he vigorously pumped Luke's hand.

"Luke Anderson," he introduced himself and grinned boyishly.

"Please to meetcha, Luke. Big Daddy Brubaker. I was just tellin' the little missus here—" he pointed at Judith "—why I fired my last ad agency. Bunch of scrapping jackals."

Luke shot a pointed look at Judith. "I think you've made…" he attempted to correct Big Daddy's false assumption about his and Judith's relationship, but Big Daddy seemed to be a verbal steamroller when he got fired up.

"A wise choice! Yes, y'all don't have to tell me that!" Luke took a seat between Judith and Big Daddy. "I'm a family man, myself, and I must tell y'all that I'm lookin' forward to doin' business with a family-run operation."

Luke cleared his throat. "I can appreciate your interest in working with a family-run business, however…"

"I'm glad ya see it my way! Family is the most important thing a man can have in this world. Numbah one. I know. I have a bunch of oil fields, a giant ranch, cars, helicopters, buildings and a couple billion bucks stuffed in various bank accounts around the world. But none of that, and I mean none of it, is as important to me as my family. Did I mention Ah have nine kids?"

Big Daddy leaned forward, pulled a bulging wallet out of his hip pocket and flipped out a string of pictures as tall as himself. "These are my young'uns. All boys, except Patsy there. The light of my life." He held her picture up so that they could admire her pretty blond looks. "And heah's their Mama, Miss Clarise. Still lovely as the day I married her," he boasted.

"Yep," he continued, folding his mini-picture album up and shoving it back into his pocket. "Family is where it's at. That's why, after careful consideration, I chose Anderson and Anderson to be my next ad agency. I like the idea of workin' with a young married couple as in love as you two obviously are."

Judith and Luke exchanged incredulous glances.

Feeling duty bound to set Big Daddy on the right track, Judith again attempted to enlighten this modern day Yosemite Sam.

"Big Daddy, Luke and I may have the same last name, but we are not..."

"I know, I know! I'm no chauvinist. Y'all women don't ride on youah husbands' coattails anymoah. Obviously, y'all are a brilliant *team*. The work that comes out of this agency is nothin' less than first rate. I'm sure we'll get along fine, and I'm willin' to make it worth youah while. I'm not braggin' none when I say that I'm stinky rich. Ya kids do the job right for me and y'all will be, too. Hell's bells, excuse me ma'am—" he tipped his hat again, in deference to the presence of a lady "—but when ya work for Big Daddy Brubaker, y'all don't need any other clients."

He looked expectantly back and forth between the gaping Andersons. "Well, folks, what'll it be? Will you help me with my little image problem?"

Judith stood up and gripped Luke by the sleeve of his shirt and smiled brightly at their tiny visitor. "Um...Big Daddy, could we just...excuse ourselves to discuss...your generous offer?" Clutching Luke's shirt, she nearly dragged him to the door. "We won't be but a second," she whispered confidentially, her smile pasted firmly in place.

"Why, sure! Take youah time. Just keep that Soder woman outa heah, heh-heh-heh. She'd like to have talked a couple of inches off me earlier today."

"Am I hearing things, or did that Southern leprechaun just tell us he wants to make us stinky rich?" Luke, still in shock, dumbly followed Judith into his office.

"You heard right," she muttered, pacing over to the window to watch the bustling city down below. "We have to tell him no."

"No? *No!* Are you *crazy?*" Luke snarled and stormed over to where she stood. "Why the hell not?"

"Because he's a sweet, little man and he thinks we're married."

"So what? He's rich. Filthy rich!"

"I just don't think we should lie to a nice man like Big Daddy. It doesn't seem fair."

"Since when are you so interested in being fair, Mary Poppins? This could be the answer to all our problems! I can't believe you want to turn away the biggest account in the history of Anderson and Anderson! Of course, I shouldn't be surprised." He plunged his fingers through his hair. "That's all you've done since we took over."

"What a crock!" Judith exclaimed. "You had just as much to do with losing the Dalton account as I did, and you know it. Don't go pulling that holier-than-thou act with me." She spun around to face him, eyes blazing.

"You're right. What the hell was I thinking? I could never be married to you, even in name only."

"Well, the feeling's mutual!" she flung back at him.

Luke's eyes narrowed and his voice became dangerously low, as he came within an arm's reach of her. "You know what your problem is? You're frustrated!" he accused, taking a step closer to her, his body language threatening.

Judith went rigid. *What did he mean by that?*

"You're so cantankerous and obstinate, I'd be willing to bet you don't even have a personal life. Who could take you for more than a few minutes at a time? And now that your precious career, the only thing on this earth that means anything to you, is on the skids, you're taking it out on me! You're just mad because you know it's all your fault."

He was so wrong. There were other things in her life besides her career she cared a great deal about. Loved. He didn't know her at all. "How *dare* you." She tore into him, gasping with rage. "You can take your amateur psychoanalysis and shove it!" she spat, fairly vibrating with anger. "You're the one who's mad because I won't con that sweet little man in the next room. *I* have morals."

"Is that what you call it? *Morals?*" he roared. "You call driving our fathers' lifelong dream straight into the ground *moral?*" Volts of electricity seemed to spark from his every pore.

"I didn't drive it there by myself." She reached out and clutched a fistful of his white button-down dress shirt. "Listen to me, buster, and listen good. You don't own this business, or me for that matter, and I am *sick* of you telling me what to do."

Luke pried her fingers off his shirt and held them firmly, almost painfully in his hand. "No," he growled, and a muscle in his jaw jumped with fury. "You listen to *me,* and you listen good. I am sick and tired of you fighting me at every turn. Like it or not, we have an obligation, a legal duty, may I remind you, to make a go of this sorry excuse for an ad agency. We have an agreement, and come hell or high water, you're going to stick to it, you little barracuda." He tightened his grip convulsively and Judith yelped in agony. "So. What'll it be, *partner?*" His voice was a harsh whisper. "You throw this opportunity away and you can kiss Anderson and Anderson goodbye. Is that what you want?" He yanked on her hands and drew her up close. "Well, I don't. And I swear to you, Judith Anderson, if you fight me on this Brubaker decision, I'll turn you over my knee and paddle your shapely little butt." With that, he roughly released his painful grip on her fingers.

"Bull!" she challenged furiously.

"Don't push me," he shot at her, taking a step closer and backing her up against the wall.

Nose to nose, they stood glaring at each other, both of them breathing hard. Then, without warning, the storm in Luke's eyes took on a hot wind of desire. An imperceptible change in the angle of his mouth had him a hairbreadth from kissing her. Slowly, he leaned into her soft body, crushing her against the unforgiving wall.

Judith knew that if she breathed any faster, she'd hyperventilate. Where was a paper bag when you needed one? she wondered hysterically. That Luke intended to kiss her was clear, and much to her chagrin she found that she wanted him to.

A force as old as time itself lured Luke into the mysterious vortex of Judith's beauty. He knew that he was going to kiss her, and knew that he would probably regret it. But try as he might, he could hold himself back no more than he could hold back the tide. Inching closer, he was tantalized by her full lips and deep, sea green eyes that were lowered in confusion. He grasped her firm upper arms lightly for support.

His eyes held a question that was almost painful in its intensity. Judith Anderson, the little spitfire he'd known all his life, seemed at this moment a perfect stranger. What was she thinking? Would she fight him in this, too? At this point he didn't give a damn. He'd fought her so hard, for so long, all the fight had gone out of him. He wanted her. There was a volatile attraction between them, and he knew that Judith, though she wouldn't admit it, felt it as well.

Numbly, she lifted her eyes, and responded to his probing stare. She was terrified of what was about to happen, and gloriously thrilled at the same time. Her conflicting emotions warred within her, and common sense lost to longing. The gentle touch on her arms was combustible, fanning the flames of passion that had existed between them since the very beginning, igniting an unfamiliar white-hot desire.

She was going to faint. Her arms slipped around his waist of their own volition, holding on tightly for support as he drew her away from the wall and crushed her to his chest. He held back for just a second, his eyes flashing, his hands tracing the sleek lines of her slender waist.

Then he leaned her back, ever so slightly, so that

she was helpless in his arms, depending on his strength to hold her up. He was in control.

"Damn, Judith," he breathed. Frustration and determination tinged the words that were barely audible to her ears. Twining his fingers in her wild auburn mane, he cradled her head in his hands and lowered his mouth to hers.

There was no violence in this kiss, only years of forbidden unacknowledged passion. Sliding her hands up Luke's broad back, she filled her curious fingers with his thick, silky hair. She was melting. Melting into Luke, becoming one with him in spirit, in body. Unable to get close enough, she shifted her body more firmly into his, snuggling, seeking his warmth, his strength, his power.

Opening herself up to him, she became vulnerable, receiving from him, giving to him, matching him passion for passion. She surrendered everything to Luke in that moment, willing for the first time in her life to submit. To bury the hatchet, however briefly. To let him know with actions, rather than words, the feelings she'd never been able to share with him before.

Their desire was voracious, their kiss frenzied, greedy. Hands and mouths moved, explored, probed, searched insatiably, struggling to quench this fire that was bigger than either of them.

Slowly, Luke pulled her upright, his hands slipping behind her back and ended the kiss, several times, before opening his eyes. Through the heavy fringes of her hooded gaze, he could see into the depths of her being. They stood, amazed, completely taken back by what had just happened, as if they had broken some unspoken taboo.

Luke was the first to regain his power of speech.

"Come on," he said raggedly, running a hand over his face, as he led her, still stunned by the impact of their kiss, to the leather sectional.

Judith followed him on rubber legs, and sat down beside him. Never, in all of her years of girlish fantasy, had she ever dreamed kissing Luke could be like that. It had been nothing short of an out-of-body experience. He had literally kissed the anger out of her.

Luke studied her uncertainly for a moment before he spoke.

"I'm sorry," he said and rubbed his jaw regretfully.

Judith's heart, like a child's kite caught in a crosscurrent, plummeted. *He was sorry?* How could he be sorry? Good Lord, she thought, beginning to panic. Hadn't he felt the roller coaster thrill in his stomach, too? It had started at the union of their lips, roared down her throat, around her heart and into her stomach, where it ran a course of wild curlicues.

"Sorry?" she whispered, stricken by the word.

"Yes. I should never have said those things to you. I didn't mean any of it. I...I was afraid."

He didn't say what he was afraid of and Judith didn't ask, somewhat relieved that it was words and not actions he was apologizing for.

He sighed. "I saw all that cold, hard cash, and I guess I just sort of lost it. I was wrong."

Wrong? Luke was admitting that he was wrong? Had hell frozen over? Stunned, Judith searched for something to say that wouldn't lead to an argument. After all, Luke had apologized.

"I know," her voice quavered. "I thought about the money, too. We could really use it. The way things are going now, we'll have to give the agency back to Ed and Ted to sell to some stranger,'' she said wistfully. ''That makes me sick.''

''Me, too.''

''Really?''

''Of course. I've waited all my life to step into my dad's shoes at Anderson and Anderson. This place means everything to me.'' He shrugged in defeat. ''What's this image problem that Brubaker is having?'' he asked changing the subject, as he continued to hold her hand loosely in his lap.

It was so difficult to think with him absently toying with her fingers that way. ''Uhh…one of his oil tankers hit the shore. There was uh…a pretty big spill, and the environmentalists are after him. I remember reading about it when it happened several months ago. He fired his last agency because all they ever did was bicker and fight.''

Luke chuckled. ''I guess you're right, then. He did come to the wrong ad agency. Might as well go tell him no now, and get it over with.''

It was strange, having a conversation with Luke that wasn't peppered with accusations. She hadn't realized it could be done.

Judith hesitated. ''Too bad we have to let all that money go…. Can you believe he said we wouldn't need any other clients if we worked for him?''

''No. Sounds too good to be true.'' Luke stood, pulling her up with him. ''Come on. Time to tell Big Daddy goodbye.'' He kept her hand in his as he led her to the door. ''I meant what I said earlier…I'm sorry about the marriage comment. I didn't mean it.''

''Me, neither.'' Judith smiled ruefully. This felt so strange, him treating her like an adult. She didn't know how to react. "Luke." His name came out as a whisper. "Do we have to tell him goodbye?"

"I thought that's what you wanted." His grip tightened imperceptibly. "You didn't want to lie to him."

Judith smiled mischievously. "I never told him we were married. Did you?"

"No."

"Maybe we should take this account. For Ed and Ted's sake, of course," she added quickly. "I mean it would be sad to let the agency out of the family...."

"And family is everything...." Luke teased.

"I just have one concern." Judith's green eyes were sober as she leaned against the door with Luke. "I'm not so sure we'll ever be able to get along long enough to come up with a decent campaign."

"You're probably right. But, when you consider he wants to make us 'stinky' rich..."

"Maybe we can keep it to a dull roar?" she asked hopefully.

"Hey, for this kind of money, I can get along with..." unable to think of anyone that he couldn't get along with, he kissed her on the tip of the nose "...you."

"Don't bet on it," she advised and shoved her niggling worries aside as she followed Luke back to her office.

Judith and Luke returned to find Big Daddy spinning in her swivel chair. Eyebrows raised, they waited for him to notice their return.

"Ah-hemm..." Luke cleared his throat.

Big Daddy grabbed Judith's desk and screeched to a halt, grinning sheepishly. "Excuse me, ma'am, sometimes I'm just a big kid."

Well, a kid anyway, Judith returned his grin. "Big Daddy, we've discussed your image problem and our client load and decided we'd be delighted to handle your account. Isn't that right, dear?" Judith sidled up to Luke and smoothed an errant lock of hair from his brow.

Startled, Luke's eyes glazed over for an instant before regaining his composure. "Oh, yes, of course, dear, delighted." His hand slid down over shapely derriere, where he patted her, lovingly. Eyes wide, she gripped his roving hand firmly and planted it up at her waist.

"Hot diggity dog!" Big Daddy, unable to contain his pleasure, bundled them all in a three-way hug. "This calls for a celebration! I'll send my car for ya tonight and we'll discuss the particulars over supper. Where do ya'll live?"

"Mount Linn," Judith answered.

"West Lake," Luke replied at the same time.

"Which is it?" Big Daddy boomed.

Nodding slightly at each other, they tried again.

"West Lake."

"Mount Linn."

They said in unison, and shot each other aggravated glances.

Luke pinched Judith's arm. "We are house-sitting for our parents while they spend the year traveling around the world. You can pick us up tonight at the house in West Lake. I'll have our assistant give you a map."

"That Soder woman? Tarnation, man! Heh-heh-heh. The way she goes on, kinda makes ya want ta hang yourself, don't it?"

* * *

"Judith! Hurry up. Brubaker's car is here." Luke had arrived at Judith's parents' home only moments earlier. He'd let himself in at her distracted and muffled call from her second-story bedroom.

They'd agreed to dress for the occasion, so while he waited, Luke wandered around Ted's study in a rented tuxedo. He'd tamed his overlong hair the best he could, as there hadn't been time for a decent haircut. And though he usually avoided tuxedos like a root canal, he had to admit that tonight he was feeling pretty dapper. Hopefully, Judith would be impressed. He'd always enjoyed showing off in front of her, but for some reason tonight her opinion of him mattered more than ever before. Must be that blasted kiss. What on earth had possessed him to kiss his partner? How unprofessional of him.

Giving Ted's globe a spin, he thought back on the sensual explosion they'd shared in his office. He'd kissed a few women in his time, but he'd never, ever experienced anything like that. He grew warm just thinking about it. Judith, the girl, had always been able to make him feel the entire spectrum of emotions with an intensity that scared him. Judith, the woman, was no different. Yes, he was going to have to watch himself with her, just as he had when they were growing up. Or before he knew it, he'd be in over his head.

"Judith!" he called impatiently, watching the driver maneuver the limo into a too-small parking space on the street.

"Right here," she said smoothly, as she stood in the doorway, fastening a diamond stud into her ear.

Luke stood stock-still and gaped at the vision before him. Images of a princess on her way to the ball flitted through his head. She was mind-alteringly beautiful. Woodenly, he moved closer for a better look. Her hair was piled regally on top of her head, showing off her beautiful swanlike neck. Wispy tendrils of hair curled softly around her high cheekbones, creating an appealing halo. Her breasts swelled gently over the top of her green satin off-the-shoulder evening gown and a diamond teardrop necklace adorned the hollow of her throat.

"You," he croaked, and tried again. "You look beautiful," he said moving over to her cautiously. *Careful, old boy,* he warned himself. *You're playing with dynamite here.* He took a nervous step back.

Judith felt curiously shy at his penetrating hazel caress. Lowering her eyes bashfully she said, "You, too. Handsome, I mean."

Actually, he looked fabulous in formal attire. Peeking through her long lashes, she gazed hungrily at the striking image he presented. His powerful shoulders were square and broad in the firm lines of his jacket. The elegance of his dress could not obscure the raw masculinity that threatened to undo her composure.

Ever since Luke had kissed her this morning, she'd been on an emotional seesaw. What if he'd only kissed her to shut her up? He'd seemed as upset as she had been. Maybe it was just his anger taking another form. She'd heard of men who used kisses as punishment. If that was the case, why didn't she feel chastised?

Instead of putting her off, his kiss had made her more aware than ever of her schoolgirl crush on the high and mighty Luke Anderson. Remembering what a goofball she'd been in front of him as a kid, and then how she'd reacted to him in his office today made her cringe with humiliation. After all these years, she was still playing the fool with him. Sadly she knew she wasn't in his league and never would be. To let her infatuation with Luke get out of hand would only lead to a broken heart. Years ago, she had vowed she would never give Luke the power to hurt her feelings again. It was a promise she intended to keep. She crossed her arms protectively in front of her.

The doorbell rang and abruptly brought them back to the planet Earth.

"Ready?" Luke's question was cool.

"I guess" her answer was aloof. Tucking her hand in the crook of Luke's strong arm they headed out the door to begin life as Mr. and Mrs. Luke Anderson.

"I *love* this place!" Big Daddy shouted above the din, and tossed yet another spotless rib on the discard plate in the middle of the table.

The Jubilee truckstop had been the last place Judith had expected Big Daddy to take them to celebrate their deal. They were ridiculously overdressed. Feeling like the prize heifer at the state fair, she valiantly ignored the slobbering, wolfish stares of the patrons at the Jubilee Rib-O-Rama. At one point, in the middle of the meal, a country-and-western band had struck up what sounded to Judith like a four-lane car crash and the vultures started to circle. The last thing she wanted to do was dance with one of these leering, potbellied good-time boys, she thought, as she leaned forward, straining to hear Big Daddy. This was no easy task. For one thing, Big Daddy liked to talk with his mouth full. For another, she was incredibly distracted by Luke's thigh, resting lightly against hers.

Poor Luke. Tugging at his bow tie, he looked like

a fish out of water amidst the swarm of truckers and cowboys in blue jeans and T-shirts. Unfortunately, it had been her idea to dress formally and she was paying for it dearly. She winced at Luke's pained expression. *For crying out loud.* How was she supposed to know that a man as wealthy as Big Daddy preferred ribs to lobster? Wriggling in misery, she smiled and nodded at something she couldn't hear Big Daddy say.

Luke shot a dangerous warning look at one of the truckers who'd been ogling Judith, obviously screwing up the nerve to approach her. *Come on, buddy, make my day,* his fierce, possessive expression cautioned. He was itching for a fight, and for once it wasn't with the stunning beauty seated at his side. Her thigh was burning a hole in his rented trousers. She seemed to be burning up several pairs of trousers tonight, he thought jealously, his hands tightly balled into deadly fists. Dammit, anyway, why couldn't she have stayed the gawky, homely kid she used to be? Her outrageous beauty was most certainly going to kill him or get him killed one day. Thank God the music was so loud. No one could hear him groan at the memory of their heated kiss. Yes, Judith Anderson would most certainly, without a doubt, be the death of him.

Mercifully, the band took a break and Judith and Luke could almost hear themselves think.

"Don'tcha just love it?" Big Daddy cried, grinning like an idiot.

"Oh, yes!" Judith shouted. She hated country-western music with the intensity of a rabid dog.

"The best!" Luke yelled. He did, too.

"We've got a place just like this 'un down in

Texas. I'll take y'all when we get theah.'' Big Daddy screamed.

"What did he say?'' Luke thundered in Judith's ear.

"I think he said he'd take us out when we get to Texas!'' Judith exclaimed at the top of her lungs. Her throat was raw from the effort.

"That's what I thought he said,'' Luke yelled, looking none too pleased at the thought of heading south with this multimillionaire munchkin. If the Jubilee Rib-O-Rama was any indication of what he was in for, he'd sooner stay here and take his chances with Judith and their shrinking client list.

She wanted to be sure they'd heard him correctly. Using elaborate hand motions to emphasize her words, she turned to Big Daddy and spoke slowly. "What … do … you … mean … 'when … we … get … to … Texas?' ''

"Just what I said, little gal! I want the two of you to be my guests at the Circle B.O. Patsy named the ranch when she was just a tyke. Stands for Brubaker Oil. Y'all can stay with us! Miss Clarise and I have an extra room that you kids can have while you get the lay of the land, so to speak. Y'all didn't think I'd want ya to be workin' on my account long-distance now, didja?'' Big Daddy's rubbery grin sported speckles of rib sauce.

Horrified, Judith avoided looking at Luke. "Well … I … no, I mean, yes …'' she stammered.

Big Daddy expected them to *share* a room? *Alone?* Together, just the two of them? What if they couldn't get along? What if they *could?* They had to get out of this trip to Texas. No way in hell was she spending one single night in a room with a man who could turn her into a blithering idiot with the lift of an arrogant eyebrow. Let alone a kiss.

Good. Good, Luke thought, resting his fingers lightly at his throat. His heart was beating again. This was a good sign. There was a small chance that they could pull off this marriage charade and even put together a halfway cohesive, imaginative campaign for Brubaker Oil. But not if they had to spend very much time in the same room together. Not to mention alone in the same room together. Overnight. Over several nights. He would lose his marbles. What was left of them.

"Big Daddy..." Luke bellowed, in an attempt to be heard over the band, freshly back from their short break. "Thank you for the generous offer! But—" Luke glanced at Judith's stricken face "—there is no way that both of us would be able to leave the agency for so long! I'll be glad to go alone."

Exhaling mightily, she looked at him and smiled her relief. He was brilliant. Of course. Someone had to stay and run the office. But then...why did it have to be her? she bristled. Why couldn't *he* stay and run the office? In any other circumstances, wild horses couldn't keep her from going to Texas to work on this account.

"No way! I insist! Why son, you'd have to be a fool to leave a pretty gal like this all alone and unprotected. No, sir. Miss Clarise would have my head if she evah found out. Besides, you two are a *team*, that's why I want Anderson and Anderson and not that silly-assed, pardon my French, agency I just fired. They couldn't agree on nothin'. They came ovah to the Circle B.O. and turned it upside down, with all theah quarrelsome bickerin'. Like to have drove us all nuts! When I turned 'em loose, I decided then and theah I wanted an A-numbah-one creative team with love in theah hearts! Why, just like y'all!'' Big Daddy brandished his rib fiercely, and Judith leaned back to avoid being hit.

Sighing, Luke threw up his hands and turned to Judith. "Well, dear, what do you say?" he shouted.

Judith looked at the two men who sat waiting expectantly for her reply. She owed it to Ed and Ted to try. Dammit, she was damned if she did and damned if she didn't. Dreading the outcome of the decision she was about to make, she swallowed nervously. Surely their people at Anderson and Anderson could run the place for a few days in their absence. She hadn't built her excellent reputation in the ad industry by shying away from challenges. Why should she start now? Hoping that someday her father would appreciate her sacrifice, she smiled bravely and yelled, "What are we waiting for?"

"Yeehaa!" Big Daddy hooted and pounded the table with joy.

"Yee...haa," Judith echoed under her breath.

Chapter Four

"All this is mine!" Big Daddy shouted over the deafening cacophony of the helicopter blades, and swept his stubby arms to indicate the flat stretch of land that rolled out endlessly beneath them.

Luke raised his eyebrows at Judith and mouthed the word "stinky." Smiling, she watched Big Daddy point out various important landmarks as they flew over his property.

Big Daddy had picked them up at a Dallas airport earlier that evening in his personal helicopter. It would have taken them hours to get to his place by car, he'd said. Why bother when he could get them there much faster in one of his choppers? Besides, he wanted them to get a good night's sleep tonight, because he had big plans for them tomorrow.

The sun was balanced precariously on the edge of the horizon, a huge orange beach ball, hovering lightly above the vast golden sea of land. So, it was true what they said about Texas, Judith mused. Everything was huge. Except for Big Daddy, she amended to herself. And that was only if you didn't count his heart. His heart was as big as the entire state, and he didn't care who knew it. Coming off the plane, he'd nearly knocked both of them over, tackling the pair with his effusive welcome. It had been good to see his cheerful, little face.

Planning for this trip had been the first test of Judith's tentative truce with Luke. Big Daddy had only given them a day to prepare for their trip to Texas after he'd gone home, and that didn't leave much time for arguing. But they'd managed to find time for one argument, anyway, she reflected, watching Luke and Big Daddy shout at each other and point at something interesting on the ground.

Since it was important that they appear married, Luke decided that they would need matching luggage. Their parents had taken every available bag with them to the reunion, so they were forced to go shopping.

Judith wanted a beautiful floral-tapestry set she'd fallen in love with on sight. Luke wanted Samsonite, because it was durable.

How durable did it have to be? she'd demanded, annoyed with his practicality. Unless, of course, he'd planned on throwing it at her. He'd thanked her for the suggestion and stuck to his guns on the flimsy tapestry. Eventually, much to the relief of a harried luggage clerk, they settled on a set of flowered Samsonite, which they both hated.

From the luggage store they'd gone to the jeweler's and purchased a set of matching plain gold wedding bands. They were wearing them now.

"There she is, ovah theah" Big Daddy pointed excitedly at the gates to the Circle B.O. As the aircraft lost altitude, his huge antebellum mansion roared into view. It was breathtaking. Pillars, like sturdy sentinels, guarded the house proper, supporting what looked like acres of veranda on the first and second floors. The long driveway was lined with shade trees and a half dozen other buildings dotted the surrounding area. From where she sat, Judith could clearly make out the servants' quarters, a giant garage, the pool house, a gazebo, a greenhouse and the stables. Horses! Judith shivered with excitement. If they had time, maybe Big Daddy would let her dust off her years of horseback-riding lessons.

At the approach of the helicopter, a stream of people came pouring out of the house and stood in a large group to watch it land. Must be the official Brubaker welcoming committee, Judith thought, watching them wave excitedly at their approach.

Once the pilot had landed the helicopter, Big Daddy flung open the door, leapt to the ground and turned to assist Judith and Luke.

Miss Clarise was the first to reach them, followed by her army of children. She was even tinier than Big Daddy, and had to stand on her toes to kiss his leathery cheek. Her bright blue eyes twinkled and danced as she greeted her guests.

"My land!" she exclaimed after Big Daddy had introduced them. "You two could pass for movie stars!" Her Southern drawl was soft and low.

Miss Clarise must not get out much, Judith mused, glancing self-consciously at her equally star-struck brood. Big Daddy's daughter, Patsy, gazed wantonly at Luke, watching his every move with bold fascination. She made no secret of the fact that she found him to be fair game, shooting Judith a look of arrogant challenge. Remembering her own crush on Luke, Judith attempted to swallow her petty jealousy. The three oldest boys were grinning at their beautiful guest and nudging each other.

"We're delighted to be here," Judith said, making an effort to ignore Patsy's insolent attitude, and Luke nodded. "I've never been on a ranch this size before, and I know I'll enjoy learning all about the Circle B.O."

Patsy rolled her expressive eyes. "Circle Bow!" she corrected. "I named it when I was just a little thing." She smiled prettily at Luke.

Luke returned her smile and said, "Since neither of us has ever spent much time on a spread like this, I'm sure we will make a few mistakes."

The three older sons snickered and Judith thought she caught the words "greenhorn" and "city slicker." Shooting them a quelling stare, Miss Clarise began introducing her children.

"Judith, Luke, I'd like you to meet our three oldest boys, Conway, Merle and Buck. They are twenty-four, twenty-three and twenty-two years old."

The three sandy-haired men stepped forward, shook hands with Luke and tipped their Stetsons shyly at Judith. How could Miss Clarise and Big Daddy have three such lanky sons, Judith wondered, smiling up at the eldest Brubakers. All three were rugged, well-built and handsome in a Marlboro Man kind of way.

"And, this is our only girl, Patsy." Miss Clarise tugged at Patsy's vest and drew her forward. "She's our little dancer, aren't you, honey?"

Ignoring Judith and focusing her attention on Luke, Patsy nodded and batted her baby blues.

"Patsy will be twenty-one, day after tomorrow," Miss Clarise continued, "so we're having a little party. You're invited, of course."

Judith would rather muck out the stalls than celebrate the spoiled Patsy's twenty-first birthday. Blond curly hair, perfect teeth, baby blue eyes, Judith disliked Patsy immediately. Tiny, like her parents, something about the little dancer made Judith feel like a klutzy, perspiring buffalo. Luke seemed inordinately pleased to meet her, she noted, irritated at Patsy's transparent attraction to her new husband. For heaven's sake. He was old enough to be her father. Maybe not, she thought looking at Big Daddy. Okay, a much older brother.

"This here is Johnny. He's eighteen." Miss Clarise pointed at her cool, dark, handsome son. "He wants to be a singer and already has his own band" she grimaced. "And this is Kenny—he's seventeen. Kenny plays the drums in Johnny's band." Another pained expression.

"Over here, we have the twins, Waylon and Willie. They're thirteen" she pointed at two identical redheads, wearing identical mischievous grins. "And last, but not least, little Hank here is six."

"Pleathed to meet ya," he lisped, his smile revealing several missing teeth.

"As you might have noticed by now, Big Daddy named all of our children after his favorite country-and-western singers." She looked fondly at her husband. "He's always saying that the only thing he loves more than country-western music is his family."

"Isn't that…nice?" Judith made a mental note not to make disparaging remarks about country music. Or his family, she added, watching Patsy stare longingly at Luke.

"Well, as much as I hate to break up this little party, it's gettin' late and we've got ourselves a big day tomorrow. Y'all kids go on and do your chores now," Big Daddy ordered. Moaning and groaning in disappointment, they shuffled off to do as they were told.

"We don't get that much company out heah in the middle of nowheah, so havin' y'all stay is a real treat," Big Daddy said as he and Miss Clarise led them into the house. "Out heah, we get up with the chickens, so y'all will probably be anxious to hit the hay. Miss Clarise will show you to your room, so I'll say good-night." Smiling, he removed his hat and bowed slightly and disappeared up one end of the impressive double staircase.

Judith was anything but anxious to hit the hay with Luke. Would Miss Clarise think it was unusual if she asked for separate rooms? Probably. You don't end up with nine children by sleeping at opposite ends of the house. She stole a glance at Luke as their tiny hostess led them through the house's opulent interior to the room they were to share upstairs. He didn't look too comfortable with this situation, either, she noted, watching him nervously crack his knuckles.

Miss Clarise stopped in front of a pair of wide double doors at the end of the hall. There, neatly stacked off to the side was the newly purchased set of flowered Samsonite.

"Looks like Conway's been here already," Miss Clarise observed as she opened the doors. "Hope you'll be comfortable in this room," she said and turned on the lights to reveal a spacious, tastefully decorated bedroom suite with an adjoining bath. "At least you have your own bathroom" she chuckled. "That's important in a family this big."

"I'm sure we'll be fine," Judith assured her, warily eyeing the king-size bed. Its imposing presence seemed overwhelming, nearly mocking her with its enormity. Her palms felt suddenly clammy as she tried to think of ways to keep Miss Clarise from leaving her alone with Luke.

Miss Clarise gave Judith a quick minitour while Luke brought in the luggage. Fresh towels and extra blankets were in the linen cabinet—don't worry about picking up, the maids would do that—and breakfast was at 6:00 a.m. downstairs in the dining room. After dozens of questions, Judith was unable to stall any longer and finally allowed Miss Clarise to go. Hugging each of them warmly, the motherly woman bid them good-night, shutting the doors behind her as she left.

"Well…" Judith wandered over to the fireplace and ran her hand lightly across the marble surface. "Here we are."

"Um," Luke groaned, flopped down on the huge bed and kicked his shoes off. "I'm beat," he mumbled and drew an arm up over his eyes. Almost immediately his breathing became deep and regular.

Judith stood uncertainly for a moment, wondering what to do next. How like a man to sprawl across a strange bed and slip into unconsciousness without a care in the world, she fumed. Deciding he wouldn't be much help in the unpacking department at this point, she began unloading the Samsonite and putting away their clothes. When she had stored the last of their luggage in the huge walk-in closet, she ambled around the beautiful room, admiring its rich, romantic decor. Glancing at Luke's relaxed form, she almost wished they were married and could enjoy the romance of this charming room as a couple. Luke snored softly and rolled onto his side, dead to the world. Well, one of them would enjoy the romance of the room, she thought wryly and headed to the bathroom for a quick, soothing shower.

Luke was still asleep when she came back into the room, clad in a short peach nightie and matching robe. She'd been hoping her blow dryer would wake him up.

"Luke," she whispered. "Are you awake?" She grabbed his big toe and shook his foot. No response. Moving closer, she perched on the edge of the bed and watched him sleep for a moment. He looked so defenseless and young lying there, nearly angelic. Sleep had relaxed the tiny laugh lines around his eyes, and suddenly Judith was a teenager again. Any second now, Luke the bossy, arrogant boy wonder would wake up and begin teasing and torturing Judith the insecure, awkward girl. Shuddering at the feelings of pain these memories dredged up, she punched him viciously on the arm.

"Luke!" she hissed. "Are you awake?"

"Oww!" he yelped and rubbed his arm. "Yes! I was just lying here drooling and snoring to pass the time."

"You have to get off the bed!" she whispered harshly.

"Why?" he whispered back.

"Because I want to go to sleep."

"Go ahead." His eyes slid shut.

"No! I'm not sleeping in the same bed with you, so forget it!"

"Then sleep on the floor."

"*You* sleep on the floor."

"I'm not sleeping on the floor. You sleep on the floor." He opened one eye and admired the shapely legs that were not covered by her skimpy nightie and robe.

"No way!" she shouted and quickly lowered her voice. "Get off this bed," she ordered, pushing at him with her feet.

Luke's hands shot out and grabbed her ankles. "I'll flip you for it," he whispered, and for a moment Judith thought he intended to flip her off the bed.

"No." Judith kicked her legs, trying to loosen his tight grip on her ankles. "*You* got Ted's office, *I* get the bed." She picked up a pillow and smacked him in the head.

Eyes gleaming with the challenge she'd issued, Luke pulled her across the bed by her ankles. Her nightgown rode up in a most embarrassing fashion and Judith grabbed at it frantically, trying to preserve her modesty.

"Um...nice" he grinned in approval at her slender thighs before he clobbered her with his own pillow.

"Damn it, Luke. I mean it, get off this bed," she demanded as loudly as she dared.

"*You* get off this bed," he mimicked and pinned her underneath him with his legs and joyfully pummeled her with his pillow. She looked up at him, hovering above her, his powerful body overshadowing hers, making her feel soft and feminine. In one swift movement, Luke dropped his pillow and grabbed her wrists, pulling them up over her head.

"Hmm... Seems like you lose," he taunted, binding her wrists together in one hand and running his other hand down her side where it rested lightly on her rib cage. "I don't suppose you're still ticklish?" he mused and lightly probed her side.

Giggling, she writhed beneath him. "No. Stop it. Luke. Damn it!" she laughed and squirmed in a frantic attempt to escape his torturous fingers.

Letting go of her wrists, Luke lowered his body on top of hers, still tickling her sides, and growled into her neck. "What's this?" he asked, drawing one of her earlobes into his mouth. "Yummy," he teased, as her squeals and shrieks of laughter increased in volume.

Judith brought her shoulder to her ear in an attempt to dry it out after Luke had thoroughly explored it with his tongue. "Yuck," she yelped, as he playfully licked her cheek. "Gross." She drew a knee up between his legs. "Quit it right now," she ordered, "or I'll do serious damage to your...um...."

"Oh, now is that anything for a bride to say on her honeymoon?" he asked, sounding thoroughly wounded as he shoved her knee back down.

"This is not our honeymoon, you big goon, and stop licking my ear. Luke. This is not a good idea."

She was right, he thought, inhaling the clean scent of her newly shampooed hair. This was not a good idea, for lots of reasons. The very least of which was the fact that the sexy woman who writhed so appealingly beneath him was his business partner. Never before had he done this with one of his partners. High business ethics were one reason why—that and the fact that his previous partners had all been stodgy, old men. Reluctantly, Luke levered himself up to a seated position, and willed his body to calm down.

Suddenly he sat perfectly still, his bottom resting lightly on her thighs. "Shh!" he commanded, laying a finger across her lips. "What was that?"

"What?" Her heart pounding, she struggled to sit up. There it was again, a soft knock at their door. "Oh, great, I bet we're in trouble now." Judith eyed him accusingly.

"Come in, it's open," Luke called.

"*Luke!*" she cried, alarmed at being caught in this compromising position.

Miss Clarise's bright blue eyes peered through the double doors. Her short gray hair was loaded with pink sponge curlers and her flannel nightgown hung clear to the floor.

"I hope y'all weren't asleep yet" she smiled and stepped into the room. "I noticed your light on under the doors."

"Oh, no, not at all, were we, dear?" Luke pulled Judith upright and threw an arm around her.

Pushing her tangled hair out of her face, she nudged Luke off her lap. "Please, come in Miss Clarise. We were just…talking. Is anything wrong?"

"No, no. I was only wondering if y'all brought any riding gear with you. You'll probably need it, as we travel around this place on horseback quite a bit."

"I don't know." Luke shrugged and looked to Judith for an answer. "Did you bring all that riding gear we keep in the garage, dear?" he asked, frowning as though deep in thought.

"I um…there was so much," she mumbled.

"I always leave the packing to the little woman, I

guess she wasn't thinking." Luke grinned winsomely at Miss Clarise.

"Isn't that just like a husband?" Judith asked and pinched him roughly on the cheek.

"Never mind," Miss Clarise said breezily. "That answers my question. Don't worry. Tomorrow Big Daddy will take you to town and get you outfitted. Our treat. You two get back to your talk. Night, now," she whispered and left, shutting the doors gently behind her.

"Night," Luke called.

Judith tossed a pillow on the floor and pointed at it. "Go to bed."

"But, dear, I'm in bed." He nuzzled her neck.

"Luke." Her tone was menacing.

"You're no fun any more," he griped, and rolled onto the floor. Judith stripped a blanket off the bed and pitched it over the edge after him. "What if Miss Clarise comes back?" He sounded pitiful.

Judith switched off the lamp on the nightstand. "I'll take my chances."

The silence in the darkened room was interrupted from time to time by Luke as he struggled to find a comfortable position on the floor.

"Luke?" Judith whispered into the night.

A sigh. "*Now* what?"

"What are their names? I can't remember their names."

"Who?"

"The kids. Big Daddy's kids."

Luke was quiet for so long, Judith thought he'd fallen asleep.

"Luke!"

"*What?*"

"What are their names? This is important!"

"I know," he grumbled. "I'm thinking…Let's see, there's Gomer, Goober, Barney…."

"That's not right!"

"Yes it is. Didn't Aunt Bea tell us that Big Daddy named all his kids after people who lived in Mayberry?"

"Dammit, Luke! I'm serious!"

"Okay, okay, already. Let's see…Sneezy, Dopey, Doc, Grumpy…I can never remember the rest. It's the same at Christmas. Dancer, Prancer, Donner, Blitzen…."

Judith moaned. "You don't know, do you?"

"Uh…no."

Rolling over to the edge of the bed, she peered into the pitch-blackness and tried to make out Luke's form.

"Maybe we can figure it out."

"Look, Judith, I'm dead. Can't we do this in the morning?"

"No!" she whispered loudly, her head hanging over the edge of the bed, her hair falling into Luke's face.

She had such soft hair. He played with the ends, twisting them around his nose and pulling them across his lips.

"Okay…." She was thoughtful. "Name some country-western singers."

"Dolly Parton" he supplied helpfully.

"Yeah, right. Which one of those boys is named Dolly?" her voice dripped with sarcasm.

"You didn't say name *male* country-western singers."

"Big Daddy only has one daughter, in case you hadn't noticed."

"Is that right?" he feigned innocently.

"Yes, that's right," she echoed. "It doesn't seem to matter much to her that you are a happily married man, I might add."

"She's a sensitive girl. Maybe she picked up on our bad karma."

Judith snorted in disgust.

Luke tugged on a lock of her hair. "What about you with old Curly, Moe and Larry there? I saw how they were falling all over themselves to get a better look at you."

So, he'd noticed. For some reason, that pleased her. "What are their names, anyway?"

"I'm not tellin.' I don't want you running off with those three goons and leaving me to do all the work."

"Patsy would be happy to help."

"I'll keep that in mind." He yawned loudly. "Judith, I'll tell you what. Tomorrow, we'll keep our ears to the ground on this name thing. Don't worry. Everything will be fine. We just have to pay attention."

"But…what if something goes wrong? What if…Luke, what if they figure out that we aren't married?"

His heavy breathing told Judith that she'd lost him for the night. Listening to the comforting sound lulled her worries, and before she knew what hit her she was breathing as deeply as Luke.

The alarm clock went off at 5:00 a.m. on the dot. Judith slapped at it groggily and sat up. Swinging her feet over the edge of the bed, they met with something warm and soft. Stifling a scream, she inspected the floor and found Luke tangled up in his blanket, sleeping like a baby.

That's right. She remembered now. They were in Texas. Stumbling over Luke, she made her way to the bathroom and quickly showered. She was putting on her makeup, when Luke staggered in, stretching and yawning. He was wearing nothing but a pair of jockey shorts as he stood blinking at her, trying to orient himself. His hair stuck out at crazy angles and his jaw was darkened by a day's growth of beard. He looked so incredibly cute, she longed to take him in her arms for a cuddle and a kiss.

Knowing that thoughts like that would only get her into trouble, she smiled at him and said, "Good morning, dear. The bathroom is all yours."

Luke stared at her blankly as she left.

Obviously Luke wasn't much of a morning person, she grinned, and padded to the closet to dress. Blue jeans, a soft cotton blouse and tennis shoes would have to do. As an advertising executive, she didn't have much need for riding gear. That was all right. According to Miss Clarise, they were going shopping today, anyway. Maybe she'd get a pair of cowboy boots and a Western hat. Not too excited about the idea, she figured if you can't beat 'em, join 'em. She wondered absently what Luke would look like in Western attire, as she pulled her hair up into a loose ponytail. Probably wonderful, she thought sourly. So what else was new?

Luke stepped out of the bathroom, freshly showered and shaved. A large bath towel was tucked loosely at his hips. Judith averted her eyes as she heard it thud damply to the floor and listened as he proceeded to dress. She would never get used to sharing a room with him, especially if he was going to be this uninhibited.

"I've got it," he said and walked over to the edge of the bed where he sat down to put on his tennis shoes.

"Got what?" she asked curiously, able to look at him now that he was dressed. Luke was wearing an outfit that was very similar to her own. Jeans, a cotton shirt rolled up at the sleeves and running shoes. That was good. They say the longer you're married, the more alike you begin to look. It was certainly true in Big Daddy and Miss Clarise's case.

"The names. Conway, Merle, Buck, Patsy, Johnny, Kenny, Waylon, Willie and last but certainly not least, little Hank."

"Wow!" Judith looked at him in admiration. "How'd you do that?"

"I had a dream that I went to country-western hell, and they were all there. Singing, no less. It was a nightmare."

"Sounds like it," she agreed sympathetically. "What were they singing?"

"I don't know. But it wasn't country-western. More like a Zulu chant or something. Patsy was getting ready to fix me for dinner and her brothers were plotting about how they were going to string me up."

"Where was I?"

"Preparing a light béarnaise sauce." He grinned.

"Sounds good." She grinned back. "I'm hungry. It's almost six, are you ready?"

"Yes, ma'am. Let's ride."

After making several wrong turns, they finally made it to the spectacular entryway that Judith had been too tired to appreciate the night before. Crystal, marble, mahogany and stained glass all combined to give the feel of understated wealth.

"Where is everyone?" Judith whispered to Luke, wondering if they'd overslept and missed out on Big Daddy's big plans. "It's like a tomb in here."

Luke gestured to the impressive living room situated just off the house's grand entrance. "I thought I saw someone move in there. Come on, maybe they can tell us where everyone is."

Entering through the archway to the vast living room, Luke stopped abruptly and stared. Judith followed his line of vision to discover what he found so fascinating.

There, seated on her neck, in the middle of a huge Oriental carpet, was Patsy limbering up for her morning dance lesson.

"Holy cow," Luke murmured, as he watched Patsy disentangle her legs from around her shoulders and roll into Chinese splits.

Some husband he was turning out to be, Judith stewed. If his eyes got any glassier, she was going to have to take him out and hose him down. Although, she had to admit, Patsy's contortions were pretty interesting. Judith had never known anyone who could wrap her feet behind her neck like that. With that much flexibility, the possibilities were endless. She wondered what Luke was thinking. They must be some very intense thoughts, because he was practically standing on his head to get a better look.

"Good morning, Patsy," she said and calmly strode into the room.

"Hi." She gazed aristocratically past Judith to Luke and gracefully stood up.

"Where is everyone this morning?" Judith was determined to remain friendly with the light of Big Daddy's life.

Balancing delicately on her toes, Patsy arched her arm in the direction of the dining room. "In there, through those doors." Ratty sweats, leotards and torn leg warmers only served to enhance Patsy's perfect, tiny figure. Her sleek, curly bob danced and bounced, matching the perpetual motion of her body as she stretched.

"Thanks." Judith grabbed Luke by the hand and headed in the direction Patsy had pointed. "Come on, dear. Let's go get some breakfast."

Once they were out of earshot, Judith slowed her pace. "You didn't have to act so gaga in there. We are supposed to be married! What's Big Daddy going to think about you flirting with his precious daughter?" she muttered under her breath.

"I wasn't flirting. She was." Luke defended himself, his expression was wounded. "Besides, you were staring at her, too. You have to admit it *was* interesting. Can you do that?" He leered at her over his shoulder as he stepped around her on his way to the dining room.

"None of your business," she snapped, marching after him.

"I can't believe you're jealous of little Wynonna back there," he goaded.

"Her name is Patsy, and I'm not jealous."

"Jealous, jealous, jealous," he sang under his breath as they arrived in the dining room.

"Shut up."

Big Daddy looked up from the plate he was loading at the long sideboard. "Good mornin'!" he called cheerfully. "Grab a plate and belly up to the chow bar," he ordered and took his place at the head of the largest dining-room table Judith had ever seen.

The Brubaker clan was in various stages of loading and unloading their breakfast plates. The formal dining room had all the ambience of a grade-school cafeteria, the way Big Daddy's brood pushed and shoved, jockeying for pole position at the huge buffet.

As an only child, Judith was somewhat intimidated by the grab-and-stuff style the Brubaker children practiced. Seemingly unaffected by the presence of the Andersons, the family laughed and shouted and ate. Miss Clarise sat calmly at the opposite end of the table from Big Daddy, undisturbed by her rowdy, ravenous offspring.

"Go ahead, darlin'." Miss Clarise nodded warmly at Judith. "Better get in there before it's all gone."

Conway, Merle and Buck took it upon themselves to shove Kenny, Johnny, Waylon and Willie out of the way to clear a path for Judith. Conway shyly held her plate, while Buck and Merle generously loaded it and escorted her to her place between them at the table. Conway held her chair for her, and much to his red-faced joy, she thanked him graciously. Luke was all but forgotten in their effort to display the manners Miss Clarise had spent years pounding into their thick heads.

Not even in the finest restaurants in Seattle had Judith ever received more personalized service. Conway poured her coffee, Merle poured her juice, Buck poured her water. Buck and Merle scuffled over who got to spread the napkin over her lap, until Conway stepped in and settled it for them by doing the honor himself.

Feeling abandoned, Luke took one of the two remaining empty seats, situated across the room from Judith, and tried to ignore the three-ring circus unintentionally created by his lovely wife.

Little Hank looked up as Luke sat down next to him and smiled his toothless smile. "Thee thure ith purty" he sprayed, over a mouthful of toast and grinned in Judith's direction.

"Umm-hmm." Luke rolled his eyes and attacked his eggs. Wasn't anyone immune to her charms? Even the youngest Brubaker was smitten.

"Settle down, everyone!" Big Daddy hollered, and clapped his hands for silence. "Let's show ouah company that we've got some mannahs." The room was suddenly quiet, and it was clear that when Big Daddy spoke everybody listened. "That's bettah" he nodded and continued eating. "When we're done heah, I'm takin' Mr. and Mrs. Anderson on a tour of the spread. I want y'all to help out wheah you can and make 'em feel at home heah at the Circle B.O."

"Bow, Daddy, Bow!" Patsy contradicted, and slid into the empty seat next to Luke. "I don't want people thinkin' that we live in a smelly, old shoe," she simpered, scooting her chair closer to her hero.

Luke smiled into his juice glass and glanced at Judith to gauge her reaction. She didn't seem to be paying the slightest bit of attention, much to his dismay, as she enjoyed the pandering of the three stooges at her side.

"Aftah the tour, I'm takin' these folks to town to get them outfitted for life on the ranch. My treat," he said magnanimously, grinning happily at his guests. "Sneakahs just don't cut the mustard out heah."

* * *

Breakfast was over nearly as soon as it began, and the next thing Luke and Judith knew they were bouncing along in a military-style jeep, taking in the sights with Big Daddy and Miss Clarise. Mile after endless mile, they toured the Brubaker domain. Miss Clarise regaled them with tidbits about Big Daddy's history, while Judith scribbled furious notes.

Big Daddy's lengthy career in the oil business was impressive. A self-made billionaire, he started out working on oil rigs as a young man, and when he was able, he slowly accumulated the property that made him rich. Now, a few thousand acres of prime ranch land, several productive oil fields and a couple of *Fortune 500* companies later, Big Daddy was one of the most widely respected, beloved businessmen in the world. *Was* being the operative word. His unfortunate tanker accident had gone a long way toward damaging the public image he'd worked so long and hard to achieve.

But Big Daddy was not one to take bad press lying down. He'd handle this problem the way he approached any challenge life handed him. With integrity, hard work, humor and the best dang ad agency money could buy.

As they zoomed over the miles, Big Daddy and Miss Clarise held hands like a couple of love-struck teenagers. They chatted and reminisced, chuckling over fond memories of the good, old days, when the kids were babies and they were just starting out.

Judith almost felt like an intruder, listening to their sweet, intimate memories. She tried to picture herself and Luke in thirty years. Undoubtedly they would be arguing about who got to drive.

Traveling past the oil wells, Big Daddy told Luke

and Judith that he'd kept copies of all the negative press that came out around the time of the accident. Newspaper articles, magazine articles, news broadcasts on videotape, you name it, he had it. They were welcome to make themselves at home in his personal library, to research the entire oil-spill incident.

Judith and Luke agreed that the library would certainly be the best place to start, and made plans to meet there that evening after dinner.

Half the day was gone by the time they made it back to the house. The four of them ate a light lunch out on the lower veranda, and when the last dish had been cleared away by the staff, Big Daddy announced that it was time to head to town.

Much to Luke's annoyance, Conway, Merle and Buck decided at the last minute to join them, declaring that they all needed new boots for Patsy's birthday party tomorrow.

"That's right," Big Daddy informed them. "Y'all can't do the two-step at Patsy's party without boots."

Luke squinted at Judith and whispered, "What's the two-step?"

"I'm not sure." She frowned. "I think it's a Western dance."

"Oh, great. Now we have to *dance?*"

"Hey, it's not my idea," she snapped, insulted by his attitude toward dancing with her. "Don't worry. We can probably fake it," she said and went outside to join Big Daddy and the others.

Luke shook his head and wondered what Ed and Ted would do in a situation like this. They certainly wouldn't be two-stepping together.

Chapter Five

"What time is it?" Luke asked, and put the article they'd been reading about Big Daddy's oil spill on the stack with the dozens of others they had waded through that evening.

Glancing at her watch, Judith stood and stretched. "Midnight. I'm tired. We've been at this for six hours now. Let's call it a night."

"Sure." Luke sat back in his chair and stretched, watching Judith wander around Big Daddy's massive, old library in her new country-western garb. He admired the way she looked in the stiff dark blue denim, and so nicely filled out the soft chambray shirt. The little silver snaps that held her shirt together, now those would probably be easy to open.... His mind drifted lazily over visions of Judith at the Western outfitter that morning. Big Daddy had bought them both a mountain of clothes, and he'd actually found himself having a good time. Judith looked delectable in everything she tried on. Luke, on the other hand, had ended up with a pile of the ugliest, tackiest Western shirts he'd ever laid eyes on. No thanks to the Brubaker boys.

It seemed as though Judith had been born to ranch life. He, however, wanted nothing more than to take off these damn snake skin cowboy boots and toss them out the window. His feet were killing him. It was so cozy here in Big Daddy's library, just the two of them, working side by side all evening long. He was surprised at how well they'd gotten along. At how much he enjoyed working with Judith. Better not start enjoying it too much, he mentally warned himself. When this year was up, one of them would undoubtedly leave the agency. The thought made him sad. Shaking his head slightly, he tore his eyes away from the pockets that hugged her firm, little behind so perfectly and concentrated on straightening up the mess they'd made on Big Daddy's desk.

"What do you think? Did we find anything we can use?" she asked, her back to him as she perused the library's endless collection of books.

Luke carried an armload of files over to the filing cabinet and began putting them away. "I don't know. There is certainly a lot of information. Something will undoubtedly come to us. We can't do any worse than his last agency," he chuckled over what Big Daddy still referred to as the "scrapping jackals" campaign. None of his first agency's avant-garde ideas had pleased Big Daddy, and he'd made it clear to Judith and Luke that he wanted something that reflected *his* views and beliefs.

Judith pulled a large volume on the history of Texas off the shelf and flipped through its pages. "We won't have much time to work on Big Daddy's campaign tomorrow. Patsy's party will probably take up the whole day,'' she complained, snapping the book closed and sliding it back on the shelf. ''Miss Clarise said it starts in the afternoon and lasts until midnight. It's supposed to be the social event of the year for this family.''

Luke ejected a tape of the news broadcasts that they had studied and turned off the VCR. ''I know *I* can't wait. Just the thought of all that country music gets my engines running.'' He said sarcastically and slipped the tape into its case, putting it away with the others.

''Good. You'll need 'em to motor around the dance floor.''

''Why didn't anyone tell me back in Advertising 101 that I'd have to know the two-step to do my job?''

''They didn't? Maybe you were sick that day.'' She scanned the titles on the shelf, looking for something interesting to read at night. Something that would keep her mind off the man sharing her room. ''We may not get much work done, but we will learn a lot about the Brubakers. It'll probably come in handy.''

''I really don't want to go to this thing tomorrow, especially the dancing part. Maybe I'll call in sick.''

''Ha. Very funny. You can't get out of it that easily. Big Daddy would be crushed if we didn't at least try.''

''I know, I know. It was all they could talk about at dinner tonight.''

Judith pulled another volume from the shelf. ''Patsy was pretty adamant about getting a dance with you.''

''You noticed that too, huh?'' he groaned and began stacking their notes. "I'm going to feel like an idiot."

Glancing up from her book, Judith studied him in surprise. Luke was worried about looking silly? She'd never thought about his human frailties before. Maybe because she'd never thought he'd had any. "Since it's a birthday, we should probably get her a present before the party tomorrow."

"Hmm. Probably the politically correct thing to do. Any ideas?"

"I'm partial to a good spanking."

Luke laughed. "You don't like her much, do you?"

Judith shrugged noncommittally.

"I don't know why. In some ways she kind of reminds me of you." Luke sat down and lifted his aching feet up onto the desk.

"Me?" Judith nearly dropped her book in shock.

"Umm-hmm." He nodded and rubbed his bleary eyes. "You're both talented, spoiled, headstrong and beautiful," he mumbled, shutting his eyes. "No wonder you don't like each other."

Luke thought she was beautiful? No. The fact that he thought Patsy was, too, negated that compliment, took the specialness out. And spoiled?

"I resent that. We're nothing alike. The reason she doesn't like me is because she thinks I'm married to you, her hero."

The same way she hadn't liked any of his girlfriends when they'd been growing up. It suddenly dawned on Judith that maybe Luke was right. Big Daddy's sullen, spoiled daughter was making a fool of herself with her obvious crush on Luke, and the love-struck girl served as a constant irritating reminder of Judith's own ridiculous behavior in the past. Roughly shoving the book onto the shelf, she wondered why he always had to be so smart.

Luke yawned. "Whatever. Are you ready for bed?"

Something about the sexy, low tone of his question had her stomach crowding into her throat. Trailing her finger along the rows of books, she made her way over to where he sat.

"I guess so," she answered when she could speak. "Hey!" Pausing at a fat book that stuck farther out on the shelf than the rest, she pulled it out and turned it over. "Luke! Listen to this. *Texas Two-Stepping Made Easy.* How about that!" Opening the cover she read, "Ten simple lessons that will have you two-stepping like a pro."

"Just what I always wanted." Luke opened his eyes and looked at her with derision.

"Come on. This is perfect. Maybe it will keep us from being complete klutzes on the dance floor tomorrow." Her eyes pleaded with his. "Let's take it to our room. I'll read it to you. You don't have to do a thing."

Groaning, Luke swung his feet off the desk. "Why do I have a feeling I'm going to regret this?" he grumbled and followed Judith upstairs to their bedroom.

"One, pause, *two,* three, four. Not one, pause, three, four. Let's try it again," Judith instructed.

"For crying out loud, Judith. It's three in the morning. My feet are killing me."

"Oh, quit yer bitchin'," she crabbed and pulled his

arm around her waist. "We've almost got it. We can't quit now."

"Yes, we can," he complained and danced her over to the bed and looked at it longingly. "Let's just take a short break. You and me." He wiggled his eyebrows at her in invitation.

Judith caught her breath. "Let's not. Come on now...for Big Daddy," she wheedled and pushed him back to the middle of the bedroom floor. "Ready? And one, pause, two, three, four, one, pause... Ouch! That's my foot!"

"Sorry," Luke mumbled. How anyone ever got used to these pointy toed, foot-torturing devices, he'd never know.

Limping slightly, Judith started again. "One, pause, two, three, four," she counted slowly, steering Luke around the room.

"Hey, isn't the man supposed to lead?"

"Who cares whose leading? We're dancing aren't we?"

"If you can call it that," he griped. "It says clearly on page two that the man is supposed to lead."

"Then lead!" she snapped.

Luke's eyes narrowed as he shot her a poisonous look. Grasping her firmly in his arms, he roughly pushed her through the steps. "One, pause, two, three, four," he counted and gained momentum. "One pause two three four, onepausetwothreefour..." They were two-stepping! *Hot Damn.* He grinned cockily at her. "And you said I couldn't lead." Losing his count, he steered them into a floor lamp and knocked it over with a crash.

"Uh oh." Judith bent to examine the fallen fixture. "It's okay. We didn't break it." She set it back up and stepped into Luke's arms. "That was pretty good. Let's try it again, while we have the hang of it."

Luke grasped her hand and led her through the simple steps. "Get ready," he warned, grinning at her.

"For what?"

"Lesson seven."

"What's lesson seven?"

"This." Grasping her hand tightly, he released her waist and spun her out in a swing step and smoothly pulled her back to his chest and continued the simple steps around the room.

Judith giggled. This was kind of fun. "Cool. Do it again!" she ordered, her face flushed with pleasure.

"I don't know if you're ready yet," he teased. "I don't want to overwhelm you."

"I'm ready, I'm ready," she laughed, nearly drunk with exhaustion. "Do it now."

Caught up in the moment, Luke spun her out again, this time her arm caught the instruction book on the dresser and sent it sailing across the room, where it crashed into the wall.

"Oops," she giggled, and collapsed into his arms. "You're pretty good." She lifted an insolent lip.

"You're not bad yourself," he admitted grudgingly and swayed slowly back and forth, her head resting comfortably on his shoulder.

"Come on, just a couple more times and we can call it quits," she cajoled sleepily, pulling her head off his shoulder and giving him her best imitation of a sprite, energetic smile. "You can do it."

How could he refuse? Her full lips smiled easily at him, her deep green eyes sparkled with fun. Here and there he was able to catch glimpses of the cheeky brat she used to be in her mischievous expression. Nothing had changed really. She was still able to get her way with him. Her approach was just a little more sophisticated now.

Sighing with exasperation he said, "Woman, you're going to kill me."

"No I'm not. You're a big, strong man." She ran her hands lightly, teasingly over his large upper arms. "Please? Just one more time?" she pleaded.

Judith knew that they should quit while they were ahead. But the sheer, unadulterated joy of spending time in Luke's arms was too big a temptation. Just as she'd suspected, he looked wonderful in the clothes that Big Daddy had insisted on buying for him today. The navy Western shirt with the silver snaps accentuated his broad, imposing build. His strong legs appeared even longer in the snug denim jeans and new cowboy boots. With his rugged good looks and thick, dark hair, Judith knew that he would turn heads tomorrow. Patsy was probably the least of her worries.

"Okay, you asked for it," he said gamely, and proceeded to thump and crash his way through another twenty minutes of two-stepping with the saucy beauty in his arms.

"Land sakes!" Miss Clarise looked at Big Daddy with wide eyes as they stood outside the doors of their guests' bedroom suite. The third crash of the night had finally brought them running in concern.

Big Daddy grinned and raised his eyebrows as their voices drifted out into the hall.

"Let me rest a minute," Luke begged.

"No." Judith insisted. "We're almost there." she panted, her breathing heavy.

"Lord, woman. You are going to kill me."

Another crash. A grunt. A giggle.

"That's good," Judith praised. "It just keeps getting better."

"I wish you'd at least let me take these damn boots off," Luke moaned.

"No, it's better with them on...more traction."

Big Daddy put his arm around Miss Clarise and headed back toward their bedroom. "She's a little hellcat, ain't she?"

Miss Clarise blushed.

"Kinda reminds me of when we were first married," he chuckled and kissed the top of her head. "I knew they were mad about each other from the moment I laid eyes on 'em. But, I had no idea... Nosiree. That's what I call love."

Miss Clarise smiled up at her man and closed the bedroom door.

Luke stumbled with Judith over to the king-size bed, where he fell down on top of it, bouncing Judith along with him.

"That's it. I'm done for." Turning on his side, he tucked Judith into the curve of his body, spoon fashion and pulled the bedspread up over them.

"Umm-hmm," she agreed sleepily and snuggled into the warmth of Luke's strong body. It felt so good, just lying there with him, exhausted after their hours of joint effort. She would enjoy this fantasy she'd longed for her entire life for just a few minutes before she came to her senses, kicked him out of bed and went to sleep.

Luke's arm found its way around her waist and tightened possessively.

"Luke?" she mumbled dreamily.

"Hmm?" His breath was heavy in her ear.

"Thanks."

"Mmm." He nodded and patted her flat tummy. He kissed her lightly on the cheek as she turned her face toward him. Their sleepy eyes locked, and for the longest time neither of them moved. Luke brushed a chestnut curl away from her lower lip with the back of his hand and ever so slowly replaced it with his mouth. Judith lay perfectly still, wondering at the almost magical sensations of Luke's soft, warm lips on her own. As though drugged by lack of sleep, she gave herself to the moment, turning her head to fully give him access to her mouth. It wasn't until the sleepy tempo of his kiss began to change into something different altogether, that Judith realized what they were doing.

"Luke," she murmured, the tone in her voice bringing his desire-laden eyes open.

Sighing, he laid his head down next to hers. "I know, I know. This is not a good idea," he said and pulled her back against his body. "Just..." he exhaled deeply "...just let me calm down a second here, and then I'll get...outa...here."

Too bad this was all just a game, Judith mused sadly, savoring the only time she would ever be able to lie for a moment in the delicious security of Luke's arms. Her old room at her parents' house suddenly and forever lost its appeal. Luke's breathing deepened, and once again Judith drifted off to sleep, lulled by the comforting sound.

Judith woke to lilting birdcalls outside their bedroom window. The sun was streaming brightly through the lacy drapes and she burrowed deeper under the covers into the warm cocoon that surrounded her. Just a few more minutes and then she would get up, she thought hazily, wondering why she felt so exquisitely comfortable. Luke stirred sleepily, stretching the leg he had flung casually over her body. Wriggling beneath its weight, she pondered this new sensation thoughtfully. The blankets were awfully heavy. And they moved. Opening her sleepy eyes with a start, she found Luke draped contentedly on top of her, still deep in slumber.

Ohmygosh! They'd slept together. Judith was appalled. How could she have let this happen? Floundering under Luke's heavy weight, she strained to see the alarm clock. Eleven o'clock. They should have been up hours ago!

"Luke," she yelped, her eyes wide with fear. "Luke. Wake up." Pushing at his leg, Judith attempted to wake him.

"What?" Luke blinked blankly and stared at Judith. "What happened?" he yawned sleepily and tried to focus on her.

"We overslept," she cried. "We should have been up hours ago."

Abruptly, Luke sat up, his eyes wild. "Wha'd we miss?"

"Breakfast for starters." She pounded her forehead with the palm of her hand. "How are we going to explain this?"

"What's to explain? We're married. We decided to stay in bed. I don't see the big problem." He flopped back down on the bed.

Judith turned and stared down at him in disbelief. "But it's so...tacky."

Luke laughed at her and gripped her shoulder.

"What are you doing?" she asked suspiciously.

"Nature's call," he answered, and pulled himself upright.

Oh, no, he didn't. They were late enough as it was. He could forget any crazy ideas about taking advantage of this situation.

"Not that call, you goose." He looked ruefully at her shocked expression and levered himself off her shoulder to stand up painfully. Limping toward the bathroom in the new cowboy boots he still wore, he turned and grimaced at her. "This call" he winced and shut the bathroom door.

By the time Judith had showered and dressed for the party to be held later that day, it was nearly noon and Luke had already left the room. Donning a deep forest green Western shirt that brought out the color of her eyes, she gave one last twirl in front of the mirror and decided that she must be ready. Never having been to a birthday barbecue, Texas style, she wasn't sure what to expect.

Passing through the foyer on her way out the front door, she heard the low tones of Luke's voice waft toward her from the living room. Patsy was with him, spread-eagled on the living-room floor in the Chinese splits, giggling hysterically at something Luke was saying. Leaning forward on her elbows, she pushed her arms together tightly, to display her delicious cleavage to its best advantage. Tossing her head so that her flaxen hair floated angelically around her face, Patsy angled her profile at Luke in her best imitation of a cover-girl pose.

Patsy symbolized everything Judith wished she could have been, when she was growing up with

Luke. And to have had him look at her the way he was looking at Patsy right now...well, maybe she would have sold her soul. But not any more. She'd accepted the fact that she wasn't the kind of girl boys looked at, the way they looked at girls such as Patsy. Why was it then, years later, after having come to terms with who she was, and finding happiness and confidence there, did a stabbing pain shoot through her heart at the sight of Luke and Patsy having such a cozy conversation?

Patsy looked up and caught Judith staring but did not acknowledge her presence. Luke turned to discover what she had seen.

Smiling warmly at Judith he asked, "Ready?"

"If you are."

"Let's go, then." He stood and ruffled Patsy's hair. "See ya at the party, kiddo."

"Don't forget our dance," she simpered, smiling coyly at him.

Luke groaned and laughed.

They found Miss Clarise outside directing an army of servants and hired help as they set up a multitude of tents and tables for Patsy's little birthday party.

"There you are," she greeted them warmly. "I was wondering if maybe I shouldn't send the troops out after you. I hope y'all slept well." Her knowing wink had Judith blushing furiously. "Did you have some breakfast?"

Luke shook his head. "We thought we'd grab some in town, Miss Clarise. We have an errand we need to run before the party."

"That would be just fine. You don't mind driving

yourselves, I hope? As y'all can see, I've got every available man busy with the party setup.''

The rolling lawn was rapidly turning into party central. A group of musicians set up their instruments on the bandstand that was provided next to the large parquet dance floor. They tested the microphones, strung miles of electrical wires and cords and noisily tuned their guitars. Caterers carted food warmers and Sterno cans by the boxload, and unfurled dozens of red-and-white checkered tablecloths in the breeze. The gazebo was adorned with streamers and balloons and the gift table was already piled high with a mountain of gifts for the birthday girl. Several sides of beef were turning slowly in a huge barbecue pit.

''Can we do anything to help?'' Judith asked, watching the swarm of activity in awe.

''Goodness, no. You two run along. I have everything under control.'' Reaching into the pocket of her apron, she withdrew a set of keys. ''Here. Take my car. It's the black Lincoln, sitting over there by the garage.'' She pointed at her car, and with a wave of her hand slipped into the mass of activity, calmly orchestrating the huge event with ease.

''She thinks we slept together.''

''We did. So what?''

''We did *not!*'' Judith stared out the window as Luke sped down the highway toward the small town nearest to the Brubaker ranch. She was growing tired of all the lies. Okay, so maybe he had her on a technicality, but they had not done what Miss Clarise seemed to think they had done.

Impatiently, Luke glanced at Judith, annoyed with her prim and proper attitude. Why was she trying to make him feel guilty for something he hadn't even done? Not that he hadn't thought about it.... Still, she was overreacting. Criminy sakes. Let her sleep on the floor and see how long her Puritan attitude would last.

"Judith—" Luke schooled his voice to not reflect any emotion. "Don't you think that the Brubakers would think it was strange if we didn't sleep together? That's what married people do. Sleep together." More than that if they're lucky, he thought, suddenly remembering how right it had felt having Judith curled so sweetly into his body last night. It was a lucky thing he'd been so exhausted or he just might have given her a reason to be so up in arms.

"I know all that," she snapped. "I just don't feel right about lying to these people in the first place. And in the second place, sleeping in the same bed with you, my partner, my business associate, is bad news. They don't say 'no fishing in the company pond' without a reason. It's just a plain dumb idea."

"But we didn't *do* anything."

"That's not the point. People talk. I'm sure someday this fake-marriage business will get out and shed a bad light on us. You know what a big gossip Mrs. Soder is. She'll have this juicy tidbit spread all over the Northwest as soon as she catches wind of it."

"Then she's fired," Luke said grimly.

"You can't fire someone for telling the truth. At least she's telling the truth. That's better than I can say for us."

"Judith, would you get off this lying jag? Frankly, it's starting to bore me. We did not lie to Brubaker. We both tried to tell him the truth, but he wouldn't stop talking long enough to hear it. Neither of us set out to deceive him. He's believing what he wants to."

"How convenient."

"Dammit, Judith, would you just shut up about it? It's a little late to do anything about it now."

Judith turned her face away from him and watched the miles roll by. What he was saying was perfectly logical, but that didn't make it right. However, one thing was true. It was too late to do anything about it now.

Luke finally broke the silence as they pulled into the small rural town and found a parking spot. Shutting off the engine, he turned to face her. "We just have to get through this miserable party tonight. Then maybe we can dig in and get some work done and get the hell out of here. Go back home. Get back to normal," he sighed, staring out the windshield at a beat-up store front.

"Fine," she said curtly and got out of the car. That was fine with her. Obviously, he couldn't wait to get back home. Away from her. Well, that was fine.

Luke slammed his door and locked it. Great. What had he said now? Grinding his teeth in frustration, he followed Judith into the nearest store to look for the delightful Patsy's birthday gift.

After what seemed like an endless search, Judith was about to throw in the towel on Patsy's birthday present. Why bother, anyway? If she were really into being honest, she'd admit that she couldn't stand the girl and stop wasting her time on a meaningless token.

"Let's go," Judith sighed, wandering out of the sporting-goods shop where Luke had become like a kid in a candy store. While she waited for him outside on the old-fashioned boardwalk, she passed the time by peering into the jewelry-store window next door. A beautiful diamond engagement ring caught her eye, and she cupped her hands on the glass to get a better look.

"Find something?" Luke asked curiously over her shoulder.

"No, not really." She shrugged wistfully. "Wait. Look." Pointing past the ring, Judith drew his attention to a tiny silver charm in the shape of a ballerina, suspended from a delicate silver chain. It was enchanting and she knew Patsy would love it.

"That's it," Luke agreed. "Come on, let's go get it gift wrapped and head back. We're going to be late as it is."

By midafternoon, Patsy's birthday guests were beginning to arrive. Judith and Luke drove up to the gates of the Circle Bow only to discover that they needed to park nearly a mile away from the house and walk in. The strain of their earlier argument was still with them, but they agreed before they got to the party that they would set aside their differences for the time being and make every effort to appear the loving creative team that Big Daddy had hired. For Ed and Ted's sake, if nothing else.

Judith was amazed at the number of friends Patsy seemed to have, and said as much to Luke.

"A lot of these people are probably friends of Big Daddy's," Luke said as they followed the multitudes over to the party area.

"I thought Miss Clarise said this was going to be a *little* party. There must be several hundred people here."

They made their way through the throng to the gazebo, where they left Patsy's gift on the table with the others. From across the yard they could hear Big Daddy calling them.

"Theyah they ah!" he cried and threaded his way through the crowd to get to the Andersons. "I'd like you to meet some of my friends," he told them and winked. "Could mean some more bidness for y'all."

Judith gave up trying to put names to faces after about the twelfth introduction. Big Daddy, it seemed, knew almost everyone who was anyone in the entire state of Texas. She had never seen so many rich, powerful, influential people in one spot before in her life.

After an hour of tiresome chitchat with fat, balding men, who held Judith's hand about a minute longer than necessary, Luke began to lose his patience. He'd never enjoyed mingling with strangers at large social events, even less so when the strangers were eyeing his wife like some kind of juicy tenderloin steak.

Judith was smiling and shaking the hand of the mayor of the small town they'd visited that morning.

"The pleasure is all mine, little lady," he said, squeezing her hand and massaging her upper arm.

Unable to stand another second of this old coot coming on to his wife, Luke stepped up and grabbed Judith's arm out of the dumbfounded mayor's roving hands and yanked her through the crowd without a word. He didn't stop until they reached the food line at the buffet.

"What a lech." Luke turned to make sure the old geezer hadn't followed them.

"What in heaven's name did you do that for?" Judith cried, and jerked her arm out of Luke's firm grip. "He was a nice man. Not to mention a friend of Big Daddy's!"

"Fine. See if I care. Let every idiot at this party

come on to you. What's it to me? I'm just the stupid husband.''

"May I remind you that you are *not* my husband?" she hissed.

Their eyes locked viciously. "At this party, tonight and for the rest of this pseudo-business trip, I am your husband, and you'd better not forget it."

His double standard infuriated her. She couldn't even carry on an innocent conversation with a nice, little, old man, yet he found it perfectly acceptable to flirt his gorgeous head off with their host's coddled nymphet. The injustice! *Ed and Ted. Ed and Ted,* she chanted in her head.

Picking up a plate, she pushed it roughly into his chest. "Here, dear," she said sweetly. "Have a plate."

Loading their plates with every kind of Southern delicacy, they found seats at an empty table and ate in silence.

A static voice announced over the loudspeaker that Patsy's gifts had been opened and were being displayed on several tables by the gazebo, if people would like to wander over and have a look-see. But first, a toast to Patsy Brubaker, and then the dancing would begin. Waiters dressed as cowboys dashed through the crowd with plastic champagne glasses and magnums of fine imported champagne, as Big Daddy and Miss Clarise made their way up to the gazebo to join their daughter.

Big Daddy adjusted the microphone down about two feet, and lifted his glass in salute. "Hellooo, theyah! Glad y'all could make it to my little darlin's party. I can't believe she's all grown-up now. Just yesterday, she was runnin' around heah in pigtails…''

he sniffed. "Well, honey, heah's to my beautiful, talented, little dancer. We're so proud of ya. Happy birthday, darlin'." Big Daddy tossed back his glass of champagne and kissed Patsy on the cheek. "Let's get this party rollin'!" he roared, and laughing gleefully, he pointed at the country-western band who took the cue and began to play.

Luke refilled their champagne glasses, several times, with the bottle the waiter had left on their table. After two or three glasses of the stuff, the music was beginning to sound almost palatable. No wonder cowboys had reputations for being such hard drinkers, he thought muzzily and slugged down another gulp. Standing up, Judith nodded at the rest of the people seated at their table and excused herself. To Luke she said, "I'll be right back, dear. I have to go powder my nose."

"Take your time, dear." He waved and wondered if the lyrics to this last song, about a man in love with more than one woman and his horse, had made her ill.

The tabletop vibrated with the rousing ditty coming from the bandstand. From where Luke sat, he could see Patsy in her spangly party shirt and skintight blue jeans, shaking her little booty. He'd been wrong when he'd compared Judith to Patsy last night. Patsy would never be even half the woman Judith was. Not even close.

Slowly the immense parquet dance floor that was situated beneath half a dozen huge black speakers at the bandstand's edge became crowded with couples. Everyone, it seemed, knew how to two-step. Luke watched them with new interest. An interest he hadn't had before dancing with Judith late last night. As far as he could tell, they'd been doing it right. He counted under his breath. *One, pause, two…* At a light tap on his arm, he turned and stopped counting. Patsy.

"Hi." Leaning into him, she hugged his bulging bicep to her bulging bust. "You haven't forgotten, I hope?" she pouted prettily.

"Forgotten?" Luke scanned the crowd for Judith. What the hell was taking her so long? She could have powdered every nose in the bathroom by now. "Uh…no…"

"Good!" she said, tugging excitedly on his arm. "Come on, they're playing our song!"

They were? He wasn't aware they had a song. The tune was unfamiliar, but that didn't mean anything— so far all the tunes had been unfamiliar. Listening to the mushy, depressing lyrics Luke got scared.

"Ah go crazyeeee
Knowin' you'll never be freeeeeee
But now she is your wi-ee-i-ee-i-fe
For the rest of your li-ee-i-ee-i-fe
Wish you'd waited for meeeeee
Just drives me crazyeeee…"

It was clear from the beginning that Luke was no match for the tiny dancer. She had obviously waited for her turn with him to show off some of her favorite moves. Much to his credit, Luke valiantly struggled to keep up with her as she led him through a bump-and-grind routine that bordered on the obscene.

Finally able to escape from the overcrowded ladies' room, Judith discovered that her husband was no longer waiting for her at the table. Glancing around, she spotted him out on the dance floor with Patsy.

And not just with Patsy. Under Patsy, over Patsy, around Patsy.

Big Daddy clapped and whistled at the light of his life, thoroughly impressed with her fancy footwork. It annoyed Judith that he seemed oblivious to the fact that Patsy was having *dancercourse* with her husband, right there in front of God and everyone.

As the music grew more frantic, so did Patsy's gyrations. Hips swaying, pelvis thrusting, legs kicking, she did everything but moonwalk. Patsy brought the phrase "dirty dancing" to life.

It was all Judith could do to keep from running out to the dance floor and snatching the birthday girl bald. She knew she should be sympathetic toward Patsy, as she had acted nuttier than that, on occasion, when it came to Luke Anderson. But for some reason, on this lovely starlit evening, Judith searched her soul and could find no charity in her heart. Not even a speck.

Conway appeared at her side. Holding out his hand to her, he nodded at the dance floor. She was on the verge of refusing, when Patsy grabbed Luke, who was by now just standing there, too astonished to move, and rubbed him up and down with her entire, limber, nubile body. Spasms of jealousy seared ruthlessly through Judith's brain.

Two could play at this game, she decided and slapped her hand into Conway's, yanking him out to the middle of the dance floor behind her. Luckily for her, Conway was no slouch in the dancing department, and before she knew what was happening, the crowd parted and formed a circle around the two zealous pairs.

The rowdy mob cheered and clapped with raucous, carefree abandon as the band struck up a rousing version of "Dueling Banjos." Judith felt herself suddenly lifted into the air in Conway's beefy arms and spun around until she was sure she would lose her supper. Setting her down on rubber legs, he then proceeded to lead her through a series of complex steps that left her blind with dizziness.

Poor Luke was faring no better. Not to be outdone by her older brother, Patsy, egged on by the encouraging spectators, shifted into high gear. Luke stood his ground solidly, the eye of her acrobatic hurricane. At one point he was able to catch Judith's eye and mouthed the word "help."

Judith vowed that as soon as the room stopped spinning, she would rush to his aid. He had suffered enough. Come to think of it, so had she.

Finally, when the music slowed to a human pace, Luke strode over to Conway and claimed his wife. Staggering into his arms, she looked gratefully up at him and murmured, "Thank God!"

Sulking, Patsy finished the dance with her brother, and when the song ended the jubilant crowd cheered wildly. They could always count on the Brubakers for an excellent party.

The next song was a slow ballad, and Judith clung to Luke as they swayed to the strains of the sad, soulful tune. The comforting beat of Luke's heart matched the rhythm of the deep bass. Amazed at how jealous she still was of Luke after all these years, she wondered when it would ever end. Probably when he settled down and got married, she mused unhappily. The thought of Luke married to someone such as Patsy made her stomach churn, and she squirmed in misery. Tightening his arms around her waist, Luke rested his chin on the top of her head and sighed. She wondered briefly what he was thinking. He probably couldn't wait for this dance to end, while she could go on like this forever.

"Come on," Luke ordered, taking Judith by the hand and leading her off the brightly lit dance floor and out onto the lawn, away from the crowd. The last rays of the sun had disappeared, leaving them alone under the huge, dark, star-filled Texas sky. Holding her hand tightly, as if she might try to escape, Luke kept walking, no particular destination in mind.

"What were you doing with that jarhead?" Luke demanded, once they were out of anyone's earshot. "Trying to get yourself killed?"

"Me?" Judith laughed sharply. "You were the one dancing with the human corkscrew."

"I wasn't dancing. I was watching. Big difference." He stopped walking and turned to face her. "How could you let him grab at you that way?"

"I don't know how you could tell he was grabbing at me with Patsy wrapped around your head," she groused.

Luke's eyes flashed angrily in the moonlight. "You're supposed to be my wife."

"Well, you're supposed to be my husband," she shot back, annoyed again with his double standard.

Reaching out, Luke took her face between his hands and drew her to him, tracing her cheekbones with his thumbs. Oh, how he wanted to kiss her. To hell with the fact that she was his business partner in another life. Tonight she was his wife, and she would damn well start acting like one, even if he had to kiss some sense into her stubborn, beautiful, wonderful...head. He heard himself groan as she sighed sweetly and ran her hands around his waist where they locked behind his back.

Judith knew she should run. He was doing it again—casting his magic spell on her, so that she couldn't think straight. This would never work. Pretending to be his wife for the sake of the business. It was surely going to blow up in their faces, and they would never work in this industry again. Luke would blame her for the end of his remarkable career, and she would probably end up jobless, homeless, senseless.... She looked at Luke's haunted face and knew she should run, now. But she couldn't. Her feet were made of clay. With all her heart and soul, she wanted another one of those mind-blowing kisses that she'd relived every moment of every day and night since that episode in Luke's office. Her body wouldn't obey the dictates of her rational mind. *Traitor!* Her brain screamed at her treasonous body. *Turncoat! Judas! Judas! Judith!*

"Judith? Luke?" Patsy's voice filtered through the darkness and penetrated her muddled mind. Luke cursed under his breath in frustration. "Oh. There you are," she said silkily. "Big Daddy says come on now, it's time to cut my cake, and I didn't want to do it without y'all."

Stepping away from Luke, Judith seized this chance to escape. "I'm sorry, you'll have to go ahead without me, Patsy. I seem to have developed a splitting headache, all of a sudden. I'm going to bed." Without a backward glance, she headed toward the house and the safety of their empty bedroom.

Luke watched her retreating form, and fought the urge to go after her. The way he was feeling now, he might end up saying or doing something they would both regret. Well, that Judith would regret, anyway.

"That's okay, Luke, Big Daddy will understand. I'm sure she'll feel better after a good night's sleep," Patsy cooed.

More frustrated than he'd ever been in his life, Luke set his jaw rigidly and walked back to the party with Patsy. Maybe Judith would feel better after a good night's sleep, but for him relief would only come in the form of a long, freezing cold shower.

Chapter Six

"Judith, are you awake?" Luke whispered and turned on the bedside lamp.

Eyes shut and breathing deeply, Judith pretended to be asleep. She felt Luke lift a spare pillow and a blanket off the bed and toss them onto the floor. Moments later, she heard the bathroom faucet running as he brushed his teeth and prepared for bed.

It would be foolish to try to have a heart-to-heart with Luke before she had a chance to sort out her jumbled mix of emotions, she rationalized, and turned over on her side, away from the bathroom. For the past three hours, Judith had lain awake, tossing and turning, trying to make some sense out of her feelings toward Luke. Unfortunately the only thing she'd managed to accomplish was getting irreversibly tangled in her nightgown and more confused about him than ever before.

Judith was sure that something was happening between them. But just what that something was, remained a stubborn mystery. One minute she was sure they were forming a bond, and the next they were at each other's throats. One minute she was sure that he found her to be an attractive, desirable woman, and the next, Patsy would smile and all bets were off.

Mashing her pillow into a more comfortable shape, she sighed deeply and listened to Luke's bedtime sounds. Gargling, spitting, flushing, he moved through his routine without a care in the world. What on earth had he been doing at the party without her for the past three hours? she wondered miserably. Probably living it up with Patsy, not giving good old Judith another thought. As much as Judith tried to convince herself that she didn't give a damn what Luke did with his free time, she knew deep down that she did. Always would. Forever. And not just because they were trying to pull the wool over Big Daddy's eyes. No. She cared because she...cared about Luke. A lot. More so now than ever before. Dammit, anyway. Why was she doomed to spend her life caring about some guy who would never feel anything for her? Suddenly exhausted, she squeezed her eyes tightly shut and willed herself to sleep.

Luke paused at the edge of the bed and watched Judith sleeping in the subtle glow of the lamp on the nightstand. She looked ethereal in the dim light, her hair fanned out behind her on the bed, her gauzy white nightgown twisted tightly around her perfect curves. Peaches-and-cream complexion and long, thick eyelashes resting lightly on soft porcelain cheeks...she was truly an angel. At least while she's asleep, he smiled to himself. Reaching down, he adjusted her covers up over her shoulders, and couldn't resist stroking her soft, luxuriant hair. She might look and feel like an angel, but he knew better.

Judith Anderson had become an amazing woman. He'd come to admire her greatly over the past few weeks. She had spunk…drive…beauty… brains.…

Hell, he more than just admired her. It had gone way beyond admiration, and he knew it. Backing away from the bed, he stared down at her as a sense of fear and dread mingled with his desire. What was happening to him? It seemed that for every minute he spent in her presence, he grew more jealous and possessive. What the hell was that all about? He usually didn't have a jealous bone in his body.

Luke ran a shaky hand over his face and groaned. Turning off the nightstand lamp, he moved through the dusk-filled room toward the window. The full moon illuminated the dwindling party as the hired help began the arduous task of cleaning up. Grasping the molding on either side of the window, Luke leaned forward and stared, unseeing, at the activity below.

He'd fulfilled his obligatory cake-cutting duties with the birthday girl and made good his escape, claiming he wanted to check on Judith. But he knew if he went back to their room, the way he was feeling, it would be a mistake. One look at her ripe, pouty lips and he'd be a goner.

Never before had he been so uncomfortable in his own skin. Wanting to work off some steam, he found an old dirt path that ran out behind the stables, down into a gully and beyond for miles. For three hours and more than a dozen miles, Luke wrestled with his feelings about Judith and what was happening to their relationship. He was no closer to knowing now than before he left. Maybe he should discuss it with Judith, he thought, tucking his chin into his shoulder and looking back at her. Maybe not. Talking was the furthest thing from his mind at this point.

Pushing off the window casing, he walked over to the bed and stood opening and closing his hands, fighting the urge to wake her. Lord, how he wanted her. Dropping to his knees on the floor, he fell forward and buried his face in his pillow, trying to smother the audible groans of frustration. Punching the innocent pillow several times, he fumbled with his blanket and searched for a comfortable sleeping position. Unfortunately, he wasn't able to find it until shortly before dawn.

Judith set her napkin in her lap and turned her head ever so slightly, to find one large blue eyeball staring deeply into her left green one. Hank. Leaning back, she smiled at her breakfast companion. His toothless grin was shy.

"What'cha doin'?" she asked him playfully.

"Lookin'."

"Oh." She pursed her lips thoughtfully, and so did Hank. "What are you gonna do for the rest of the day?" she asked him, solemnly.

"Horth-back riding."

"That sounds like fun."

"Wanna go?" He sat up and wriggled expectantly.

"I would love to. I have some work to do first, so maybe you could go with me later this afternoon?"

"If Mom leth me." He shrugged, disappointed that she wasn't throwing down her fork and bolting out to the barn after him this very second. "I have chorth in the afternoon."

"Well, maybe we can go tomorrow morning. You can show me around."

"Okay." Hank grinned.

Judith suspected that the party yesterday could account for the lack of Brubaker attendance at breakfast this morning. She must have missed out on a wild time, because she and Hank were the only two who seemed willing or able to make it to breakfast.

Chewing her cereal thoughtfully, she decided that with or without Luke she was going to get some work done on Big Daddy's campaign this morning. Luke was right. The sooner they got down to business, the sooner they could go home. Get back to normal. Toss off this phony marriage charade and resume their life of antagonism. Maybe then she would be able to put all of these unnatural feelings of longing for Luke behind her and concentrate on her career. This close proximity to him was intensifying emotions she thought she'd successfully laid to rest years ago. Emotions which, left unchecked, would leave her open to Luke's rejection. Even now, as a fully grown woman, she couldn't stand the idea of being rejected by him. She shuddered at the images of herself as a homely nuisance who would do anything to be noticed by her hero.

Yes, she thought, blowing on her coffee as Hank blew on his milk, the sooner they went home, the better her chances of getting out of this mess with her heart in one piece.

Judith set down her coffee cup and turned to Hank. Hank set down his milk and smiled bashfully up at her.

"Hank, when you see your daddy, will you tell him that I'll be in the library doing some work?"

"Yeth."

"Thanks. You're my pal." She winked at him and, after several concentrated attempts, Hank managed to blink at Judith in return.

Judith thought surely her heart had dropped into her shoes. The sight of Luke and Patsy entwined in a ravenous embrace, lips locked in passion, quick froze her feet to the foyer floor. Feeling as though she were down for the count in a kick-boxing match, it was all she could do to gasp for air and force her feet into action. Backing slowly out of the foyer, she turned around and moved, as though in a trance, toward the library.

Walls swayed, time bent, her mind hallucinated over the image burned there. Had it been a dream? No. The image was too real. A cold, shivery wave of nausea swept over Judith, causing her to lean against the library door's cool surface, fighting the bile that rose in her throat. Opening the door, she stumbled inside, and made it over to Big Daddy's couch, where she lay down and prayed for the room to stop spinning. She opened her mouth, but no sound, no scream would come out, only tiny, pitiful moans. Her eyes were dry, and she wondered absently why. People who'd been hit by a Mack truck rarely cried, she reflected. They were either too stunned or dead. She wondered which one she was. Couldn't be dead, she decided, the pain was too intense. Closing her eyes tightly, Judith lay on the couch, and breathing deeply waited for the hellish pain to end.

Luke pulled Patsy's arms from around his neck and firmly pressed them to her sides. The woman was part

boa constrictor. He'd been looking for Judith when
Patsy had blindsided him with her lips, murmuring
something about loving her birthday charm.

Some thanks. A simple handshake would have
served the purpose just as well, but how do you tell
that to the rich client's nympho daughter? Luke ran
his hands across his jaw and wondered what he could
say to Patsy that would discourage her, but not cause
any problem with the agency's relationship with Big
Daddy.

Patsy took a step forward and walked her fingers
up the buttons on the front of Luke's shirt. "What's
wrong?" She smiled beguilingly. "No one saw."

"That's not the point, Patsy. I'm a happily married
man. I don't go around kissing other women, because
I happen to love my wife." Luke was pleased with
the sound of that. It sounded as though he meant it.
It sounded as though he loved Judith and wasn't wild
about having this pretty, little sex kitten wrap her nubile body around his. He sounded like a faithful husband, in love with his wife. He was getting good at
this husband thing.

Patsy stepped back and looked up into his face, her
eyes flashing, probing into the depths of his, searching
for a crack in the veneer. At last she sighed and
smiled to hide her disappointment.

"You really mean it, don't you? You really love
her." She looked down at the floor, laughed and
shook her head. "When you first got here, I thought
maybe I had a chance. You two seemed so…unusual.
I don't know how to explain it. You just didn't seem
to connect all that well, like you were always uptight
with each other or something." Tossing her hair out
of her eyes, she cocked her head at him and shot him

a resigned look. "I was wrong, wasn't I? You are in love with her."

Luke nodded and shrugged. "Patsy, I grew up with Judith. I've known her all my life. I don't think there was ever a time that I didn't love her. Maybe I didn't always know it...but I loved her. And..." Luke realized what he was saying and took a deep breath "...I'm afraid I always will."

"She's a lucky woman." Patsy smiled at him. "Friends?"

Luke grasped her outstretched hand and shook it firmly. "Friends."

Patsy left him in search of breakfast and Luke stood in the large, quiet living room and thought about what had just happened. In the course of a few short minutes, his life had changed irrevocably. The fact that he truly had no desire for Patsy's eager advances, came as something of a shock to him. Usually, even if he wasn't interested in the woman, he took pleasure in being noticed by her. But not any more. Never before had he been so consumed with a woman that all others ceased to exist for him. When he'd explained to Patsy how he felt about Judith, he was shocked to realize that he'd been telling the truth. He did love Judith. And in spite of their tumultuous past, he always had. Something about Judith Anderson had always been exciting. Over and above the fact that she was usually driving him out of his mind, he found her fascinating. Yes, even in the past, there had been something about her that drew him to her, drove him half-wild. Pushed him to the absolute limit of his endurance. And she was still doing it to this day. Only now the rules had changed. Now, she was a fully grown woman, and he was a fully grown man. And he was running out of patience.

Judith breathed a sigh of relief that Elizabeth and not Mrs. Soder had answered the phone at Anderson and Anderson. "Hi, Elizabeth, how's it going?"

"Oh, hi, Judith! Fine. Just fine. Quiet. Well, that is except for Mrs. Soder.... Don't worry about us though, everything is under control. How much longer are you guys going to be gone?"

"If I had my way, we'd be coming home tonight." Judith struggled to keep the despair out of her voice.

"Really? Why? Texas sounds like fun. It's raining oodles of poodles here. Is anything wrong?"

Elizabeth had a wonderful, sensitive, trustworthy nature and Judith longed to spill the whole sordid tale to her sympathetic friend, but she couldn't seem to form the words. "No, not really. I'm just tired."

"Hmm. How are you and Luke getting along?"

Judith grinned weakly. Elizabeth was too smart for her own good. "Our relationship is changing."

"You don't sound too happy about that."

"Umm, um," she mumbled, too miserable to respond. "I just wish this whole thing was over and I was safely at home, in my own room. Alone."

"Well, hang in there."

"I will. You, too. Call us if you have any questions or problems. And remember, no one knows about this marriage thing except you. Don't let Mrs. Soder find out."

"Mum's the word. Speaking of Mrs. Soder, she's been waiting for you to call. She has a couple of things to discuss with you or Luke."

Judith moaned. "Only a couple? Go ahead and transfer me...and Elizabeth? Thanks."

The door to the library opened and Judith's heart constricted painfully as Luke entered and joined her on the couch. Judith forced her lips up, baring her teeth at Luke, and hoped he believed she was smiling. "It's for you," she said sweetly. Handing him the phone, she left the library to search out some private place to lick her wounds.

The stable seemed like the perfect sanctuary. Besides, trying to concentrate on the Brubaker account after what she'd seen in the living room that morning was useless. The vision of Patsy wound around Luke, clinging for dear life, filled Judith's head, obliterating all else.

Entering the dark, musty stable, she hoped maybe Hank would serve as a distraction. The smell of horse, hay and leather greeted her and immediately she was a child again, attending her Saturday-morning horse-back-riding lessons. Dust floated slowly in the slanting rays of sunshine that filtered through cracks in the barn's walls, illuminating the stalls and their curious occupants. Soft nickers and whinnies welcomed her, beckoning her to come rub a velvety nose.

Smiling, she walked over to a handsome steed and stroked his smooth, whiskery nose. He nudged her hand, looking for a treat, and Judith felt her mood lighten considerably. To heck with men. There were other lovely things in life, she decided and looked around for Hank. He was missing, and the only other person in sight was Conway. Ambling down the barn's broad hallway, he raised an arm in greeting.

"That's Lightning," he said, nodding at the horse

Judith was petting. "You ride?" he asked around the straw that dangled between this teeth.

"Yes. I took lessons for seven years as a kid. Western and English." She scratched the top of Lightning's head. "I have a couple of little ribbons back home." She offered shyly.

Conway nodded, clearly impressed. "You'd do well on him. He's gentle. But fast," he added and winked. "A real handful out in the open."

A ride was just the soothing balm she needed for her wounded soul. "May I ride him?"

"Sure. What about Luke? Does he ride, too?"

"Uh, no, I don't think so." She hesitated. "I doubt if he'll want to anyway, he's on the phone." And unless Mrs. Soder wasn't feeling well, he would be for the rest of the day, she thought with grim satisfaction.

"Well, okay, then." Conway shrugged agreeably. "Looks like I got you all to myself, for a few minutes anyway...." He chuckled and winked lazily at her again. "Let's get you ready to ride." Leading her to the tack room, he helped her find Lightning's saddle and bridle, showing her where his curry comb and other paraphernalia were, for after her ride. Conway slipped a halter over Lightning's head after they returned from the tack room, and tied him to a post outside his stall so that Judith could saddle him.

"You look like you know what you're doing." Luke's low voice sent shivers up her spine as he leaned against the wall, watching her make adjustments on the stirrup.

Dammit. She'd hoped to be out galloping across the pasture by now, leaving her husband and his girlfriend in the dust.

"Mmm," she answered noncommittally.

"Where are you going?"

"Out back."

"Can I go?"

"I don't care."

"What's your problem?"

"I don't have a problem. What's yours?" she asked churlishly. Conway grinned into his sleeve.

Ignoring her, Luke looked at Conway. "You have a horse I can borrow?"

"Sure. You ride?"

"Yeah," Luke lied.

Conway sized him up and decided he was lying. "Got just the horse for you." Jutting his chin out toward the end of the barn, he indicated Luke's mount. "Come on. I'll getcha outfitted." Grabbing a saddle and bridle out of the tack room, Conway led Luke to his horse. "Name's Burrito," Conway said and began saddling the sorriest piece of horseflesh Luke had ever laid eyes on.

Luke stared at the poor crowbait nag in disappointed wonder. Why did Judith get the macho horse? He narrowed his eyes at Conway, as the cowboy kneed the horse's belly and tightened the saddle's cinch. Luke was having a hard time liking the Brubaker offspring today. And what was the burr under Judith's saddle? Maybe he should go back to bed and start this lousy day over again. He was just considering this idea when Conway led the flea-bitten plug from hell out of the stall and into the yard where Judith stood, getting ready to mount up.

"Come on," he called over his shoulder to Luke. "Burrito's ready and champin' at the bit."

Sure. Ready for the glue factory. Disgusted, Luke

followed Conway to the yard. Handing the reins to
Luke, Conway deserted him in favor of Judith. Un-
necessarily assisting her with the saddle, his large
hands lingered on her back as he moved around her.
Conway turned, nodded at Luke, and wished them
luck.

"How do I get on this thing?" Luke asked once
Conway was out of earshot.

"Why don't you ask *Patsy?* I'm sure she'd be
happy to help," she snapped angrily.

"What's that supposed to mean?" Luke asked suspiciously. What was she talking about? What had she
heard? Or worse, seen?

"Nothing," she bit out, stepping up into the stirrup
and swinging her leg up over Lightning's broad back.
"Just try to remember one thing, *dear,*" she sneered
at him. "For the rest of this pseudo-business trip, you
are my husband. For Ed and Ted's sake, if nothing
else." With one last meaningful, furious glance, she
tossed her wild auburn mane over her shoulder,
spurred Lightning and galloped out of the corral and
down the dusty road.

She had seen. Damn. Setting his jaw with determination, he copied what he'd seen Judith do on
Lightning and swung his leg over Burrito's swayed
and bony back. He had to catch her. He had to tell
her the truth. "Come on you old nag!" he yelled at
the horse, and proceeded to bounce out of the corral,
and down the road after Judith at a brain-jarring pace.

It was immediately apparent to Judith how Lightning had earned his name, as she soared over the Brubaker outback. The wind whipped her hair painfully
into her eyes as she turned in her saddle to check on
Luke. Bobbing along like a cork on the ocean in a

storm, she could see him hanging on for dear life, furiously calling her name.

Someday, she was certain, she would look back on this experience and laugh. Howl with hilarity that for once she was the one in control, looking good, riding like the champion she'd once been, while Cool Hand Luke, somewhere behind her, rode Burrito like a pogo stick. Yes, someday when she wasn't so hurt and angry, she'd laugh. But not today. Today she just wanted to escape. Turning around, she dug her heels into Lightning's sides and leaned forward, urging him on, faster, further away from her pain.

There was no way Luke was going to let Judith believe that he'd been kissing the client's daughter. He would set her straight if it was the last thing he did, and judging from the pain that shot through his groin every time he landed on Burrito's bony back, it just might be. Gritting his teeth, he aimed the poor old bag of bones in Judith's general direction and slapped Burrito's skinny behind as hard as he could with his reins. Snorting in surprise, Burrito reared back and upon landing, took off at the speed of light. Luke's ride smoothed out considerably at Burrito's change of gait and before he knew it, he was gaining on Judith. *Heaven help her when I catch up with her,* he muttered under his breath, filled with righteous indignation. He'd barely had a chance to adjust to this new pace and pull himself up from somewhere south of the saddle where he'd been riding, when Burrito, misinterpreting a cue from his rider, turned sharply and left Luke lying in a heap on the ground.

Judith felt as if she were watching a slow-motion action scene in a spaghetti Western. Luke flew off Burrito's back, ever so slowly, and rolled even more slowly end over end, until his head met a large, sharp rock. With a sickening thud, Luke was out cold.

"Luke?" she whispered in horror, pulling Lightning up short. "Oh my God. *Luke!*" This time she screamed. Terror spurred her across the ground that separated them, and sliding off her mount, she dropped to her knees and crawled frantically over to Luke's lifeless and bleeding form. Adrenaline flooded her veins, causing her heart to roar deafeningly in her ears. "You'd better not be playing some kind of trick on me...." Her voice was thready, shaken.

"Luke!" she cried impatiently, patting his pale cheeks, "Answer me." Walking her hands over his legs, she probed for broken bones. She prodded and poked his stomach, chest and arms, unsure of exactly what she was searching for...unsure what to do about it when she found it. A feeling of complete helplessness washed over her.

A soft moan brought her eyes back up to his face, where a nasty bump, the size of a small egg was forming over his right eye. Somewhere she'd heard that head wounds bled a lot, even minor ones. But nothing had prepared her for this. Fighting a feeling of lightheadedness, she gently searched the strong contours of his neck with her fingers. He was still breathing, his pulse was steady she noted, filled with relief. At least he was still alive.

Fumbling frantically with the buttons to her blouse, she quickly stripped it off and carefully dabbed at his bleeding wound with it. "Come on, baby," she coaxed to his ashen face. "Don't die on me," she begged, wrapping the blood-soaked blouse firmly around his head.

Judith's mind was whirling. *No.* This couldn't be

happening. Fearfully whispering an earnest prayer, she took his large, limp hand in her warm, red, sticky one.

"Oh, Lord," she moaned, "Lord, I'm so sorry for being such a jealous idiot. Please. Please, don't let my stupid temper cause anything bad to happen to Luke. Let him be okay. I promise to be good from now on. I'll go to church every Sunday, I'll give everything I own to charity, I'll...I'll be nice. Really nice, even to Luke...especially to Luke. Just don't..." her voice choked as she attempted to get the words out over the lump in her throat. "Just don't let him die." She wiped her running nose and eyes on Luke's shirttail.

Burrito ambled up and nickered curiously as Judith knelt crying over Luke's supine body. Reaching up, Luke grasped her by the wrists and pulled her down on top of his chest. "I'm going to hold you to that," he mumbled thickly, sliding his hands over her bare back. "Say hallelujah, Judith. Your prayers have been answered."

"Let go of me." Judith struggled to get out of Luke's death grip.

"Are you kidding? Just when I finally have you exactly where I want you?" He ran his hands over her bare shoulders, feeling the soft, smooth skin, burning an erotic trail with his fingertips. "Now where were we? Oh, yes. You were promising to be very nice to me if I didn't die, right? Feel free to begin anytime now...." His voice was raspy.

Fuming with indignation, Judith wriggled out of his grasp and tried in vain to shield her skimpy bra from his probing gaze. "You're contemptible," she spat, confused at the feelings Luke's hands were igniting on her bare flesh. For heaven's sake, the man was practically at death's door, not to mention the fact that he'd spent the morning cheating on her with their client's daughter, and here she was, thinking how delicious his hands felt on her body. Just how sick and depraved had she become?

Luke winced in pain as he struggled to sit up. "First, I nearly kill myself trying to catch you, and then you insult me. I don't know if I want you being nice to me. I may not survive it. Besides, I have a headache." With a cocky grin, his eyes rolled back in his head and he slumped to the ground.

"Luke?" Abandoning her attempt at modesty, Judith leaned over him, smoothing his hair away from his injured forehead.

"Hmm?" he asked dreamily.

"Are you all right?"

"Righty-ho," he murmured. "Right as rain."

She smiled tentatively. "Well, I wouldn't go that far, but I imagine you'll live." Gently she lifted his head into her lap and cradling it on her thighs, asked, "Luke, how many fingers am I holding up?"

Grimacing with effort, he slowly opened his eyes and contemplated the three fingers she held up. Sliding lazily lower, his eyes fastened on her generous cleavage.

"Two." He smiled happily.

"Yes. You'll definitely live," she sighed.

Chapter Seven

The restless moans finally penetrated Judith's sleep-drugged mind. Someone was moaning. Maybe it was her, she thought groggily, tentatively prodding the stiffness in her neck. There it was again. No, it hadn't been her. Who, then? A decidedly male voice muttered some nonsensical phrases and moaned again.

Luke. It all came flooding back. Every bloody detail. Flinging off her comforter, she climbed out of the makeshift bed that she had fashioned out of two parlor-area chairs and tiptoed over to where Luke lay, tossing feverishly in his sleep. Moonlight streamed through the bedroom window, illuminating the man who lay sprawled across the giant bed. He had kicked his blankets off, onto the floor, and the top sheet was clumped around his ankles.

Clad in nothing but a pair of cotton briefs, he appeared the picture of robust health, with the exception of the bandage that covered his forehead. She stood, shivering in the cool, predawn air and watched his

smooth chest rise and fall. Even in repose, he exuded
strength. Shivering again, she wondered whether it
was from the chill in the room, or the man who posed
as her loving husband.

She could feel the heat radiating off his traumatized
body as she straightened the top sheet and covered
him. A light film of perspiration gave his skin an ir-
idescent sheen in the eerie white light.

"Judith! Wait! I can explain!" Luke muttered, and
angrily kicked the top sheet back down around his
ankles. Wrapping her arms around her waist, Judith
leaned forward, curiously, waiting for the explanation.

"Go. You stupid nag." Flailing his arms wildly he
swung at the air. "Get away from me…"

Startled, she stepped back. He was either talking in
his sleep or he was delirious. Whichever, she didn't
like the sound of what she heard. She still couldn't
believe what had happened. It was just lucky that
Hank had come along and spotted them crouched together on the ground.

"Whath wrong?" the boy had asked, his childish
face mirroring Judith's anxiety.

"Luke fell and hit his head, honey. Do you think
you can ride back to the house and get some help?"
Judith still sat with Luke's bleeding head cradled in
her lap.

"Yeth," Hank nodded wide eyed and openmouthed.

"Hurry, but be careful," she ordered.

Hank had taken off like a shot, yelling all the way
that Luke was dead. The entire Brubaker cavalry had
come galloping back with Hank in the lead, all grim
with fear and worry about Luke. Merle and Buck
knew first aid, and Conway, ever aware of their lovely
guest, peeled off his flannel shirt and handed it to

Judith. Nodding absently, she slipped it on, too worried to care that she hadn't been wearing a blouse. Removing his hat, Conway smacked the twins, Waylon and Willie, soundly about the head and shoulders with it for staring at her state of undress. That was his job.

Once they all arrived back at the house in one of Big Daddy's Land Rovers, the family doctor met them and examined Luke, after the Brubaker brothers helped him to the bedroom suite. The doctor had assured Judith that it would be all right to let him sleep, that his concussion was mild, and to keep an eye on him for signs of complications.

Watching Luke sweat and ramble deliriously, she wondered if this constituted a complication. Maybe she should wake him up and take his temperature or something.

"Luke?" she whispered, touching his damp shoulder.

"Get away from me, and don't kiss me!" he ordered angrily, his glassy eyes blazing at her.

Well, dammit, it's not like I'm trying to seduce you here, she fumed, jerking her hand back. He looked really strange.

"Luke? Are you awake?"

"Mmm."

"Is that a yes?"

"Mmm." He blinked several times, trying to focus.

"You were moaning and I wanted…" What did she want? Now she wasn't so sure, as she stood next to the bed, watching him watching her. "I wanted to make sure you were all right."

"Mmm." He reached up and gingerly felt the lump over his eye. "My head feels like I've just partied nonstop for a week."

Judith smiled at him in sympathy. "Ouch. I know that feeling."

"You do?"

"Don't sound so shocked. I wasn't always the twerpy, little kid you used to know. I'll have you know I attended a party or two in college."

"No way," he mumbled.

"Way." She grinned. "Can I get you something? An aspirin?"

"Miss Clarise left me some on the nightstand." He gestured weakly to the bottle and his half-filled glass of water. Propping himself up on his elbow, he ran a hand through his hair, finger combing his shaggy locks into place. He watched as Judith reached over and shook two tablets into her palm. Nowhere was he able to glimpse even a ghost of the former Ms. Judith Anderson. Her fluid movements were graceful, down to the way she refilled his glass with water from the pitcher. The oversize sleeveless T-shirt she wore did little to hide her long, lithe shape from his interested stare. Her curves moved gently under the soft fabric, tantalizing his libido into overdrive.

"You're sweating," she observed, feeling his neck with the back of her hand. "Hot," she muttered to herself.

If she only knew. "Mmm," he said, glad that the room was dark enough to conceal the effect her touch had on him.

"Here, sit up," she said, dropping the aspirin into his hand and reaching behind him to plump his pillows. The soft cotton of her nightshirt grazed his overheated flesh, causing a riot of goose bumps to stand at attention.

Married life wasn't so bad. "Thanks." He took the

aspirin and the glass of cool water. It would take more than water to quench this blaze.

She took the empty glass, set it on the nightstand and stood for an awkward moment, looking down at him.

"Well, I…uh…guess I'll just go back to bed." The soft light that filtered through the window backlit her cascade of chestnut curls, turning it into a cloud of wildfire, flowing over her moon-kissed shoulders. The thin fabric of her shirt was nearly transparent and her coltish body, firm and shapely, appeared and disappeared within its shadows. Even in the gloaming he could see the beauty in her face, celestial in its perfection.

"No. Please." He leaned forward, beseechingly. "I'm awake now. Talk to me." He patted the edge of the bed in invitation.

She hesitated. "You need your rest." More than that, she needed to get away from him.

Rest was not what he needed. "I'm rested. Sit. Talk to me," he implored again. He moved over, under the sheet that now covered him to the waist.

"Luke…"

"Judith." His voice was firm, brooking no argument.

Sitting down warily, she avoided his eyes. "What did you want to talk to me about?"

"I want to explain something I think you may have seen today." Gripping her arm firmly, he pulled her back down to the edge of the bed when she tried to stand up. He wished she'd stop acting like a scared deer about to bolt.

Heart thrumming wildly, Judith looked at the wall above Luke's head. She had no desire to hear the details of his little tryst with Patsy.

"It wasn't what you thought," he began, and tipped her chin down so that her eyes met his. "I was looking for you and poked my head into the living room to see if you were there. You weren't, but Patsy was."

"I don't need to hear this." Judith turned her head, pulling her chin out of Luke's grasp. "You don't owe me any explanation."

"Of course, I do—I'm supposed to be your husband."

"Luke—" Judith shot him a pointed look. "We both know you're not my husband, and no one is here to witness our conversation, so you can cut the act."

Luke blew a sharp, impatient breath and looked around the room as though searching for the words he needed. "Will you just shut up and listen to me for once?" he demanded sharply. "You know as well as I do, that everyone here believes we are married. How would it look to the client, if I came on to his daughter? Especially a client who loves the fact that we are so happily married and is willing to pay us a ton of money because we are. Come on, Judith, do you really think I'm that stupid?"

"I know what I saw," Judith declared, her laugh was brittle. "Who could blame you? She's adorable."

Luke looked at her sadly. "No, she's not. She's not nearly as attractive as you are, and she never will be."

"You don't have to lie to me. I wasn't going to kill you in your sleep or anything," she said defensively.

"I'm not lying." Sliding his hand down her arm, he took her hand in his. "She doesn't do anything for me."

The rhythmic stroke of his thumb on her hand was distracting. She knew she should pull her hand away, move off the bed and go back to sleep. But her body would not obey the commands of her mind and she sat, rooted to the edge of the bed, her hand firmly planted in his.

"What was it then? A pity kiss?" she asked sarcastically. "Do you kiss all the girls that you're not attracted to?" she wondered aloud, her voice sounding unsteady in her ears. Is that why he'd kissed her in his office that day? Because he felt sorry for her?

He tightened his grip on her hand convulsively. "Damn it, Judith, I didn't kiss her!"

"That's what it looked like to me."

"She kissed me. End of story."

"Why?"

"She said she wanted to thank me for the charm we got her for her birthday."

"She didn't kiss me." Her eyes narrowed suspiciously.

Luke laughed. "I just happened to be in the wrong place at the wrong time." He took advantage of the confusion he saw in her face. "We had a little talk about it and I think we came to an understanding."

"What understanding?"

She looked so vulnerable, his heart swelled with the desire to protect her from all the hurt in life. These were the same feelings he'd tended to have toward her as a boy, only now they went much deeper. He would pulverize anyone who so much as hurt one fiery red-gold hair on her lovely head, Patsy included. "We understand that I care about my wife and I don't fool around with other women."

"Oh." Judith sat paralyzed, afraid to look into Luke's eyes. Afraid that he meant it. Afraid that he didn't. Afraid to find out. She pulled her hand away from his and rubbed her chilly arms in an effort to get her blood moving.

"You're freezing. You should put something on." He lifted the sheet in invitation. "Or you could get in here with me. I could warm you up."

Said the spider to the fly. "No, thank you," she answered primly.

"Where's your sense of adventure?" he yawned. His eyes drooped, unable to fight the sleep he needed any longer.

"I left it out in the barn with Burrito." She grinned, watching him lose his battle with fatigue.

"Good idea," he slurred. His long, dark eyelashes rested against his cheeks and his breathing became slow and even. "Judith?" he breathed, smiling slightly.

"Hmm?"

"Thanks for listening about Patsy…" His eyes fluttered open. "I have to tell you about a dream…I had…when I hit my…head."

Drowsiness carried him off to sleep and Judith sat watching him, thinking about what he'd said. She wanted to believe him with all her heart, and deep down she knew he was telling the truth. But admitting it would mean opening herself up to Luke. And that was the one thing she just couldn't let herself do.

The next morning Luke's head felt as though a tiny road-construction crew was blasting for a tunnel through his brain. The doctor had come early at the Brubakers' request and checked him out again. Everything would be fine with plenty of bedrest, he'd assured them, and he made Luke promise not to get out of bed for at least four or five days to give his injury ample time to heal.

Disgruntled, Luke sat propped up in bed and watched Judith from their bedroom window. As she walked from the stable toward the house, Hank trotted along beside in an effort to keep up with her long-legged stride. He chatted a mile a minute, mimicking her purposeful walk, his hands tucked into his pockets in the same manner as hers. When she stopped, he did, when she adjusted her hat, he followed suit in the same fashion. If Hank could have his way, Judith would move to the Circle Bow permanently and he would never leave her side.

Judith crouched down in order to better hear what her new buddy was saying, and nodded seriously. After a moment she threw back her head and burst out laughing at the punch line to one of his childish jokes. Much to his rapturous delight, she picked him up, swung him around and carried him toward the house on her back.

She looked like something out of a damn shampoo commercial, Luke thought, amazed by the gentle tenderness that Judith displayed with the young boy. Never, even in his wildest imaginings, had he ever been able to picture Judith as somebody's mom. Until now. Down there with little Hank, she looked positively maternal. June Cleaver in Western garb. The sight stirred something deep in his gut. A feeling that left him with a haunting sense of emptiness that he could not explain. Something about picturing Judith with a husband and children stuck in his craw, and he wasn't even sure why. Maybe because they'd grown up together, and the idea of her starting her own family was just one more step away from his youth. Then again, maybe the idea of her starting her own family was just one more step away from him.

* * *

"You're awake." Judith's face was flushed from the exertion of swinging the youngest Brubaker around in circles till they were both dizzy. Hank had wanted to come back to the room with her, but Judith told him that he must wait until Luke was feeling better before he visited. She lifted her hair off her neck and fanned herself with her hand. "How do you feel?" she asked, coming over to perch on the edge of the bed.

"I've had better days," he said, tentatively exploring the bandage that covered his head.

"I don't suppose you'll be doing any more trick riding while we're here, hmm, dear?" Judith lifted a lazy eyebrow at him.

"Very funny. I should have remembered what a hotshot equestrian you used to be as a kid, and waited for you to come back."

"Weren't you the one who always used to say, 'If it doesn't have an engine, it's not worth riding'?"

"Yes. And I still do."

"Oh, come on. You have to admit that flying across the pasture that way was kind of exhilarating."

"Judith, my head was not the only thing that suffered on that so-called ride. I may never father children," he lamented and stared ruefully down at his blanket-covered lap.

Judith laughed. "I didn't know you even wanted children."

He scowled defensively. "Not now, but you never know…" Very slowly and very carefully he settled back into the pillows that were stacked against the headboard and closed his eyes. It was nice having Judith here to talk to. It distracted him from the throbbing in his head. Unfortunately, it reminded him of the throbbing in other areas.... He groaned and rear-ranged the covers.

"I should let you get some sleep," Judith said and started to stand up.

"No," he complained childishly. "That's all I've done since yesterday afternoon. I'm bored. Stay and talk to me."

"Well, okay..." Judith eased uncertainly back down onto the bed. "Can I get you anything?"

Luke opened one eye and contemplated her question. Better ignore it, he decided, she might not like the answer. "So. What about you?"

"What about me what?"

"Do you plan on getting married someday and having a bunch of kids?" He tensed, bracing himself for whatever it was she was about to say.

"I don't know about a *bunch*," she laughed and then seeing that he was serious, grew thoughtful. "I wouldn't mind having more than one, though. I was an only child and sometimes it got pretty lonely."

"What are you talking about? You always had me."

Judith stared at him as if the bump on his head were causing his delusion. "Not really." Frowning, she refuted his curious statement. "As I recall, you were busy with your friends."

"That's not how I remember it. I can't recall a single thing about my childhood that you weren't a part of. We were *always* together. The Anderson kids. Wherever we went... 'You kids go play,' 'You kids get out of here,' 'You kids run to the store for us.' Don't you remember?"

Judith smiled. "I remember driving you nuts."

Luke laughed. "Yes, you did. But as I recall, I was pretty rough on you myself. For some reason, I used to love getting you all riled up. I'd look forward to it. Don't ask me why I enjoyed getting you so hot and bothered, but I did.'' He paused and studied her through his half-opened eyes. ''I still do.''

Staring at her hands, she darted a quick peek at him and tried to decipher the meaning of his suggestive words. She sat silently, digesting this new light Luke had shed on their relationship as children. ''I thought you hated it when I acted so crazy. Now you're telling me you *enjoyed* riling me up?'' she asked in amazement.

''Sure,'' he said, surprised to realize that he had. ''It beat the hell out of being lonely.''

Her large green eyes were wide with disbelief. ''You were lonely?''

''Judith, I was an only child, too, you know. You may have been a pain in the butt, but you were my pain in the butt and I'd probably have done just about anything for you if the chips were down. In fact, if you'll think about it, I saved your hind end on more than one occasion,'' he laughed. ''You had a way of getting yourself into some pretty funny jams.''

Judith reddened. ''I always thought you hated me.''

Luke hooted. ''Ha! That's a laugh. You hated *me.* And you went out of your way to let me know it, I might add. I never could figure that out. I can't remember doing anything to provoke you half the time....''

''Neither can I.'' Her voice was small, ashamed.

Luke regarded her with interest. Judith was embarrassed? He'd never seen this side of her before. The things you learn about someone when you move in with them, he mused. He'd seen more sides to Judith Anderson over the past several days than he had in an entire lifetime with her. If he were honest, though, in the past he hadn't given her much of a chance.

They sat in silence for several minutes, each lost in his own memories, trying to align his own perspective with that of the other.

Judith's mind was reeling. He'd always thought that *she* hated *him?* If he only knew, she thought in shock. Pride prevented her from spilling her guts and confessing her girlhood crush on him right then and there. What good could it possibly do now? It still didn't change the fact that she'd been a pesky, ugly, little twerp. And heaven only knew what he really thought about her now. No. They were partners now, and she was through making a fool of herself over him. Time to change the subject.

"You asked me to remind you about a dream you had when you hit your head," she said, hoping with all her heart that it wasn't one of those erotic dreams, starring Patsy and her many and varied contortionist abilities.

"Oh, yeah." Luke frowned and squeezed his eyes tightly shut. "It was so weird. I can only remember parts of it, but I think I dreamed it when I hit my head on the rock. I saw stars." He opened his eyes and smiled at Judith. "Just like in the cartoons, and then Big Daddy came riding out of the sky on a huge American flag with a billion shiny stars exploding everywhere. He looked really hacked and he asked me if we had thought up an idea for his campaign yet. There was smoke coming out of his nose and ears and his eyes were shooting sparks. I told him yes, because I didn't want to tell him that we'd been here all this time and we hadn't done anything. Then he breathed fire at me and said it had better be good, because he killed his last agency for having dumb ideas. I asked him how he killed them, and he said he let them ride a horse named Burrito. Then I said, 'Sir, I think I must be dreaming,' and he said, 'Of course you are, don't you recognize an American dream when you're in one?' Then he gets on the flag and takes off into the horizon yelling, 'I am the American dream!' and a huge crowd of people gather and look up at him, dazzled by the fireworks.''

Judith stared at him.

"The end," he said, wondering why she was looking at him so oddly.

"That's it?" she asked.

"Yes, that's it. What did you expect? *Gone with the Wind*?" he huffed, irked by her strange reaction to his dream. He thought she'd at least laugh a little. He guessed you sort of had to be there, as he tiredly rubbed his aching temples. It had seemed funny to him, Big Daddy riding around on an exploding flag. Oh well, last time he'd tell her anything.

"What?" he demanded as she continued to stare at him. "For crying out loud, Judith, it was just a dream."

"The American dream," she said, still staring at him.

"Yeah. So what?"

"You know why Big Daddy killed his last ad agency?"

What the hell was she talking about? "Why?"

Judith leaned forward on the bed, her eyes locking into Luke's. Excitement fairly radiated off her. "Because all of their ideas drew attention to the spill." Drawing both of her legs up underneath her, Indian style, she wriggled closer to Luke and grinned.

He knew that look. He'd seen it hundreds of times

as a kid, usually just before she pulled some outrageous prank. "What are you talking about?"

"The spill. The problem." She lifted her palms to the ceiling and raised her eyebrows at him expectantly. At his puzzled expression she continued. "As opposed to Big Daddy. The solution." Dropping her hands in her lap, she looked at Luke with an intensity, a passion, that startled him. Intrigued him. Taking a deep breath, she launched into her explanation.

"While it's true that Brubaker Oil suffered from an unfortunate oil spill, that is now in the past. It can't be undone, so why dwell on the negative? Even explaining how Brubaker Oil paid for the entire cleanup and promised to open a wildlife preserve for endangered wetland birds and animals still reminds people that there was a spill. And no matter how you look at it, an oil spill is bad news. But the fact that Brubaker Oil provides jobs for thousands of Americans is good news. An American company. American jobs. American oil."

Luke was beginning to see where she was headed with this and caught her enthusiasm. "Brubaker Oil, helping you realize the American dream." He traced the words with his hand along the bottom of an imaginary television screen.

"Yes!" she screamed, grabbing his hands and bouncing on the bed. At his pained expression, she stopped bouncing and whispered, "Yes!" and kissed him on the cheek.

Luke looked at her out of the corner of his eye, his upper lip curling in pleasure. "You're pretty smart, you know that don't you?"

"Me?" she squealed in delight. "It was your dream!"

"I thought you didn't like my dream."

"What? I thought that's why you were telling it to me. It was some brilliant concept you dreamed up. Real symbolic stuff, riding in on the American flag and all..." she teased.

"Now for the hard part."

"What's that?"

"Finding an exploding flying flag."

Judith giggled. "Get real," she whooped and rolled back toward the foot of the bed. It felt great to have the solution to Big Daddy's image problem, and she was giddy with joy. Uninhibited laughter bubbled up from deep within as she gave in to its intoxicating release.

Luke pushed at Judith's bottom with his foot. "I'll bet they have one at the Western-outfitter store," he joined in her contagious laughter, forgetting how badly his head hurt.

"Why not?" she kicked her feet happily in the air and wiped at her streaming eyes. "They have every other tacky, gaudy thing ever made."

"True. And an exploding flag is nothing compared to some of the outfits I tried on before Patsy's party." Their peals of laughter echoed in the quiet bedroom.

"You were exploding all right." Howling in earnest now, Judith gasped, "Why do you suppose you dreamed Big Daddy's flag was exploding?"

Luke guffawed. "I don't know. Must have had something to do with that Burrito."

"Aaahhh!" she shrieked.

"Maybe," Luke laughed, "Maybe it wasn't the flag that was exploding after all. I told you that horse had an uneven gait."

"Ooowww! Stop it. Please, it hurts," she begged and held her sides, as she rolled back and forth at the end of the bed. "Quit it, I mean it," she ordered between peals of laughter. By now Luke was laughing nearly as hard as she was, which didn't help matters.

Crawling over to the edge of the bed, she snatched several tissues from the nightstand and tried to catch a glimpse of herself in the bureau mirror.

"Do I look like a raccoon?" Judith asked, looking at the smudged tissue she was using to mop the tears that streamed down her face. "I bet I do," she giggled and blew her nose.

"No. You look beautiful. A beautiful raccoon..." Luke grinned.

Pulling herself up on her knees she caught her reflection in the mirror and screamed. "Good ha-ha-heavens!" she shrilled and doubled over with laughter again. "Luke you are a ha-ha-horrible liar!"

"I'm quite serious," he raised his eyebrows in comic appraisal. "You should do your makeup that way all the time."

Collapsing into a fetal ball, she lay and waited until the convulsions of hilarity subsided. When she had finally regained partial control, she sat up and scrubbed at her eyes and cheeks with a fresh tissue.

"How's your wound?" she sniffed.

"What wound?" He grinned.

Judith rolled her eyes and flopped back down next to him on the bed. "Ohh," she groaned. "I haven't laughed this hard since...well, ever."

"Me, either," he sighed contentedly.

Propping herself up on an elbow, she rolled on her side to face him. "Can't you just see it?" Her cheeks were pink from all the scrubbing, and her eyes glowed with unbridled enthusiasm.

"Yes," he said, smiling at the secret creative connection that only the two of them shared. They were of one mind on this idea, he could feel it deep in his gut. They were in tune, one mind, one soul, one heart. Luke closed his eyes and took a deep breath, because it was at that moment he knew for sure that he was in for the long haul. Not just with the Brubaker account, but with the woman at the end of this bed. He groaned at the laughable irony of the whole situation.

Reaching over, he hauled her up and across his broad chest. Plunging his hands into her thick tangle of curls he pulled her face up close to his and just stared, his eyes flashing, her head anchored firmly in his hands. Should he ask her to drop the business-partner rule? Hadn't they crossed some invisible office-protocol line by now? Couldn't they forget business etiquette and celebrate with a kiss? No. He knew they couldn't. Not the way he was feeling now. Not with her lying here next to him in this bed. The celebration, at this point, would entail far more than a simple kiss.

"Are you all right?" Judith asked, alarmed at the pain she heard in his shuddered groan.

"Yeah. I'm fine," he answered and shook his head. "Go get a pad of paper and a bunch of pencils, and let's get down to work."

Mrs. Soder's childish voice echoed from the depths of the trash can, where Luke had tossed the receiver after one particularly vicious attack on his ear.

"Is that right?" Luke leaned over the side of the bed occasionally, to respond to her nonstop diatribe. "Umm-hmm." He tossed into the can's buzzing depths and nudged Judith with his elbow.

"Hand me those notes will you?" he mouthed, and said, "Oh? Umm-hmm," to Mrs. Soder.

Judith giggled. For the past four days they had done nothing but work nonstop on Big Daddy's account.

The campaign was progressing beautifully, and the crew at Anderson and Anderson was kept hopping night and day. The art department prepared storyboards for Big Daddy's commercials, and print pieces for national magazines that they expressed overnight to Texas for approval. Judith and Luke faxed rough ideas up to the creative team to polish into a prepared presentation to propose to Big Daddy when the time came. Conference calls enabled them to brainstorm copy for the entire campaign; radio, print, television and whatever speeches Big Daddy might wish to give in person.

All in all, it was the most comprehensive and superior campaign to ever come out of Anderson and Anderson. Everyone on the entire staff agreed that this was the one that would most likely push them over the hump to the top. They were all thrilled and excited about the whole campaign, most especially Judith and Luke.

"Umm." Luke winked at Judith as the buzzing continued from the trash can. "This is perfect," he whispered, handing her the script for the television spot she'd been working on.

Growing warm under his praise, she watched him fish the phone out of the garbage and haul it up onto his lap. He looked almost a hundred percent again, she noted, as he plumped the pillows up behind his back and tucked the phone between his shoulder and ear. With his unshaven face and tousled hair, he looked the picture of masculine health in his old military sweatshirt. She loved the way the soft, aging fabric clung to his rock-solid build.

A deep, frustrated sigh shuddered through her body as she realized that these thoughts were becoming more and more powerful with each passing day. Set-

tling back at the foot of their giant bed, she smiled
ruefully and watched him roll his eyes heavenward at
Mrs. Soder's overbounteous conversation and thought
about the last four days.

The professional connection that she and Luke had
formed since they agreed on the American-dream idea
was nothing short of phenomenal. They worked together with the timing and smoothness of a high-
performance engine. Everything clicked and fell into
place with an ease and precision that thrilled Judith
to the tips of her hot pink toenails. She had never
before, in her professional career, experienced such
an interlinking…such a harmonious meeting of the
minds…such an extension of her creative self, em-
bodied in another human form, as she had with Luke.
The look she caught on his face from time to time
told her that he felt it, too.

At no time during the past four days had there even
been the slightest hint of a disagreement. Their styles
complemented each other perfectly, bringing a new
and exciting flavor to the project that neither of them
had been able to achieve in the past. This experience,
this melding of the creative mind on a professional
level with another person, was completely unfamiliar
to Judith, and as wonderful and sexy as it felt, she
was also afraid. What would happen to her now?
Would she lose her sense of self? Would she grow to
depend on Luke, only to end up brokenhearted when
he moved on and took his career to new heights without her? Once again, Judith was vulnerable to Luke
Anderson. And above all else, the thing that terrified
Judith about being vulnerable to Luke now…was her
absence of malice. Where were the shrewish fits of
anger? Try as she might, the only thing she seemed

to be able to work up toward him was a sickening display of sweetness and light.

Yes, she decided, heaving another heartfelt sigh and shifting to a more comfortable position at the end of the bed, she'd changed. And there was nothing she could do about it. Not a thing. Luckily for her, Luke's head injury had kept her from making a complete fool of herself with him. Keeping his health uppermost in her mind, she was able to abstain from grabbing him and kissing the daylights out of him—while he sat there in his sickbed looking so adorable—as he worked them both into an exhausted stupor each day.

No, he wouldn't go into a coma over her unrequited love, if she had anything to do with it. However, if he were to make the first move, it would have to be at his own risk, of course, but she would have no objection. Unfortunately, he'd been the perfect gentleman. On occasion he would wink or lift a flirtatious eyebrow, but Judith was sure that there was no way he was suffering from the sexual tension she imagined growing between them the way she was. Maybe she was imagining things. Maybe it was just being locked in the same room for four days with a brilliant man who was teaching her things she'd never dreamed of about her chosen profession. Then, again, maybe she was falling in love. She shuddered and wrapped her arms tightly around her waist.

"Sounds like you have everything under control, Mrs. Soder. Like Dad always says, you're the boss, so keep up the good work and we'll see you in a week or so." Luke nodded and umm-hmmed into the phone a few more times before he slammed the receiver down in utter exhaustion. "That woman could talk the legs off a centipede," he said and grinned.

Judith smiled. "What'd she say?"

"What didn't she say?"

"Are the final drafts of the proposal and storyboards on their way?"

"Yes. We should get them this afternoon. If you feel up to it, we can present our idea to Big Daddy tonight."

Judith shivered with excitement and nervousness. "Are we ready?"

Luke shrugged and stretched, running his hands through his thick coffee-colored hair. "Honey, I'm ready now. I'm so keyed up about this whole thing, I could burn down city hall." He beat on an extra pillow with pent-up energy. "It's without a doubt the best work I've ever been associated with."

Honey. In all the time she'd known Luke, he'd never used a term of endearment with her, unless she counted the sarcastic "dear" he'd used since they met Big Daddy. *Honey.* It was a melody.

She was proud of the casual way she was able to continue their conversation. "Me, too. I've worked on some exciting projects before this one, but never anything that I felt so sure would be so big. Okay. Tonight it is, then. I'll go tell Big Daddy."

A light knock at the door drew their attention. Scooting off the edge of the bed, Judith padded barefoot to the door and pulled it open. Miss Clarise stood in the hallway behind a shy, little Hank, who held a rather sketchy bouquet of wildflowers and a handmade card.

"Hiya, buddy boy." She beamed at her young paramour, and drew him into the room and over to the bed by his arm. "Whatcha got there?"

"Flowerths," he lisped, his tongue protruding through the vacant spots in his toothless smile. "And a card for Uncle Luke.'' He peeked at Luke from under his eyelashes and waited expectantly.

"For me?" Luke was visibly touched by the construction-paper-and-crayon get-well card that little Hank had fashioned for him. "And flowers, too?"

"Yeth." He grinned and held them out.

Luke ruffled the boy's hair affectionately. "Thanks, pardner, you're the best." He set the card on his dresser and popped the flowers into the pitcher of water on his nightstand.

"When are you guyth gonna come downththtairth and have thupper with uth again?" Hank's freckled face puckered with inquisitive hope.

"Well, now, how does tonight grab ya, buddy?" Luke looked at Judith and winked.

Hank's eyes lit up, and he jumped up and down in glee. "Oh, boy!" he cried.

Miss Clarise put a gentle restraining hand on her bouncing son. "That's wonderful. We'll set two extra places." Moving forward, she patted Luke on the knee. "We're so glad you're feeling better," she said, her concern for him genuine. "We'll just be on our way now. Hank?" She took his dirty, sticky hand in hers and tugged him off the end of the bed, where he was preparing to mount and ride the footboard.

"Miss Clarise?" Judith followed her out the door and into the hallway. "We were wondering if we could present our idea to Big Daddy tonight after dinner.",

"Why, of course! You're done already?"

Judith nodded. "We've been working pretty hard for the past few days, and we have a wonderful support staff in Portland, so I guess we're as ready as we'll ever be."

"Wonderful. I know Big Daddy will be thrilled.

You can set up in the library, dear, and we can all just go there after our evening meal.''

Judith drew a deep, fortifying breath. She hadn't considered that the whole gang would want to attend the unveiling of their American-dream campaign. ''Sounds good,'' she said bravely. Peeling Hank from around her leg, she handed him back to his mother. ''We'll be ready.''

Luke listened to the low, sexy tones of Judith's voice as she stood in the hallway conversing with Miss Clarise. She was driving him out of his ever-lovin' mind. And not the way she used to. No, this insanity came from being confined in a room, for four solid days, with the most creatively brilliant, beautiful, amazingly alluring woman he'd ever met in his life. If he had to spend one more night alone in this room with her, he just might spontaneously combust. Thank God that Judith was such a focused professional. If she had even so much as crooked her little finger in his direction, he'd have been all over her like a cheap suit. It was obvious she was not aware of the one-sided sexual tension that was burning him up till the wee hours every night. The five lousy feet that separated her makeshift bed from his was no longer enough. Something had to be done. But what? He couldn't just go stay in a motel. What would the Brubakers say?

Oh, well, he'd worry about that after the presentation tonight. Maybe he could go for another ride on good, old Burrito. If that didn't cure him, nothing would.

Chapter Eight

"And then a slow dissolve to an old picture of Big Daddy as a little boy in bare feet and tattered jeans. Across the bottom of the screen we superimpose the words, 'Brubaker Oil. Helping America realize the dream.'" Judith dropped the pages of the flip chart and turned with Luke to face the Brubaker entourage. "Of course, these are the preliminary workups. We'll polish the entire…" Her voice trailed off as the sniffles and nose blowings of the small family audience reached her ears.

Big Daddy, tears streaming down his weathered and cracked cheeks, stood up and walked blindly forward, gathering the Andersons in one of his now famous three-way hugs. "I *love* it!" he wept openly, fumbling for a handkerchief to mop his running nose. "Howevah did you find out all those things about mah childhood? Oh, it does take me back!" He grinned foolishly and mopped at his overflowing face.

Trumpeting loudly into his handkerchief, he

walked over to the liquor cabinet and pulled out a
bottle of whiskey. To Miss Clarise he said, "Honey
pie, have someone bring us a couple bottles of that
fancy champagne we've been savin'. This calls for a
celebration!"

Judith and Luke stared at each other, numb with
shocked pleasure. *He liked it!* Not that there was ever
any doubt, but they had never expected *this* reaction.
Grinning happily at each other, they accepted their
glasses and lifted them in toast with Big Daddy and
the whole Brubaker gang. Hank and the twins shared
a bottle of sparkling cider.

"To the best dang, pardon mah French, ad agency
in the country." He laughed and pointed his glass at
the Andersons. "You two have something very special. Hang on to it. And each othah!" he advised amid
snickers and giggles from his brood. "You have both
been an inspiration to ouah family, and it's been a
pleasure having you stay heah with us. Heah's to a
long and prosperous relationship between ouah two
families." Everyone cheered as Big Daddy saluted
them with his glass and downed his drink.

Judith looked uneasily at Luke, and her discomfort
was mirrored in his eyes. Just how long could the
relationship last between the two families, when one
of the families was a fake? Luke squeezed her arm.
It would be over soon, his look seemed to say.

"Oh, now, don't get all shy on us!" Big Daddy
ordered, taking their discomfort for modesty. "I've
worked with a few creative types in mah time, but
none who had the perfect blend of inspiration, family
values and love in theah hearts for each othah. I am
prepared to offer y'all an insane amount of money if
you'll stay heah with us and set up shop in Texas."

The hopeful eyes of Big Daddy's family were all

directed at Luke and Judith. Patsy, Conway and little Hank seemed especially interested in the Andersons' answer. Luke cleared his throat and glanced at Judith.

"Uh, while your generous offer is very tempting, I'm sure I speak for my wife as well as myself when I say that it's with great reluctance that we will be returning to Portland to get back to work at Anderson and Anderson."

Judith nodded and smiled sadly in agreement. "Yes, Luke is right. Although you've become like a family to us in many ways, our family and our business is in Oregon, and that's where we belong." Luke curled his fingers around hers and gently squeezed.

"I figured as much, but you don't ask, you don't get." Big Daddy clapped them soundly on their backs. "Well, never mind. Y'all have a place in my heart." He thumped his chest with his fist. "And you'll always have a home right here at the Circle B.O."

Patsy rolled her eyes in disgust. "Bow, Daddy! *Bow!*" she whined, as she headed out the library door with her brothers.

"Thank you, sir," Luke said and shook Big Daddy's hand. "It was a pleasure doing business with you, and I know we'll both miss this place a great deal."

"Oh, I imagine y'all be back," Big Daddy drawled. His eyes twinkling he followed his family out of the room, leaving Judith alone with Luke.

Now what? Judith wondered, as she began gathering the visual aids to their presentation. Now that the presentation was over and successfully received, there was nothing to do back in their bedroom. Nothing... She caught Luke's eye and quickly glanced away,

feeling suddenly awkward about being alone with
him.

Luke took her armload of materials, dumped them
in a box and stacked the rest of their presentation
materials by the door. Grabbing Judith by the arm, he
ushered her into the hallway. "Come on," he uttered
curtly, propelling her through the foyer and out the
front door into the twilight.

Striding along in silence, Luke's long legs quickly
devoured the ground between the house and the stables and Judith practically had to run to keep up with
him. The sun's dying rays gave life to the long shadows lying across the road that ran past the corral and
beyond. Down the rutted, dusty road for more than a
mile they walked, not daring to speak, not daring to
look at each other. In each head the wheels were turning, racing, wondering what the next step would be
in this new and intimate relationship.

Luke lead the way through the shadowed grove of
trees, to the creek he'd found the night of Patsy's
party. The bubbling water rushed over a small water-
fall and pooled in a hidden pond, lined by trees and
large rocks. It was cool and dusky as the waning sun
could no longer reach into this oasis on the range.
Walking purposefully over to a grassy patch near the
edge of the creek, Luke sat down and pulled his expensive cowboy boots off and tossed them over his
shoulder.

"Come on." He nodded at Judith to follow suit.
He waded into the water, pulling the legs of his Levi's
up around his knees and smiled as an icy shock traveled up his spine. He knew he'd have to dive headfirst
into the frigid water if he was going to quell the raging inferno that Judith had set in his gut.

Judith giggled as the mud oozed between her toes,

and the icy water caused her teeth to chatter. She wobbled around on the slippery rocks for a while, enjoying the cool reprieve from the day's heat. When her neck began to ache from the chill, she headed for the shore and settled down on the grass to wait for him.

Luke knew that if he were smart, he'd stay in the cold water where it was safe. But, Luke also knew that sometimes, especially when it came to Judith Anderson, he could be a real idiot. He felt her eyes on him as he slowly waded over to the grassy area where she sat, compelling him, drawing him, magnetizing him inexorably to her. He had no choice but to answer her unspoken call.

He came to where she sat and stood looking down at her for a moment, his body an instrument, tightly strung with his need for her. Dropping to his knees between her legs, he grasped her arms in his strong hands and slowly pulled her within inches of his face.

"We can't go back," he stated, the excruciating tension between them was palpable, nearly visible.

Well aware of the double meaning behind his words, Judith was surprised by the torment she read in his eyes. Still unsure that she was its cause, she reached up and cupped his cheek in her hand. She wanted to show him that she was trying to understand, that she too had suffered in confusion over their relationship.

He groaned at the warm touch on his face. "You know what I'm talking about, don't you?"

"I...know that I'm scared," she whispered, still afraid that maybe he wasn't fighting his deep feelings for her, but instead fighting some physical urge that had nothing to do with her as a person.

"Me, too," he admitted, nuzzling her hand, with

the raspy day's growth of his beard. Pushing her back on the soft green carpet of grass, Luke eased down next to her and propped himself up on an elbow so that he could drink her in with his eyes. It felt so right, her lying there, by his side. He felt so incredibly protective and possessive of her at that moment, he wondered what he would do if she were no longer a part of his life. The way he was feeling now, he wasn't sure if he could go on living.

Exactly when she had ceased to be just a part of his childhood and had become a part of him, he couldn't be certain. But as surely as his heart was an integral part of his body, she was a part of his heart. His soul. And someday, if he were very lucky, the rest of his life.

"What now?" He had agonized over this question and couldn't answer it himself.

Judith answered uncertainly. "I don't know. It's so…complicated all of a sudden. It feels strange to be finished with Big Daddy's campaign. All of our energy was focused on that one goal, and now…"

Luke tucked his arm under his head and lay back, his face next to hers, on their cool, grassy pillow. "And now we're done, ready to move on to the next thing, but we don't know what that next thing is…"

"Exactly," she shrugged lightly, her eyes slamming into his the way a lightning bolt strikes the earth during a storm. Unable to sustain the contact, she lowered her eyes to his mouth, and fought the urge to trace his full, boyish lips with her fingertips.

Luke had to change the subject or lose his mind. "I think we did it," he said, referring to Big Daddy's reaction to their brainchild.

"That's an understatement." Judith smiled. She was still emotionally charged by what they had accomplished together and touched by Big Daddy's tears. "You were wonderful to work with. I don't know about you, but I think that Big Daddy was right, that we do have something special. Some kind of electric synergy or something."

That wasn't all they had. Couldn't she tell that he felt it? Surely she knew how badly he wanted her.

She turned her head slightly to look at him. "Which is strange, when you think about how we got along as children."

The smile lines around Luke's eyes deepened as he met her shy gaze. "You scared the hell out of me when we were kids, and I think, for some reason or another, you were afraid of me, too."

Judith nodded.

Luke continued, "You still scare the hell out of me."

"Why?" she asked surprised.

Raising his arms, Luke folded his hands behind his head and frowned in concentration. "Because you threaten me."

"I threaten you?"

"Not in the way you think, but yes. You challenge me professionally, for one thing. This last week has been one of the most stimulating, thought-provoking weeks in my entire professional career. You are sharp, insightful, quick, and you have an amazing grasp of what is going on creatively in someone else's head."

"Just yours."

"Really? Why?"

Judith wrinkled her nose in thought. "Because I've known you all my life. And for some weird reason, I have always been supersensitive to you."

Luke was silent, contemplating her words.

"Oh, I know you think I was always just an insensitive, little brat, but there was a lot more to it than that," she hurried to explain, misinterpreting his silence.

"A lot more to what?" he urged her to expound, curious now.

Grimacing, she berated herself for turning the conversation in this uncomfortable direction. How could she gracefully change the subject? she wondered, plucking a blade of grass and chewing nervously on its end.

"Judith, it's too late."

Rolling over on her stomach, she looked down at him, quizzically. "What do you mean?"

"I mean we're in too deep here. Everything between us has changed so, you might as well come clean. What is it about our childhood that makes you so angry? Why were you always so mad at me?"

Judith dropped her head, her long, wavy locks hiding the embarrassment on her face. "It's hardly worth talking about. It seems so childish and inconsequential now..." Her laugh was stilted as she lifted her head, tossed her hair back and searched his handsome face with her eyes. He nodded expectantly, compassion in his expression.

Judith sighed. "It's no great mystery, really. I'm sure you already know the answer. I was a hideous child, and you were beautiful. I was quirky, and you were cool. I was naughty, and you were nice. I hated you." Looking at some distant memory, her eyes glazed over, and as she spoke she traveled through the years. "With all my heart and soul, I hated you. At the same time, strangely enough—and I will never understand this—I loved you. With all my heart and soul, I loved you. You were my knight in shining armor, my mystery dream date, my fantasy man. And you didn't know I was alive. And it wasn't just you. Other kids taunted me, too…mostly boys. That hurt me so badly I never allowed myself to be vulnerable to a man…especially you." Her eyes refocused and she glanced at him, suddenly humiliated at what she'd admitted. She felt like crying, and much to her dismay a single tear rolled down her cheek and splashed onto his shirt.

"Hey, don't," he whispered, and grasping the back of her neck, pulled her head down onto his chest. "Shh," he soothed, as she sniffed and tried to swallow past the painful mass lodged in her throat. "I knew you were alive." He smiled and stroked her hair. "I definitely knew you were alive."

"Only because I was such a pain in the rear," she sniffed, listening to the comforting murmur of his heartbeat under her cheek and thrilling to the rhythmic stroke of his hand.

"No. Because you were bold. Fearless. Amazingly creative. Hey, next to you I felt dull. And believe it or not, I used to wish I could be more like you. You are the female version of your father, and I always had your dad up on a pedestal. I think that's why I wanted his office so badly. Sort of a talisman, I guess. Maybe I was hoping some of that creativity would rub off on me. When we started at Anderson and Anderson, I wasn't sure I could keep up with you creatively. Your daunting reputation had preceded you."

Gently tugging on her hair, he pulled her face back so that she had to look at him. "And then I saw you for the first time in twelve years, and I knew I was in trouble."

"Threatened?"

"Absolutely."

Judith was honestly puzzled. "But why?"

Luke reared back and stared at her. "Judith, when was the last time you looked in the mirror? You are without a doubt one of the most beautiful, sexiest women I've ever met."

Her mouth dropped open and she smirked at him in disbelief.

"Judith, you're so gorgeous it's scary."

She burst out laughing, and Luke saw that she clearly did not agree. "That's so strange. Do you still feel threatened?"

"Let's just put it this way…lately you threaten my sanity, but it no longer has anything to do with work. As far as work goes, I agree with you wholeheartedly—we have something very special together."

"But…when we're not working together, I drive you crazy."

Hearing the hurt in her voice he turned on his side, rolled her over onto her back and pinned her wrists above her head.

"Yes. You drive me crazy," he exhaled deeply and threw a possessive leg over hers. "And…" He lowered his mouth so that it hovered lightly above hers. "I think if we gave it half a chance, we might just have something very special together when we're not working." His cocky grin whispered feather light over her slightly parted lips.

"But…" She wiggled under his firm grasp. "I don't want to threaten you…" Her nose bumped into his as she smiled tentatively.

"I'll take my chances," he breathed, and lowered his mouth to hers. His kiss was as light as butterfly wings, slowly, gently claiming her mouth.

Judith waited, savoring the sensation, the exquisite torture causing an unfamiliar heat to begin a slow boil in her veins.

Instinctively she arched up to him, trying to deepen his excruciatingly sexy exploration of her mouth. Pushing her back down, Luke stayed in control, refusing to allow her to take the lead.

"No," he whispered across her mouth.

"Yes," she pleaded, straining against him, her inexperience creating an impatience for something she did not understand.

The note of desperation in her voice was his undoing. Twining his hands into her hair, he brought her face up to his and immersed himself in the ravishing fever of their hungry kiss.

"Luke," she implored, his name a small whimpering sound, and he felt his body quicken in immediate response. He was lost forever and he knew it and—surprisingly—he didn't care any more. Never before had Luke been so carried away by the moment, that he was beyond all reason.

It no longer mattered that they were business partners—at this point he'd gladly give up Anderson and Anderson for her. Hell, he'd give up his entire career, if that's what it took. No price was too great to pay. For Judith Anderson, he'd lay down his life.

Pulling her more firmly beneath him, he tore his mouth from hers and burned an erotic path of kisses down her jaw to the creamy hollow between her breasts and gloried in the ragged gasps of desire that he tore from her throat. She trailed her nails lightly across his corded, muscular back and he felt the tingling, burning path end at the nape of his neck where she threaded his hair in her searching fingers.

Luke was vaguely aware of the galloping rumble of his heartbeat as he settled his mouth back over hers with a deep growl. His heart thundered louder and he felt Judith grow still in his arms.

Sweet ecstasy! Was he having a heart attack? What a way to die! *No, not yet!* his mind screamed as he frantically deepened their kiss, the steady drumming of his pulse roaring in his ears.

Wrenching her mouth from Luke's insistent kiss, Judith struggled in his powerful grip.

"Luke," she hissed, her eyes wide with fear. "Someone's coming."

She was right, he decided, as the pounding of horse hooves invaded his muddled mind. That's okay, he would simply dismiss whoever it was and get back to the business at hand, he thought grumpily, kissing Judith one last time before turning to discover who was so rudely interrupting them. He stood up and pulled Judith unsteadily to her feet, helping her straighten her clothes and finger combing his own hair.

Big Daddy astride Lightning burst through the trees into the small clearing and hooted gleefully when he spotted them.

"I was hopin' I'd find y'all heah," he chortled, pulling the horse to a stop and leaping to the ground. "The little missus and I were just talkin'," and well, we've got an idea we're so excited about, I just knew y'all would share in ouah excitement."

Excitement was no problem, Luke smiled ruefully at Judith, her lips still swollen from his kisses, her cheeks pink from the abrasion of his whiskers. Privacy, now that was getting to be a problem....

"What is it, Big Daddy?" Judith asked, her curiosity piqued by the sparkle in his small, shiny black eyes.

Rubbing his hands together merrily, he tried to organize his jumbled thoughts. "Miss Clarise and I wanted to thank you for all youah hard work and celebrate the kickoff of ouah new campaign, so we decided to throw a little party."

Judith and Luke glanced uneasily at each other. When Big Daddy said "little party," was he expecting them to learn yet another form of exotic country dance?

Noting their puzzled expressions, he laughed. "A weddin' party!" he bellowed. "Yes, you two lovebirds have inspired us with your passion, and the little missus and I have decided to renew ouah weddin' vows."

Her heart overflowing, Judith stepped forward and bent to kiss Big Daddy on his craggy, old cheek. How perfectly lovely. She looked at Luke, her eyes brimming at the beauty of an age-old love, eternally young in its depth. Luke, feeling slightly misty himself, shook Big Daddy's hand and offered his hearty congratulations.

"I'm glad y'all feel this way. I was afraid maybe ya wouldn't, but the missus said you'd be all for it. I can just see it now!" he cried. Grabbing Lightning's reins and preparing to mount he exclaimed, "It's going to be the double weddin' of the century!"

Their smiles became brittle, flash freezing to their faces. *Double wedding?*

"Just think, the four of us, renewin' ouah marriage commitments to each othah on the same day! I can't think of nothin' I'd like bettah!"

Big Daddy seemed not to notice that Judith and Luke were too shocked to respond. Hoisting himself up into the saddle, he turned Lightning to face them.

"I have to get on back to the house now. Miss Clarise has a bunch of plans to make. She wants an old-fashioned affah, in the traditional sense, with bachelah pahties and showahs... Don't that sound like a hoot and a hollah?'' Big Daddy grinned like a Cheshire polecat. ''Oh,'' he said, before he spurred Lightning toward the house, ''one moah thing. Theah will be no hanky-panky between the brides and the grooms, so we'll all be sleepin' in separate rooms till the weddin' day, this Saturday. Luke, old boy, y'all will bunk with me, and Judith, honey, y'all will stay with Miss Clarise. The weddin's only three days away, so y'all will probably be too busy to miss each othah anywho. Well, I gotta ride—the missus awaits.'' Doffing his hat, he dug his tiny heels into Lightning's large belly and was off in a cloud of prewedding plans.

Judith and Luke stood stunned, staring after him in dazed wonder. *A double wedding?* Training her blank gaze on Luke, Judith was unsure whether to laugh hysterically or cry. How on earth could they renew marriage vows that they had never taken?

Running his hands across his darkened jaw and around to the back of his neck, Luke shrugged helplessly.

''I suppose I should be getting down on bended knee right about now...'' he raised his eyebrows at her, trying to gauge her reaction to Big Daddy's announcement.

''Oh, Luke,'' she moaned, sinking to the grassy spot, that only moments ago had been their haven from reality. Dragging her hands over her face and pulling her hair roughly back and over her shoulders, she asked, ''What are we going to do?''

Luke dropped down beside her and pondered her question. ''What do you want to do?''

''What can we do? Tell him the truth, I guess.'' She wished with all her heart that she didn't have to hurt the Brubakers this way, that she was really married to Luke and that renewing their vows would be just another sweet memory in their lives together. But they weren't married, and unfortunately for her, probably never would be. "What do you want to do?" She held her breath, waiting for his heartbreaking response. He'd admitted that there was something special between them, but did that mean love? Marriage…even a phony one? She still wasn't sure how he really felt, and his response to this double-wedding business could really hurt her feelings.

Luke shook his head. "It seems too bad that we have to ruin his plans…I mean we've come this far, and all." He shut his eyes, as though afraid she would berate him for continuing the deception.

"He did seem pretty happy," she agreed, thrilled that he hadn't scoffed at the idea of marrying her, even if it would be a farce. "Um, if we went through with it, would we…be…um, married when we were done? I mean, I've never done this before and so…I don't know." After all, what if they really would end up married? Was she ready for this? Did she want this? Terrified, she was beginning to realize it was exactly what she wanted. Oh, no! And what did he want? Good Lord, she was so confused she felt faint.

"I don't have much experience in this type of thing, either," he grinned at her. "I don't think so…but you never can tell."

"What, hemm—" She cleared her throat and plucked at the grass under her hands. "What if we were? Married, I mean. You know, after the ceremony and all, um what would you do?" Please don't laugh, she prayed silently.

Luke looked at her thoughtfully, a small smile played at the corners of his mouth. "Well, I guess I'd be a married man."

"And so, what would you do?"

"I'd go on a honeymoon."

"No, come on. Really, what would you do?"

"I'm serious. I don't think it would be the worst thing that ever happened to me."

"How flattering."

Luke grinned at her pained expression. "What would you do?"

"Well, I don't think we should get married just to save the business. I mean, I don't think Ed and Ted would expect that. Besides," she stammered, blushing, "I always thought I'd marry for love."

"Don't you love the business?" Luke teased.

"You know what I mean," she groused.

"Why don't we try to find out if we would really be married, and then make our decision from there," he suggested pragmatically.

"Would it make any difference?" She had to know.

"Of course, it would. I want to know what I'm getting myself into...." Noting her crimson cheeks, he relented. "But either way, I'd probably go through with it. If you wanted to, that is." He studied the myriad of expressions that crossed her lovely face.

He would marry her? But why? Just to save the Brubakers' feelings? Or, maybe it was for the money... Or the business... She could think of a host of reasons why he'd be willing to marry her and sadly none of them had anything to do with love.

No, unfortunately, no matter how she looked at it, she didn't think that she'd ever be able to go through with it. They would have to come clean. Lose the account. Lose Big Daddy's friendship. Lose the money and ultimately...lose each other. For when Judith Anderson walked down the aisle and committed her life to a man, it would be because that man loved her above all else and not because he was trying to save his business. Knowing that her decision would probably break her heart once she allowed herself to think about it, she considered the alternative.

She could go along with Big Daddy's plans, make him happy, save the account, save the business and please Ed and Ted. She and Luke could figure out what to do with their marriage, real or fake when the time came....

What if the things Luke had been saying were true? What if he really did care? What if he really were attracted to, and interested in marrying her? Did she dare to believe? To trust him with her heart? In her mind the risks were huge, no matter what she decided.

Her head began to throb with the weightiness of her problem. Surely Ed and Ted had never had to face this question.

Grasping her hand firmly in his, Luke hoisted himself up to one knee and looked deeply into her eyes, his face completely serious as he solemnly asked, "Judith Anderson, will you marry me?"

Chapter Nine

The moment Judith had been waiting for her entire life was finally here. Luke Anderson was proposing marriage. As a young girl, she'd fantasized about this moment, so many different times, so many different ways. Each time her answer would vary, depending upon her mood. Sometimes she'd fall happily into his arms, declaring her undying love, and others she'd rebuke him, scorning his audacity. This time she was at a complete and total loss for words.

"Are you sure that's what you want?" she asked, when she finally found her voice.

Luke nodded and smiled tenderly. "Judith, I've never been more certain of anything in my life."

A small coil of excitement began to unwind in the pit of her stomach and sprang through her body, dancing in her head, leaving her dizzy with its thrill. Somewhere in the back of her mind a tiny rational voice screamed that he hadn't said anything about love, but in her supercharged happiness, she squashed it and went with the moment. She wouldn't ask him why he wanted to marry her, since she really didn't have a decent choice in the matter.

For once in her life, she would take a chance, live on the edge. And, if it didn't pan out…she'd pay the price later with a broken heart. A price, at this point in time, for this man, she suddenly knew deep in her gut she was willing to pay, no matter how painful.

Searching his face for some sign that he was only going along with this charade for the account, she found instead a somberness, an almost spiritual reverence for the question he'd asked. His face was filled with childlike hope and a sense of awe at what he'd just asked her to do. And even though chances were, at the end of the ceremony, they'd be no more married than they were at this moment, Judith took his question to heart, and knew that her answer would change their lives. Agreement would signal submission, something she'd never been good at with Luke, but for some strange reason, she was eager to try.

Deep in her heart, she knew she could trust him. She believed that he would take what she gave and in turn give back to her. She needn't fear that he would use her surrender against her, but instead he would also surrender himself. Filled with a sense of power that their union would give, she knew she must do this for herself. Not for the Brubakers. Not for the agency. Not for the money. But for Judith. For Judith and Luke. And knowing that she couldn't control how he felt, she hoped with all that was within her that he felt the same way.

"Yes," she said simply. "I'll marry you."

"You will?" Luke nearly fell off his knee. Like the sun peeking from behind a cloud, his face was suddenly radiant at her answer. *Judith was going to marry him!* Or at least renew their vows....

"Yes," she repeated, as Luke dragged her into his arms and crushed his lips against hers in a kiss so exuberant she feared for her teeth.

"You won't be sorry!" he promised. "I know deep down that it's the right thing to do. For lots of reasons." He smiled gently at his bride to be. Real or not, they were getting married, and Luke Anderson was happy about it and didn't care who knew.

Pushing her worrisome doubts aside, she shyly answered his smile. "I think so, too," she said as he pelted her face with tiny enthusiastic kisses.

"We'd probably better be getting back," he finally sighed, and standing, helped Judith to her feet. "You remember what Big Daddy said, no hanky-panky between the brides and grooms."

"There's always the honeymoon," she flirted boldly, and then looked at him with doubt as the realization of her words dawned on her. Big Daddy would expect them to stay together on their wedding night.

Reading the direction of her thoughts, Luke grinned. He sensed her misgivings and kissed her lightly on the forehead. "Don't worry. We'll cross that bridge when we come to it. When the time comes, I'm sure we'll figure something out."

Bolstered by his self-confidence, she smiled. "Yes," she agreed, "we'll figure something out."

Growling, Luke grabbed her hand and marched her back to the house.

They entered the brightly lit homestead to discover wedding headquarters in full swing. A virtual swarm of activity hummed within the old mansion's walls, as Miss Clarise and Big Daddy issued orders and directed traffic.

Servants were briefed, assistants were on the phone pulling the strings of the Brubaker's endless connections—even at this late hour—and excited Brubaker offspring crowded around their eccentric parents, wondering what they could do to help plan for yet another wild party.

"Mama, I will need several new dresses," Patsy was informing her mother and lugged a stack of fashion magazines to the middle of the living room floor. "Shoes to match, of course, and some new jewelry…" She chattered on, reminding her mother not to forget the dance band, because no wedding would be complete without a dance…

"Heah they ah," Big Daddy announced, pulling Judith and Luke into the fray and slamming the front door closed behind them. Shooing Judith toward the living room, he held Luke back by standing in the way. "The ladies ah in the livin' room makin' plans and pickin' out dresses. Go on along now, honey pie, and don't worry none, I'll keep your man outa trouble." Herding Luke into the den with the three eldest Brubaker sons, he shut the door to prying female eyes.

"The men's club," Miss Clarise sniffed and beckoned Judith to join her and Patsy on the couch in the living room. Patsy seemed to miraculously have bounced back from Luke's rejection, and for the first time since they'd arrived, she was friendly to Judith.

Watching Miss Clarise and her daughter pour over the stacks of fashion periodicals, Judith suddenly and desperately missed her mother. And not just for advice on the style of her wedding gown. Barbara Anderson always knew the perfect answer to any question Judith ever posed. She was the model of womanly perfection, as far as Judith was concerned. Always poised and sophisticated, but with a special warmth that drew people from all walks of life into her circle of friends. Judith had a million questions to ask her mother now, starting with the question of her sanity.

Judith never dreamed that when her special time came, her mother would be in Korea whooping it up with an aging military platoon and that she would be in Texas with the sitcom version of the cast from *Dallas*. Deciding to make the best of this nutty situation, Judith swallowed her disappointment, threw herself into the spirit of the occasion and began hunting in earnest for—as Patsy would say—a drop-dead, killer wedding dress.

Luke wasn't a smoker, but took the proffered cigar and lit up, happily polluting the air in the den with the Brubaker men. Conway had refilled his whiskey tumbler several times, and by now, Luke, keeping pace with the rest of the boys, was feeling no pain.

"That's one hell of a filly you got youahself theah, boy!" Big Daddy roared and pounded Luke on the back till he choked on his drink. "Why, if I was twelve feet taller and a hundred years younger, I just might give you a run foah youah money theah!"

"I don't think so, Dad," Conway drew contentedly on his cigar, and blew a gray cloud of lazy smoke rings around his head. "Nope, she's a one-man woman and—" he pointed at Luke with the damp end of his cigar "—he's the man."

Luke's eyes shot to Conway with interest. What made him say that? How did he know that, when Luke himself still wasn't sure how she felt about him?

Merle and Buck nodded in agreement and Luke stared at them through his whiskey-fuzzed mind. *How did they know?*

"Yep," Conway expounded grandly, great billows of smoke pouring from his nostrils, "I'd know if she wasn't in love with him. I'd have found her weak spot by now," he bragged and chuckled comfortably with his brothers. "Lord knows, I've looked."

What was with these amoral Brubaker kids? Luke wondered muzzily. Surely they didn't learn their lecherous ways from Big Daddy or Miss Clarise, he thought. Oh, well, no point in punching Conway out now, he decided, complacently puffing on his cigar. No harm done.

He grinned cockily at Conway. "She is something, ain't she?" he asked, getting into the Southern hospitality they so easily offered. "And she's mine," he announced proudly. *At least for now,* he decided, and shoved the worries about what the future would bring to the back of his hazy mind.

"He's a fortunate SOB," Big Daddy loudly agreed as they all lifted their glasses in salute.

By the time the Brubaker clan was ready to call Wednesday a day, they were well into the wee hours of the next morning and many of the wedding plans had been settled.

Luke spent what was left of the night on a roll-away bed in his and Judith's suite, listening to Big Daddy snore in their bed and longing for Judith's delicate slumber. He spent some of the time longing for her delicate body, as well, but the buzz saw that was Big Daddy's nose kept him from getting too carried away.

Judith occupied the adjoining bedroom to the Brubaker master suite, and spent several sleepless hours tossing and turning in alternating fits of excitement and fear. During one particularly vivid nightmare, she bolted straight up in bed, her sweat-soaked nightgown clinging to her feverish body, and tried to decide if Luke had actually left her standing at the altar alone with the Brubakers.

Thursday brought a never-ending list of decisions for everyone. Flowers, food, music, minister, cake, limousines, clothes fittings, tents, chairs, hired help and more. Miss Clarise was in her element, the consummate party planner and organizer. She relegated duties to dozens of helpers and still found time to make sure that she and Judith had the perfect dresses for their unforgettable day.

Friday, all the last-minute details were sewn up, delivered, handled and checked off the enormous list, and by all appearances, the Brubakers and the Andersons were ready to get married yet again.

That evening, a swarm of Big Daddy's gentlemen friends descended on the ranch, depositing their womenfolk for the ladies' shower, and in a dust cloud of yeehaws and yahoos, nabbed Luke and his Brubaker cohorts and were off to the bachelor party in town.

Judith had never seen so much frilly, lacy, downright naughty underwear in her life. Blushing madly, she tried to squelch visions of parading around in front of Luke's probing eyes in some of the more risqué getups. Patsy positively howled at Judith's scandalized reaction to the male stripper she'd hired for the evening's entertainment. The slick-skinned, muscle-bound dancer was a personal friend of hers and went out of his way to embarrass the young, innocent bride-to-be. Miss Clarise further shocked Ju-

WIFE IN NAME ONLY

dith by tucking a couple of hundred-dollar bills into strategic nooks on the gyrating man's body.

Luke tried valiantly to enjoy the slithery, smothering ministrations of the twirly, bosomy, jiggly women who danced for him to the wild chanting of the gang at Big Daddy's favorite rib joint. After all, he was just as male as the next guy, but for some disturbing reason, visions of his beautiful Judith kept flitting through his head and ruining all the fun. Now, if it were Judith, wiggling her perky little tush and spinning her spangly pasties, well, that would be a different story. But, alas, she was in the middle of some hen party from hell, and he hadn't had a chance to speak to her since he'd proposed Wednesday night. A chance to tell her how much he loved her. Taking a deep slug of his beer, he knew that the way things were going, he probably wouldn't get that chance.

This was it. Her wedding day. Judith's hands trembled as she adjusted the beaded cap that sat on top of the pile of auburn curls she'd swept regally to the crown of her head. The antique-lace veil spilled richly down her slender back and a smaller sheath of wispy translucent netting covered her beautiful face. Matching beads on the dress's bodice shimmered gently in the morning light and a long, majestic train fell to the floor and nearly halfway across the room. Feeling like a fairy princess, she longed for the presence of her mother and the comforting, wise words of her father. Especially since she hadn't seen Luke since that day by the creek. Was she crazy to be going through this? Luke had never said anything about love, and she'd always vowed that she would never walk down the aisle for any other reason. It was too late to back out now, wasn't it? Yes. At least Luke cared, that much she knew. And she could never hurt the Brubakers by getting cold feet now.

She could hear the strains of the string quartet, playing chamber music down on the lawn, a backdrop to the multitude of voices that floated up to her room. "Something old, something new, something borrowed," she chanted to calm her nerves, "something...blue and—" she tucked a coin into her shoe "—a lucky penny for my shoe...." She'd need all the luck she could get to make it through this zany day.

Drawing a deep, steadying breath, she lifted her rosebud bridal bouquet off the dresser and went into the next room to wait with Miss Clarise and Patsy for the ceremony to begin.

Luke, having been the best man at more that one wedding in his time, had witnessed countless cases of cold feet. So where were his? Cold feet, that is, he wondered, shrugging into his jacket, taking care to straighten its long tails. He turned in front of the mirror and surveyed his appearance. Not bad, he decided, and jauntily attached his boutonniere to his lapel. He couldn't wait to get out there and take his vows. What the hell was with him, anyway? he grinned to himself. What bachelor in his right mind would so happily throw away his bachelorhood? Then, it dawned on him. Those other guys weren't marrying Judith. If this wedding wasn't real, and if they weren't really married when it was over, he was going to make sure that they were by the end of the month. Or he'd know the reason why.

Patting his pockets, he felt for the ring box that carried the diamond she'd admired in the window the day they'd bought Patsy's charm. He hoped she'd still like it. He knew her ring size because they'd purchased matching gold bands the day they bought their flowered luggage. It seemed like a hundred years ago now, he mused. As far as he knew, Big Daddy hadn't applied for a marriage license for them in the state of Texas, but knowing the mischievous Brubakers and their endless connections, anything was possible. So, if at day's end he really was a married man, well, bring on the honeymoon.

Big Daddy's rap at the door signaled it was time.

Luke suffered impatiently through a host of candle lighters and bridesmaids as they progressed with the speed of a herd of snails up the endless aisle. Then, Patsy, relishing her audience, crawled down the aisle with her own personalized variation of the march. After her were an assortment of ring bearers and flower girls. For crying out loud, concrete dried faster than this circus was progressing. A couple of operatic tunes and a poetry reading later, the audience finally stood, and Miss Clarise began her torturously slow journey toward the altar between Merle and Buck.

And then, the moment Luke had been waiting for, what seemed like his entire life. Judith, standing in all her magnificent bridal splendor, her hand tucked loosely at the crook of Conway's proud arm, began her slow-motion trip toward him at the altar. Luke wondered absently what was happening to his blood pressure. It felt as though the top of his head was about to blow off, his pride was that fierce. He had never experienced such an overflow of deep, lasting, true love toward anyone or anything in his life.

Their eyes locked, and as if there were a physical line connecting them, he drew her toward him, through the smiling crowd, down the eternal aisle to the altar, where Judith released Conway's arm and took his with the most beautiful smile he'd ever seen.

As they had planned, Miss Clarise and Big Daddy were the first to take their vows. Judith and Luke stood off to the side, between the lengthy line of attendants and the older couple at the altar. The sun sent ethereal rays of light slanting across the two aging faces, bathing them in its heavenly glow, giving them a soft, youthful quality. Their expressions were shining with their love for each other as they tenderly exchanged the promises of old—to love, honor and cherish one another until death them did part.

Big Daddy gazed at his lovely bride with such complete adoration that Judith felt the tears brim in her eyes till they spilled over and flowed down her face. She hadn't thought to bring a tissue or handkerchief with her, and as she stood witnessing the holy union before her, her nose began to run. Desperately, she tried to think of a way to stem the flow, but when Big Daddy took his darling bride's face in his weathered hands and softly kissed her lips, Judith was undone. Dabbing at the waterworks with her bouquet, she sniffed and hiccuped, blubbering like a baby.

The beauty. The holiness. The pureness of their love, rose as an emotional lump and lodged painfully in Judith's throat. She couldn't see through her tears, she couldn't hear over her hiccups, she couldn't breathe past the growing mass in her air passage. Judith Anderson was quite literally choked up.

Luke glanced at her with concern. He was no expert on the sentimental workings of a woman's mind, but it appeared to him that Judith was coming a bit unglued. Mascara flowed in dark rivers down her cheeks and her nose had turned an interesting shade of shiny hot pink. Not to mention the fact that, if he remembered his first aid correctly, she was going to need mouth-to-mouth resuscitation soon. Very soon.

Having pronounced his first couple man and wife, the minister turned his attentions to Luke and Judith. His face registered mild surprise as bride number two wadded up her veil and mopped at the torrential downpour streaming down her cheeks, wheezing all the while. Smiling kindly, he waited while she attempted to pull herself together.

She nodded and waved, smiling weakly at him, willing him to ignore her, signaling that she would eventually be okay...she hoped.

Good Lord! What on earth was happening to her? she wondered frantically between wheezy sobs and deep, racking hiccups. Each time she thought of the beautiful scene that she had just been a part of, each time she remembered how wonderful the Brubakers had been to her and Luke, each time she thought about this next deception that she and Luke were about to pull, each time she remembered that Luke, as yet, had still not mentioned anything about love...she sank deeper into her downward spiral of hysteria.

Not knowing what else to do, the minister forged ahead with the ceremony, repeating the familiar ''dearly beloved''s and ''we are gathered''s until he came to the phrase, ''if anyone knows a reason why this man and this woman cannot be joined in holy matrimony...''

This woman cannot be joined in holy matrimony... this woman...cannot be...holy...this woman...cannot be... The words echoed and reverberated in Judith's head, repeating, vibrating, resounding, till she thought she would scream...scream...scream....

Who was screaming? Judith wondered, then realized that she was. "I know," she choked, terrified at the enormity of this important moment. "I know," she cried, sobs jolting her slender body. "I know a reason why... Because...because, we're not married. We never were. And, Luke...Luke doesn't really love me...I'm so very sorry," she whispered sorrowfully to the shocked and silent group, before gathering up her voluminous skirts and running back down the aisle as fast as her wobbly legs could carry her.

"My land." Miss Clarise was the first to break the eerie silence.

Big Daddy turned to Luke, his face livid. "What in tarnation is goin' on heah?" he demanded. "What's all this nonsense about y'all not bein' married?"

Luke sputtered incoherently, still shocked and hurt over Judith's sudden change of heart. "I...I..." he stammered until Conway's beefy fist connected with his jaw.

"What the hell did you do to that little gal?" Conway yelled as the wedding guests squealed in terror. Conway pulled his arm back for another go at Luke's face, only to be thwarted by Patsy, who, calling upon her many years of ballet, gracefully flew through the air to land on her brother's back.

"Stop it, Conway!" she screamed, pounding his broad, steely back with her tiny fists. "Quit it now! You hear me?"

The audience gasped in unison as she covered her brother's eyes with her hands and rode him blindly around in circles till he crashed into the buffet table that held the wedding cake.

Miss Clarise dove for the cake in a vain attempt to save it and ended up wearing several layers on her wedding dress.

"Now look what you did to Mamath' dreth!" little Hank cried in dismay and promptly burst into tears.

The murmuring and rumbling among the wedding guests swelled as Patsy slid off Conway's back and rushed to Luke's aid.

"Are you all right?" she asked, and in her haste she slipped on a piece of wedding cake and landed with a resounding thud. "Uff!" she grunted, sliding into Luke and knocking him back down again.

Standing now and craning their necks for a better look at the fracas up front, the crowd reacted with appropriate ohs and ahs. The stripper from the bridal shower vaulted over several chairs to pick up Patsy.

"Put her down!" Conway ordered the stripper, redirecting his fists at this new source of irritation.

"Oh, shut up, Conway," Luke pulled himself to his feet and hammered the cowboy with a quick right cross. Dusting his hands, he stepped over Conway's limp body and said, "That's for hitting on a married woman."

The clamor of an already exhausted, agitated wedding party swelled into the mutinous hue and cry of a fledgling riot.

From the safety of the stripper's arms, Patsy chimed in, "Yeah, Conway, that'll teach you!"

Luke stopped on his way past Patsy. "Don't push your luck, kid. As far as I'm concerned, you're next."

Outraged, she made an ungainly effort to kick Luke's backside as he continued on. Legs flailing, she inadvertently launched one of her spiked pumps into the air where it whizzed passed Luke's ear and caught Big Daddy squarely on the chin.

"That does it!" Big Daddy roared as complete and total bedlam ensued. Swinging around to face Luke, he yelled, "Youah fired!"

A wild roar went up from the delighted crowd. Once again the Brubakers had come through with an excellent party. The string quartet struck up a rousing chorus of the University of Texas fight song as the chaos escalated. Dodging assorted hats, gloves, pocketbooks and bits of wedding cake, Luke wove through the brawling mob and into the house in search of Judith.

Chapter Ten

Luke paused at the doorway to their bedroom to find Judith inside, lying in a heap of satin and lace, crying her eyes out. His heart—what was left of it, after she'd just jilted him at the altar—went out to her. Why would she go back on her word this way? he wondered. Unless, she discovered at the last minute that she really didn't care for him, and couldn't pretend any more. His heart turned over painfully at the sorrow he felt and saw mirrored in Judith's tears.

He raked his hands wearily through his hair and wondered what to do next. They'd been fired. Their careers were over. The possibility of any future together for them was over. Judith had slammed the door on all of it. Obviously, he'd been wrong to think that she'd changed. That she'd grown up, matured. She was still up to her childish, hurtful tricks.

Leaning against the door frame, he wondered if she'd gone to these elaborate lengths to punish him for the way he'd treated her as a girl. For the way all the children in her lonely past had treated her. Well, he knew one thing for sure. She would have to come to terms with those hurts in her own way. It was clear to him now that it was beyond his power to heal her.

Suddenly angry with her, and with himself for getting into this mess in the first place, he realized it was probably for the best. Better to find out now, than to make the huge mistake of committing themselves to a business partnership and quite possibly a marriage only to have it all crumble later, after it was too late. Still, though, it hurt. Hurt like hell.

Sensing Luke's dark and brooding presence in the room, Judith lifted her bleary tear-stained face and stared blankly across the room at him. The muted sounds of the wedding riot below filtered through the open window, teasing the wispy, lacy curtains along with the breeze.

"Why?" Luke's voice was harsh, echoing the pain of his shattered dreams. "We had everything. You blew it."

"We had nothing," Judith sniffed, her words were flat, dead.

Luke felt as if Conway had just socked him in the gut. The room swayed and he struggled to remain standing. To remain calm. And dignified. He had his pride, too. He might be a laughingstock among the throng downstairs right now, but he'd be damned if he was going to let this woman drag him through the emotional wringer for another minute.

"Well, it's lucky we found that out now, isn't it?" he jeered, sharp pains searing through his head, worse now than when Burrito had so unceremoniously dumped him on the rocks.

Judith looked dully away, despair forming an impermeable wall around her. She opened her mouth to argue and closed it again, too tired and beaten to fight any more.

Luke was boiling mad now. She was scaring him. Where was her spunk? Her fight? How dared she just lie there, emotionless, when his whole world was falling apart? He was desperate to make her feel something. Anything would be better than the empty, unfeeling robot who lay sulking on the bed. He debated whether or not to drag her out of her silken heap and paddle her bottom, punishing her for her betrayal, but then wondered tiredly what good it would do. Judith was, and always would be, her own woman and not someone who could be forced. That's what he'd always loved about her.

It was only a matter of moments that he stood, watching her stare blankly, unseeing at the wall, but it felt like hours. She didn't care, or she would say something. Do something to explain her cruel behavior. *We have nothing.* The words reverberated depressingly in his head. What about their love? What about their families? What about the business that they'd both worked so hard for? What about the two charming little fruitcakes who had given them a chance for greatness?

"To hell with you," he ground out, the fury ricocheted through his body. Turning on his heel, he stormed out of the bedroom and out of Judith Anderson's life.

"Wheah's he goin'?" Big Daddy grumbled at Miss Clarise as they stood watching Luke gallop out of the paddock on Lightning. The long tails of his wedding jacked flapped in the wind, his body hunched low in the saddle, his jaw set with anger. Lightning sensed his rider's anxiousness and stretched his stride, swiftly covering the ground with an eager, soaring gallop. Luke rode like a pro, urging him on, flying away from the woman who'd taken his dreams.

"Where do you *think* he's going?" she huffed angrily. "To get away from you, you old goat! You just fired the best thing that ever happened to you without even giving him a chance to defend himself. Let's go apologize to our wedding guests, and after those kids have a chance to cool down, you go hire them back again," Miss Clarise ordered her red-faced man.

"I'll do no such thing!" he thundered.

Her bright blue eyes narrowed, shooting sparks of anger at her new—and old—husband. "Oh, yes, you will. I don't care if those kids are married or not, and neither should you. It's obvious to me that they have more love for each other in their little fingers than many of our miserable, old married friends." She took a step closer to Big Daddy and poked him in the boutonniere with her finger. "You're always preachin' about how much you value love. Well, they *love* each other! And I think they love you! And you want to throw all that away, and you don't even know why. How about practicing what you preach and showing a little love yourself? Those kids are obviously willing to go through with this harebrained wedding scheme of yours, just to please us. Well, your well-meaning plans backfired on you, Big Daddy. Come on, let's go say we're sorry about what happened to all our guests!" she shouted at the stunned man in front of her. "Now!" Miss Clarise slugged him in the arm.

"Lord, how I love it when you're frisky," Big Daddy grinned and went off to practice his vow of obedience to his wife.

* * *

Luke dropped off the sweaty, foaming Lightning once he reached the secluded stream in the trees and dragged off his coat and tie, throwing them angrily to the ground. Leading the horse to the edge of the creek, he allowed the thirsty animal to drink for a while and cool off. Too bad he couldn't cool off as easily himself. He walked over to the spot where he and Judith had agreed to marry only days ago and sat down in the familiar comforting grass. He didn't want to think. He didn't want to feel. He just wanted to step back in time, to the moment he'd pledged his life to Judith.

Unconsciously, he smiled fondly at the memory. She'd stilled in his arms for the longest moment, and then kissed him and admitted that she'd waited her whole life to hear him ask that question, and—this was the part he loved the best—that she'd always loved him. *Hot damn!* Judith Anderson had always loved him!

Groaning, he lay back on the grass. So what happened? What changed her mind? Absently, he went over the details of the ceremony and tried to determine exactly when Judith had decided not to go through with the marriage. Her unaccountable flood of tears seemed to begin when Big Daddy and Miss Clarise promised to love each other till their dying day. What was wrong with that? That was nothing to cry about, was it?

It was then that it dawned on him. Something Judith had said, the other day in this very spot, about marrying for love. *What an idiot!* How could he have been so stupid? Had he told her that he loved her? He racked his brain trying to remember, and came up blank.

"Oh, Judith," he groaned, and pounded his forehead with the palm of his hand. Of course. That was it. She'd realized what an unfeeling clod she was about to marry, and she couldn't go through with it. Knowing how important a loving marriage was to her, he didn't blame her. Now all he had to do was convince her how important it was to him. With grim determination, he stood up and brushed off the seat of his pants. It was time to go tell his bride how much he loved her. How much he'd always loved her.

What in heaven's name had she been thinking? Judith wondered, as the impact of what she'd said to Luke hit her. *We have nothing.* Nothing could be further from the truth. They had had everything together, and she'd just thrown it all away. What the hell had she done? One minute she was standing at the altar with Luke, about to realize her lifelong fantasy of becoming his wife, and the next, she was running down the aisle as though she'd been about to marry the devil himself.

"Oh, Luke," she sniffed and dabbed at her nose with the back of her hand. It was obvious that Luke loved her. If she were honest with herself, she knew that he always had. What other boy would have tolerated her tricks, rescued her from so many jams and never told a soul? And now, as adults, she knew from his touch, his eyes, the sweet words of comfort he still offered so unselfishly to her when she was in need.... Yes, Luke Anderson loved her and she'd taken that love and reduced it to nothing. Pushing herself up on the bed, Judith knew that if she let him walk away this time, she'd never forgive herself. Wearing a grim look of determination, she battled with her massive skirt, kicking at it, trying to find the opening for her legs. When she'd accomplished that, she scooted to the edge of the bed and decided that she had to find him and apologize now, before it was too late. No, nothing on heaven or earth could keep her from going after her man.

"Judith?" Luke stood in the doorway of their bedroom once again, his body as tightly coiled as a wild animal in a position of fight or flight. He opened and closed his fists nervously, wondering how the woman standing in the middle of the room, still wearing her wedding dress, would respond.

Upon hearing his voice, she tensed and turned, the light of love and hope burning in her eyes. "Luke?" she whispered, every bit of longing and yearning that she'd felt for him through the years packed into the one breathy word.

Groaning, he strode across the room and pulled her roughly into his embrace, muttering her name over and over again, as though he were afraid she might disappear.

"Oh, Luke," she breathed, sobbing, laughing, loving... "I'm so sorry. I wanted it to be so perfect, it's just that I realized..."

"Shh." Luke silenced her with a kiss. "I know. I was wrong. So very wrong." He rocked her back and forth in his arms. "We never should have lied to them. You were right all along. It's better this way, to have everything out in the open, to base our relationship on the truth..." He pulled her head back and their eyes locked. "We still have a relationship?" The question was half serious, half in jest.

Judith sighed. "Yes! Oh, thank God. I was so afraid I'd lost you."

"Never." The corners of his mouth lifted in a tentative smile. "We haven't been able to get away from each other yet, I don't know why we should start now...Judith," Luke's voice was raspy with emotion. "I should have told you this a long time ago, but for some reason I guess I thought you knew." His eyes were bright, and he looked so vulnerable Judith wanted to cry. "I love you, Judith Anderson, with all my heart."

"Oh, Luke," She smiled up at him. "I love you, too. I always have and I always will."

He fumbled in his pocket for the small box that contained her diamond. Removing it from its case, he took her slender hand in his and slid it on her finger, next to her plain gold band.

Drawing her breath in sharply, she turned her hand from side to side and admired the brilliance of the large, beautifully cut stone. "How did you know?" she gasped, full of wonder, and sank down to the edge of the bed, where Luke joined her.

"I saw how you looked at it, the day we went to town. You like it?" He smiled proudly down at her hand.

"No," she whispered. "I love it."

Luke's eyes went suddenly dark as he drew her up against his wildly thudding heart. Cradling her in his arms, he lowered her slowly back on the bed and kissed her with an intensity that left her breathless. Her arms came up to circle his neck as their bodies melded and struggled to communicate what for so many years had been left unsaid. Their whispers came in short, gasping breaths as, between frenzied kisses, they spoke of promises to continue loving each other for the rest of their lives.

"What the *hell's* goin' on in heah?" Big Daddy thundered, marching over to the edge of the bed. "Get off that little gal, boy!" Judith and Luke leapt guiltily to their feet. "Last I heard, she wasn't your wife."

"Well, I plan on changing that, real soon, sir." Luke was anxious to explain his honorable intentions before Big Daddy flipped his ten-gallon lid.

"How soon?" Big Daddy squinted at him curiously.

"As soon as possible, sir."

"*Hot* diggity dog!" he howled, and slapped his thigh so hard it nearly knocked the fringe off his wedding jacket. "If y'all will excuse me, I got a couple of strings to go pull down at city hall. Meet me downstairs in an hour," he shouted and bounded out the door.

Judith's eyes were wide with surprise as she watched their eccentric host's retreating back.

"I take it this means we have our jobs back," she giggled.

Laughing, Luke gathered her into his arms and looked down at her beautiful face. "It looks like Big Daddy is going to get his big wedding after all," he said kissing her lightly on her full, soft lips.

Judith grinned. "Well, maybe this time we'll get it right."

"You think so?" Luke began to sway with Judith to the strains of a country song that came from the party down below, now in full tilt. "You know, this stuff kind of grows on you," he said, referring to the music.

"Mmm," she agreed as he swung her out, twirled her a couple of times and pulled her back into his arms for a kiss.

"Well, what do you say, Judith Anderson, will you marry me?"

"Yes, but not for the reasons you think," she

laughed when he dipped her and pulled her back up for yet another kiss. "I'll only marry you because I won't have to change the monogram on my towels."

"Good thinking," he agreed genially, sweeping her around the room. "Think you'll hyphenate?"

"Hmm, hadn't thought about it…Anderson-Anderson. Has a nice ring, don't you think?"

Luke stopped dancing and pulled their noses together. "The nicest," he said, and covered her mouth with his.

Epilogue

The tinkling sound of silver flatware tapping against the side of a crystal wineglass finally brought a hush over the excited wedding crowd some time shortly after midnight. Ted and Ed Anderson stood in Big Daddy's gazebo with their wives and an uncommonly silent, but beaming Mrs. Soder.

Lowering his glass, Ed smiled at Ted and stepped up to the microphone. "A toast!" he announced, and a lengthy round of good-natured cheering prevented him from continuing for a moment.

After the noise died down, Ed's voice reverberated and echoed from the giant speakers the reception band had been using. "When we arrived here in Texas today, we thought we were coming to save what was left of our quickly diminishing advertising agency." Ed and Ted both grinned remonstratively at Mrs. Soder. "We'd received the news that our charges were killing the business, and perhaps each other as well."

Unable to contain herself, Mrs. Soder piped up. "Well, the last time I spoke to you, they were!" she cried defensively. This was met by rowdy laughter and good-natured catcalls, which successfully drowned out her continued explanation.

Nudging the eccentric chatterbox in blue out of the way, Ted picked up where Ed left off. "You can imagine our surprise and happiness to discover that not only was our business thriving, but our two kids were only an hour away from marriage." Ted paused as something dawned on him. "That would make us in-laws, wouldn't it, Ed?"

Ed's grin widened. "And we'll have the same grandkids, too!" he chortled, his eyes growing misty right along with Ted's.

Ted cleared his throat and dabbed at his eyes. "Anyway, to make a long story short, we've decided that our wedding gift to the kids will be..."

"Anderson and Anderson!" the parents all shouted together, and then fell into each others' arms in a tearful mass of happiness. Unable to stand it, Big Daddy rushed forward, threw himself into the parental hug, and ended up with Mrs. Soder wrapped tightly around his neck. The band began to play again and when they could finally pull themselves into some semblance of order, the parents joined the other two-steppers on the dance floor.

Having long since left the reception, Luke and Judith were having a party of their own. Just the two of them, a couple of disinterested horses and a grassy spot by a creek that was beginning to feel like heaven.

*   *   *   *   *

Receive **75¢ off** your next

SILHOUETTE *Romance*®

book purchase.

Silhouette®
Where love comes alive™

Receive **75¢ off** your next

SILHOUETTE *Romance*®

book purchase.

**Where royalty and romance
go hand in hand...**

The series continues in Silhouette Romance
with these unforgettable novels:

HER ROYAL HUSBAND
by Cara Colter
on sale July 2002 (SR #1600)

THE PRINCESS HAS AMNESIA!
by Patricia Thayer
on sale August 2002 (SR #1606)

SEARCHING FOR HER PRINCE
by Karen Rose Smith
on sale September 2002 (SR #1612)

And look for more Crown and Glory stories in
SILHOUETTE DESIRE starting in October 2002!

Available at your favorite retail outlet.

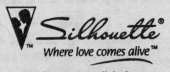

Where love comes alive™

FREE
Gourmet Garden Kit!

With two proofs of purchase from any four Silhouette® special collector's editions.

Special Limited Time Offer

YES! Please send me my FREE Gourmet Garden Kit without cost or obligation, except for shipping and handling. Enclosed are two proofs of purchase from specially marked Silhouette® special collector's editions and $3.50 shipping and handling fee.

Name (PLEASE PRINT)

Address   Apt. #

City   State/Prov.   Zip/Postal Code

IN U.S., mail to:
Silhouette Gourmet Garden Kit Offer
3010 Walden Ave.
P.O. Box 9023
Buffalo, NY 14269-9023

IN CANADA, mail to:
Silhouette Gourmet Garden Kit Offer
P.O. Box 608
Fort Erie, Ontario
L2A 5X3

FREE GOURMET GARDEN KIT OFFER TERMS
To receive your free Gourmet Garden Kit, complete the above order form. Mail it to us with two proofs of purchase, one of which can be found in the upper right-hand corner of this page. Requests must be received no later than December 31, 2002. Your Gourmet Garden Kit costs you only $3.50 for shipping and handling. The free Gourmet Garden Kit has a retail value of $17.00 U.S. All orders subject to approval. Products in kit illustrated on the back inside cover of this book are for illustrative purposes only, and items may vary (retail value of items always as previously indicated). **Please allow 6-8 weeks for delivery. Offer good in Canada and the U.S. only.** Offer good only while quantities last. Offer limited to one per household.

© 2002 Harlequin Enterprises Limited
598 KGJ DNCX

PSNCP02-OFFER

JOAN JOHNSTON

The Hazard-Allistair feud had endured for generations—and after meeting proud, stubborn Harriet Allistair, Nathan Hazard could see why. Harriet had come west to Montana, convinced that inheriting her uncle's farm offered the chance to prove herself to her family—and most importantly, to herself.

From his neighboring ranch, Nathan is counting the minutes till frustration and desperation drive her off "his" family's land. But what he hasn't counted on is an "Allistair"—least of all, newcomer Harriet—getting under his skin, making him wonder if ending the feud once and for all could mean a new beginning for them both.

"Like Lavyrle Spencer, Ms. Johnston writes of intense emotions and tender passions that seem so real that readers will feel each one of them."
—*Rave Reviews*

Available the first week of June 2002 wherever paperbacks are sold!